Praise for Ga...

'Gabby is **one**...'
Sarah Millican

'...very funny. **If you like Terry Pratchett, or think gothic fairytales should have more LOLs, 'tis the book for ye.'**
Greg Jenner

'I have read this and it is great. **Pratchetty fun for all the family.'**
Lucy Porter

'...**magical, surprising and funny.'** Jan Ravens

What people are saying about the Darkwood series:

'**Clever and funny and so very very entertaining.** I would encourage everyone of every age to go ahead and read *Darkwood*.'

'Completely **fabulous, can't wait for the rest of the series.'**

'A **fun, exciting, action-packed** story that once I started reading I couldn't put down.'

'I **loved the mix of humour and fantasy**, the tongue in cheek style of writing and the **quirky characters.'**

'I could go on and on about how much **I love this book** and why.'

'A delightful new mashup of old familiar fairy tale characters and themes, with loads of originality and memorable characters. ... I think this **may well turn into one of my all-time favourites.'**

'...incredible! It **made me laugh out loud in several places**, but also managed to pull off some intricate themes around power and bigotry – **I adored the characters and the fun, genre-savvy writing.'**

By Gabby Hutchinson Crouch
Darkwood

SUCH BIG TEETH

THE DARKWOOD SERIES, BOOK TWO

Gabby Hutchinson Crouch

This edition published in 2020 by Farrago,
an imprint of Duckworth Books Ltd
1 Golden Court, Richmond TW9 1EU, United Kingdom

www.farragobooks.com

ISBN: 978-1-78842-144-7

For Alex and Violet

Contents

1
Here Be Monsters

The land of Myrsina lies nestled snugly beneath the Great Mountains, with the kingdom of Ashtrie to its east and an expanse of western coastline twinkling with the Golden Sea. If you were to measure its area, you would compare it closely to Wales, because that's roughly how big it is, but also because for some reason Wales is the standard unit for measuring landmass, in the same nonsensical way we always measure dinosaur size in double-decker buses. Myrsina doesn't have either dinosaurs or double-decker buses, but its soil is reasonably fertile, its climate reasonably clement, and its people are very, very happy with the way it's being run, by a benevolent collective called the huntsmen, who keep the populace on the path of natural righteousness and continue to purge the land of witches and other magical beasties. No, really, the people love being governed by the huntsmen, ask any one of them, and they will tell you how wonderful life under the huntsmen is, or at least, they will if they know what's good for them.

On the border between Myrsina and Ashtrie, running north all the way to the mountains, stands the cursed forest of Darkwood, where all those terrible witches and beasties slink away to hide when the huntsmen come for them. Over the years, the Darkwood has become a haven to magical beings of all kinds, and death itself to any human who dares enter its twisted thickets. Why, two huntsmen were killed out there in separate attacks only a matter of weeks ago, and then of course there's what happened to the village of Nearby, at the Darkwood's edge. A whole human village, bewitched and brought under the influence of the wicked wood, to the point that they actually turned their backs on the rulers of their land and drove the huntsmen from their streets, right in the middle of a good old-fashioned witch burning. Dreadful scenes.

Past the very wicked and ungrateful village of Nearby is a river with a log bridge, and just beyond that is Darkwood itself. There used to be a perimeter fence in front of the line of trees, but this has recently been taken down. Even so, the humans from the village still don't actually venture into the Darkwood. If they were to go in there, they could end up wandering lost until they dropped dead from starvation and exhaustion, or they could be swiftly killed by one of the many dangers of the forest... or they could find themselves in a clearing in a hollow, where a little house stands alone and incongruous in its cosy appearance. It's not just the cheery warm firelight at the windows that seems out of place, or the pretty roses around the door or the neat little vegetable garden to the side; there's also the fact that the house's exterior is almost entirely made out of cake, biscuit and rather stale and grubby pastry. Don't be fooled by its charming, delicious aspect. Witches live in this house. With a spider. Oh, and it's haunted.

If you were to escape that sweetly scented house of horrors alive, and trek for ten minutes upstream, you would find a small opening in a hillock, around the size of a badger's sett. From out of this small and unassuming hole pops a head. It is the size of a human child's, but utterly covered in tangled, filthy hair, with eyes not unlike those of a large cat, and a mouth split wide with viciously sharp, twisted teeth.

'Yummy,' it says, quietly, and pulls itself out of the hole. The rest of its body isn't any sort of improvement on the head. It stands upright, covered from top to toe in the same matted grey hair. It wears a couple of leather belts adorned with small, hand-beaten axes, and what serve as its fingers end in large, sharp claws.

If that's not bad enough, out of the hole in the ground emerges another creature just like the first, then another, then another… until seven in all stand around the hole, waiting. These are the Dwarves, and they're waiting for the witch who lives in their cave with them to appear. After a moment, she does – a tall, dark woman in her late twenties, dressed in filthy armour that has been gruesomely adorned with the skulls of small birds and rodents. Getting out of the cave entrance is clearly more difficult for someone of such stature and impractical dress than it is for the Dwarves. Once she's out, she makes it yet harder for herself by turning around and delicately pulling a large wall mirror from the hole, utilising two grooves dug into the sides of the opening so that it will just about fit. That done, she asks the Mirror if it's OK, hefts it onto her back and sets off, trailing Dwarves behind her like a chattering, hairy cloak.

This witch, terrible in her armour, is known to many as the White Knight, the spectre of the forest who protects its beastly inhabitants using brute force and a wide selection of deadly blades. Her real name is Snow.

You wouldn't think from the state of her that she was once a princess. You wouldn't think that she's now the rightful heir to the throne of Myrsina.

You wouldn't think from how ferocious she and her party of Dwarves appear that they're actually all just off for lunch in the cake cottage downstream.

Inside the cake cottage, life is… OK. It's fine, it's passable. It would be better if it weren't raining right through the roof. Turns out, shortbread isn't particularly waterproof. Several buckets and pans, half filled with rainwater and wet biscuit, litter the floor. One of the pans is accidentally a large pie case, which isn't doing anyone any favours.

11

The whole 'house made of cake' situation is extremely impractical, any one of its residents would be quick to admit that. It's certainly not a deliberate architectural choice, it's just that its owner is Buttercup, a witch whose only known magical power is that she can turn anything that isn't alive into baked goods – and almost always accidentally so, at that. Buttercup has given up on trying to put out pans for the water now, due to the situation with the pie case on the floor, which was very recently a skillet pan. She is, instead, gazing in irritation at her fingers as Jack Trott and Gretel Mudd rush about emptying pails of water.

Jack Trott was once believed to merely be a thief on the run from the law. He has since been outed as a witch with the power to grow any plant to any size at will, and has shouldered the blame for the death of a Giant due to an unstable beanstalk thirteen years ago and, far more recently, a young huntsman accidentally killed in exactly the same way. Much to his relief, he's been exonerated of the death of the Giant, who it turns out was actually secretly murdered by huntsmen. He is still, however, very definitely a witch, and did definitely kill that young huntsman, albeit unintentionally. He has apologised to the dead huntsman in question several times now.

Gretel Mudd is not actually a witch at all, it's just that so many people now think that she is one that in the current climate it's safer for everybody concerned if she lives out in the Darkwood rather than returning home to her family's farm in Nearby Village. This is not even remotely an ideal situation for her, as much as she enjoys the company and camaraderie of the witches of the wood. She really wishes she could just go home, and the fact that bits of wet biscuit keep falling on her head only cements that miserable homesickness further.

The cake cottage has two further residents, neither of whom is helping with the buckets, on account of it being physically impossible for them to do so. One is Trevor, a largeish house spider who would be perfectly ordinary, were it not for the fact that he can talk, and enjoys wearing a range of tiny little hats, glasses and false moustaches. The other is the Ghost of Patience Fieldmouse, the aforementioned huntsman accidentally killed by Jack Trott in a beanstalk-related incident, as they were all trying to flee the monstrous Bin Men who prowl the forest every Monday night, taking offerings left outside homes and slaughtering anybody caught wandering after dark. Her death does remain a little bit of a sticking point, but she has at least accepted that it wasn't deliberate and that Jack was actually trying to help her at the time. To her credit, as underlying causes of housemate grudges go, your own unintentional killing is rather more pertinent than whose turn it is to clean the dishes.

After a lot of running about with buckets, Gretel stands back and assesses the leakage situation.

'I think this is the best we're going to manage, for now,' she says. 'Buttercup, how did you manage to accidentally cakeify the *roof*?'

Buttercup sighs. 'I was trying to fix the Battenberg chimney.'

'See now, all that answer does is lead to further questions.'

'I can start growing thatching straw as soon as this rain's stopped,' Jack says. 'Don't worry, Buttercup, we'll get it sorted.'

'I'm pretty good at thatching,' adds Gretel, with a touch of pride. 'Did you guys see the pig shed's roof on Liberation Day? I did that myself.'

There is a muted chorus of slightly bored 'yes's. The Liberation Day she refers to is the day that the witches and beasties of the Darkwood teamed up with the residents of Nearby to turn a large occupying battalion of huntsmen out of the village. There had been a party afterwards, and Gretel had shown the witches around her home village during their brief visit to her much-missed old stomping ground. That was just over two weeks ago now, and she's still going on about it.

There is a bang, and the door is kicked open.

Buttercup sighs indulgently. 'Are you *ever* going to knock, Snow?'

Snow smiles fondly at Buttercup as she clanks wetly in. The rivulets of rain dripping off her armour and the liberal spray of water from seven hairy Dwarves shaking themselves dry quickly coat the cottage's interior and leave its residents with a damp sheen and a sinking sensation that they really needn't have bothered with all those buckets after all.

'Rainy out,' announces Snow.

'Yes, we noticed.'

Snow eyes up the buckets. 'Surprised that Trott hasn't just grown a big waterproof canopy of ferns or something over the whole house, to be honest.'

Jack tuts, annoyed. 'Trousers. I didn't think of that.'

Gretel steps towards Snow, with an air of impatience. 'You brought your dad?'

Snow lets Gretel help set the Mirror down on the kitchen table. 'Yes, if only to shut you up about it. What's for lunch?'

Oh yes – the Mirror is magic, can show anything within the land of Myrsina as long as the request is made in rhyme, and contains the soul of Snow's dead father.

Buttercup looks at all of her pots and pans currently littering the soggy kitchen floor. 'I'll try to magic us up a nice pie.'

'And Snow and her dad can tell us the whole "what's going on" of it all,' says Gretel, wiping the Mirror dry.

'The rest of the forest in general's doing pretty well,' Snow tells them, taking a seat and propping her feet up on the table. 'The few beasties that were injured fighting for the village are all healing up nicely. No huntsmen scout parties to report, either. Looks like what we did in Nearby put a stop to that.'

'For now,' adds Patience. 'I know what they're like. They're persistent. They'll be back.'

'Yes, well, that's the sort of thing we can check with the Mirror, isn't it?' says Gretel. She levels a meaningful gaze at Snow. 'Let's see how things are in the Citadel and whether it isn't about time for… the other thing…?'

'There's another thing?' Trevor asks excitedly, abseiling down on a line of web from rafter to table. 'What other thing... Ooh! Is it a princess thing?'

'Trevor...' warns Snow.

'Are you going to reclaim your rightful place of the throne? With a big ceremony where the whole country bows down to you while you stand on a big rock or something?'

'Trevor.'

'And then there'll be a masked ball and I'll go in disguise and all the ladies will be like "who *is* that dashing man?" And I'll be all "ha ha! It's me! Trevor the spider and not a man at all!"'

'Trevor. Calm down. There'll be no throne-reclaiming...' Snow pauses, watching the expressions of the others. 'Well, not for now at least, we've still got a lot to do before we can even contemplate that.'

'But we can at least get the wheels in motion?' Gretel prompts.

'The "other thing" has *wheels*?' Trevor asks. 'This sounds exciting! Tell me what it is! Tellmetellmetellme...'

Snow rolls her eyes. 'Go on then, New Girl, since you're so keen.'

'Snow was talking about an excursion north, to the mountains,' Gretel tells them. 'Try to get the wolf and bear witches on board before any kind of push against the Citadel.'

The mood in the room suddenly becomes much more uneasy.

'Ah,' says Trevor, 'so... sorry, where do the wheels come in with this incredibly dangerous idea?'

'Getaway cart, I hope,' replies Jack.

'Have none of you ever been north, at all?' Gretel asks. 'Jack? Snow? Buttercup?'

'What's that, dear?' asks Buttercup, coming back into the kitchen, holding a rather sad-looking quiche. 'Sorry, I *was* trying to do a pie, it just went a bit wrong.'

'You've been out here the longest,' says Gretel to Buttercup. 'You ever met any of the witches in the northern territory?'

'Ooh no, they keep to themselves up there and the rest of us are very much not welcome. It's all wolves and bears. And a giant crow.'

'A giant crow?'

'Or a raven. I can never remember the difference.'

'Like…' Snow frowns. 'As big as an eagle owl?'

'As big as a man, dear. Or at least, that's what the stories would have you believe, but there are so many silly stories about *us* going around that maybe we should take it with a pinch of salt. Why all the interest in the northern territory, anyway?'

'Snow and Gretel want us to go up there,' Trevor tells her.

Buttercup's fingers tremble so much that she drops her quiche. 'Bother!'

In the cake cottage, dropped food very much has a five-second rule – it only lasts about five seconds on the floor before the Dwarves eat the lot. The inhabitants of the cottage watch with their usual morbid fascination as the Dwarves descend in a noisy feeding frenzy upon the smashed quiche.

'Oh dear.'

'It's fine,' says Jack, 'I'll grow us a salad.'

Snow spits. 'Ugh. Salad.'

'I'll be fine with my bluebottles, mate,' Trevor tells him.

'And I don't have to eat any more,' adds Patience, 'thanks to my accident.'

'You're… welcome?' attempts Jack.

Patience glares. 'Too soon, Trott. *Toooo soooooooonnn.*'

'Buttercup, she's doing it again!'

'Patience,' tuts Buttercup, gently pushing Snow's muddy feet off the table, 'no spooky voices indoors.'

Gretel sighs. It's been like this ever since they got back from the liberation of Nearby – extremely slow going. If she didn't know better, she might almost say that Snow's deliberately putting off making her next move. Almost as if she's worried. Almost as if she's afraid.

Gretel doesn't say any of this, of course. It's not the sort of thought one voices aloud to a woman who uses tiny throwing axes to keep her hair in place. Instead, she says, 'Can we see the Citadel, then?'

'Sure.' Snow gives the frame of the Mirror a sharp tap with her knuckles. 'Dad?'

From deep within the magic Mirror comes a man's voice – the voice, in fact, of the long dead King of Myrsina. 'Ask properly,' it says.

Snow huffs. 'This, again.'

Gretel leans in to the Mirror. 'Mirror, Mirror, here for lunch, show us the huntsmen. Er… thanks a bunch?'

There is a sudden crackle of magical energy around the Mirror, like electricity hanging in the air. The surface of the Mirror stops reflecting the kitchen ceiling and instead shows a thick static. The static quickly clears, to show an image of the streets of the Citadel.

In the Citadel, the huntsmen still patrol, and gather in groups as the rest of the population avert their gazes and hurry past. Lists of abominations are still pinned up around the Citadel – but, Gretel notices, the paper looks old and worn, as if no new edicts have been issued lately.

There *are* some new sheets of paper pinned up, and oh, this is interesting. They appear to be campaign adverts for a new head huntsman, following the death of the last one. Gretel can't make out from the Mirror's image whether all the posters are for the same candidate, or whether they're identical-looking posters for several different candidates. Considering that all huntsmen wear expressionless white porcelain masks and never use their real names, it's anybody's guess.

'They're going to have an election,' says Patience.

'That's good for us, isn't it?' asks Gretel. 'We were wondering when our chance would come to make a change… surely this means it's now?'

Patience shakes her head thoughtfully. 'I don't know. These things are weighted to keep all of the decision-making in the hands of the huntsmen. Certainly, all the candidates will be high-ranking huntsmen – as bad as each other. There is one significant upside right now, but Snow isn't going to like it.'

Snow gives the Ghost an eyebrow.

'They're in disarray,' Patience continues. 'The fact that they're having an election means that there's no clear candidate to lead, otherwise he'd have just swept in and taken over already, like the last one did. If you wanted to strike the Citadel now, they're at their weakest...'

'So are we.'

'We just liberated a village, and saved Darkwood from the brink of destruction.'

'Yes. One village. This would be different. I keep saying we need more allies.'

'We'd *have* more allies if you revealed yourself as the lost princess; the rightful heir.'

Snow scoffs. In fairness, Patience *had* warned Snow that she wasn't going to like it.

'People still have fond memories of the royal family,' Patience persists. 'A lot of the ordinary people would follow you if they knew who you are, and believed they could bring back the crown.'

'Old people,' snaps Snow. 'Everyone who looks back fondly on having a king and queen is a wrinkly, and I am not getting a load of grannies killed in battle just so that I can sit in a shiny chair.'

'We're not necessarily talking about a physical battle,' interjects Gretel. She can feel this one turning into yet another long argument that ends up going nowhere and wastes yet more time.

'*I* was,' counters Patience. She flings a fork onto the floor telekinetically, in direct contravention of the house rules re haunting. 'We can't just sit here! They'll only get more powerful again!'

'Some of us would *really* like to get out of this forest,' adds Jack. He looks across at Gretel meaningfully.

'We can come up with a way that doesn't risk lives,' says Gretel. 'Surely the least we can do is go north, talk to the witches there. You did say you wanted to get rid of the huntsmen for good,' she reminds Snow quietly.

'And I'm *going* to! Would you all just get off my case?'

'Snow,' calls Buttercup after her, but Snow is already on her feet and stomping to the door, Dwarves skittering along behind her.

She slams the door behind her, leaving Dwarf hair and water everywhere, as well as an awkward silence.

After a moment, the silence is broken by the Mirror.

'She forgot me again, didn't she?'

2
Over There Be Monsters, Too

Past the trees and over the bridge in Nearby, life is getting back to not-quite-normal. The buildings that were wrecked by the huntsmen's siege weapons have almost been fixed. Enough food resources have been salvaged to last them through the rapidly approaching winter. They all miss Gretel, of course, but at least now they know she's doing OK, and at least they all got to see her again at the party.

All of them, except one.

Gretel's twin brother Hansel spent the whole of the celebrations unconscious in bed, and continues to be extremely unhappy about this fact. The rest of the village are sympathetic, of course, and curse the huntsmen's cruelty for drugging Hansel into a comatose state when the battle to liberate Nearby had begun.

In truth, Hansel was never drugged. In truth, Hansel is a witch with incredibly potent powers that he can barely control when he gets too upset, and he found the battle for Nearby very upsetting indeed. In truth, the churning ground and grasping shadows in the village square that proved the last straw for many of the occupying huntsmen, and which had been attributed to either Gretel or a Darkwood resident, had actually been a manifestation of Hansel's distress. Releasing that much magical power in one go had overwhelmed his body, and sent him into thirty-five straight hours of unconsciousness to recover. Nobody in the village has been told that it was, in truth, Hansel who saved them all.

Hansel is OK with this. He is less OK with missing his twin sister's one visit to the village since she was drummed out by a huntsman, on suspicion of witchcraft.

'Are you all right?' asks his friend Daisy Wicker for the umpteenth time since the huntsmen left.

'Yep, of course,' he replies, and tries not to let his expression betray that he is still very much not all right.

They are on their way to the new trading post that was built at the border with the forest out of bits of wood from the old fence. The new friendship, possibly even an alliance, with the Darkwood has had certain knock-on advantages. Trade is now possible with the forest, with villagers swapping medicines, books and various home comforts in return for rare fungi, fruits and herbs picked by the Darkwood's inhabitants. Today, Hansel and Daisy are taking winter woollens of various different sizes, including a couple of old horse blankets with holes cut in them, in the hope that the Ogres might be able to use them as sort of ponchos. When they get to the post, they find that somebody from the forest has left a large quantity of ginger root, blackberries and aloe there, along with a few small particles of river gold.

'Gold, again,' mutters Daisy, swapping over the goods and packing the fresh produce into a basket. 'That'll be the Dwarves, apparently they love finding it. Gets them all excited. They nearly had my mum's ring off, at the... oh. Sorry.'

'No, it's all right,' Hansel tells her. 'You can talk to me about the party. It's fine, honestly.'

'It feels mean, after you missed Gretel.' She pauses, and Hansel knows what's coming next. 'You know, it should be safe for us in the woods. The beasties and witches are our friends now. They

21

wouldn't attack us. I was thinking, maybe we could be the ones to go and visit Gretel, this time?'

'I don't know, Daisy.'

'But we'd be fine!'

'Maybe *we* would, but… I don't know. If we went into the Darkwood, that would mean leaving the village undefended.'

'The whole village worked together to fend off the huntsmen last time,' Daisy argues. 'They'll be all right without us for a day. The huntsmen probably aren't even coming back, anyway. Gretel saw to that.'

'Hmm,' is Hansel's only reply. He doesn't tell her the real reason why he's too anxious to leave the village undefended.

He's been getting these dreams. Even as he'd lain unconscious after the battle, a terrible feeling had seeped into his sleeping mind that something really bad is approaching, something even worse than before. Since then, the dreams and the sense of dread have only become worse.

'Will you think about it?' Daisy asks, setting the jumpers and blankets out in a neat order of size. 'I think it would do you the world of good to get away for a bit. See Gretel. She's doing fine, you know. She told me she lives in a house that's mostly biscuits, so that's something interesting.'

'I already am thinking about it,' Hansel tells her gently. 'And mostly what I'm thinking is that it would still be a bad id— oh!'

'"A bad idoh"?' repeats Daisy. She turns, and sees that he has collapsed to his knees, clutching his head in clawed hands. 'Oh!' she cries. 'Hansel! What's wrong?'

What's wrong is that he has suddenly, from nowhere, been hit with a waking vision so strong and so terrible that it momentarily consumes him. He can neither stand, nor speak, nor think; he can barely even breathe. Thankfully, it stops moments later, before his magic has had the chance to slip from his control and burst out into the air and ground. Gasping, still grasping at his head, he blinks as his friend's concerned face flows back into his sight.

'Hansel, what happened?'

'I… er…' How can he tell her what he's just seen? How can he possibly explain it?

'Is it that Mirror again?'

'What?'

Daisy takes Hansel's elbow tenderly. 'When you were left in that cell with the magic Mirror, it talked to you. It showed you things.'

'Yes. But…'

'I know that the Mirror can form attachments to people – if it gets close to someone, it can create a magical link with them, even if they're at the other end of Myrsina.' Daisy pauses for a moment, proudly. 'Princess Snow told me that. She's really lovely, by the way. Very regal.'

'Yes, people keep telling me.' Hansel winces in the sunlight and tries to sit up properly. His sight is back to normal again now, but the magical vision has left him with a terrible headache. He wishes he could tell Daisy the truth. After all, he thinks to himself, Gretel always knew about his powers. She'd helped him to hide them, she'd been the one person he could talk to about it… and then, he reminds himself, she had taken the blame for the magical disturbances in the village and ended up hounded from the village by a huntsman.

No. He can't tell Daisy.

'So, is that what it was?' Daisy gazes at him earnestly.

'Mm?'

'The Mirror. Did it link with you, in the cell? Is it sending you warning visions, even though it's in the Darkwood?'

Hansel still squints at Daisy. She's really thought this one through already, hasn't she? He could explain away all of his magical premonitions by blaming them on the Mirror. Daisy couldn't have come up with a more convenient get-out clause for him if she'd tried.

'Um,' he says after a moment, 'um, yeah, maybe? I think it could be?'

Daisy's eyes light up. 'I *knew* it! I knew Gretel would find a way to make sure we could get messages from the Mirror! What did it show you?'

'It's not good...'

'The village?' asks Daisy. 'Are the huntsmen going to attack us again?'

Hansel shakes his head. 'It wasn't the village. It was the Citadel.'

'*We* were attacking the Citadel?'

'Not us. A monster, though.'

'So, the Darkwood was taking down the Citadel.' Daisy rubs his arms. 'Hansel, that's good! It showed us winning!'

Hansel shakes his head again, recalling the horrible vision. A huge beast, a Hydra, storming through the Citadel's streets. Ordinary civilians running and hiding. People trampled under its huge feet, snatched up in its many jaws. Blood and screams and pain and grief... It doesn't feel like winning. It feels like a catastrophe, something that must be stopped. He can still feel echoes of that crushing terror from all those people in the vision. So many people.

'How many live in the Citadel, Daisy?'

Daisy ponders this. Unlike Hansel, she's actually been to the Citadel, selling baskets at the craft market. 'Ten thousand?' she hazards. 'Thereabouts?'

'Ten thousand people.' Hansel can't even imagine ten thousand people; the biggest place he's ever been to was Ham, when his step-parents bought a new thresher a few years back, and he'd been so unnerved by the clatter of hundreds of boots and horseshoes on the cobbled street that he'd ended up spending most of the trip hiding in the cart. Yes, the Mudd twins were raised by both a stepmother and a stepfather. Hansel's never bothered to ask about birth parents or how the whole 'two step-parents' thing actually works. There's never seemed to be much point, since they all love one another anyway. Mudd is, after all, thicker than water.

'What I was shown was a warning,' he tells Daisy. 'We can't just leave ten thousand people to the terrible fate I saw.'

'Hansel, are you seriously saying…?'

'Yep,' Hansel tells her. 'I think… I think we need to go to the Citadel. We need to help them.'

3

And All That Other Bit Be Monsters as Well

Snow's latest strop is mercifully short-lived. She returns after half an hour or so, to Buttercup's coos of soft concern and offerings of scones. As Gretel had been expecting, Snow makes no mention of the argument that had preceded her walking out, nor of the fact that she had clearly forgotten the Mirror and needed to come back for that anyway. Gretel had not, however, been expecting Snow to demand to see the map again, or ask to see Gretel's ideas for an excursion north if they were to leave, say, tomorrow at dawn.

Gretel unfolds the map of Darkwood drawn up for her by Snow's birds. No matter how many times she uses it, she's never quite prepared for just how bad it smells. Everyone reels away from the stench of it, with the exception of Snow, who is very used to the stink, and Patience, whose sense of smell died with the rest of her.

The map is full of messily drawn details of the forest's southwest corner, but to the north and east is a blank.

Patience leans in, a piece of charcoal telekinetically raised next to her.

'OK,' she says, 'so, the huntsmen's scout parties weren't able to chart the forest's interior anywhere near as well as you have, but there are a few bits I can add from what maps of theirs I saw in my old life.'

The charcoal draws a jagged line along the top of the paper.

'The Great Mountains are up here. Nobody ever really bothers with them. All just snow, goats and collapsed mineshafts.'

The charcoal draws a wavier line down until it bisects where Nearby Village and the Darkwood's border are marked out.

'This is Nearby's river. Comes down from Bear Mountain.'

'Bear Mountain?' asks Gretel.

'Yep.' The charcoal draws a particularly large mountain shape at the start of the river's line. 'This bad boy. The huntsmen know about it because it's a biggie, you can see it all the way from Slate, but they never actually explored it, because...' Here, the charcoal draws another line from north to south, meandering over the river's line several times until it finally joins the birds' marking for the forest's boundary. Patience points at the marking for Bear Mountain, on the 'forest' side of the boundary line.

'It's in Darkwood,' murmurs Gretel.

'I stayed near Slate once,' offers Jack. 'Just for a bit. Back before I escaped into Darkwood.'

'So, while you were on the run from angry Giants, with your ill-gotten gains?' asks Patience.

Jack shoots them all a guilty smile. 'Yeah. Then. Anyway, there was a lot of talk about bear raids in the villages north of Slate. But that wasn't all. There were other stories about different creatures, stalking the mountain villages at night.'

'The wolves?' asks Trevor, gently swaying over the map on a thread of webbing, like a little leggy pendulum.

'Not just wolves.' Jack pauses with a little dramatic flourish and then says in a flamboyantly spooky voice, 'Werewolves.'

Gretel nods. 'Right, so we've gone from a bear witch and a wolf witch to a gang of bear raiders, actual Werewolves and a crow the size of a man, all apparently hiding out on a scary mountain together?'

'I did say they were best left alone, dear,' says Buttercup.

'No, I meant it in a good way,' says Gretel brightly. 'Guys. Werewolves! A gang of criminal bears! A massive crow! Imagine having magical assets like *those* on our team!'

She looks around at the others. Her smile freezes when she notices how hurt they all look.

'What's wrong with *our* magical assets?' asks Trevor.

'Oh! Nothing, of course…'

'Well, you don't have any, technically,' says Jack.

'Er, excuse you! I'm a *spider* and can *talk*.'

'Some of us can grow whole trees,' argues Jack.

'Oh wow, what an amazing and rare power. Trees. Yeah, you don't see many of *those* round here, not like talking spiders, which are ten a penny, obviously.'

'Yeah, and I can do all telekinesis and stuff since I died,' adds Patience.

Even Snow looks mildly defensive. 'I controlled an otter the other day.' She pauses, glaring around the room. 'It was pretty big.'

'Hmm,' manages Buttercup, looking down at her hands. She's managed to turn her own bit of charcoal into an éclair. She pushes it away.

Gretel sighs internally. 'Look, you're all great and powerful witches, OK? With a terrifying Ghost and a talking spider super-spy. You never know – they might all be up their spooky mountain right now too worried to come and make contact with us because they think *we're* too scary.'

Trevor raises a foreleg. 'Er, that's a point, actually. People are always saying "ooh, spiders are more scared of you than you are of them", and it's true, we are. Maybe they're like spiders. You know – adorable and friendly, like.'

Buttercup still looks worried. 'You're saying a *Werewolf* is like a spider?'

'Maybe! We haven't met one yet!' Gretel smiles brightly around the kitchen. 'So, what do we all reckon?'

Jack leans back in his chair. 'You've already decided we're all going, haven't you?'

'Absolutely not!'

'But Mum! I said I'd go!'

Ethel Wicker glares up from her weaving. 'You are fourteen, Daisy my girl; you are *not* going on a mysterious mission to the Citadel of all places!'

'It's not like I haven't been there before,' argues Daisy.

'Yeah – before the Citadel's huntsmen invaded the village, locked us up and nearly burned you alive.'

'Exactly, Mum. I got through all of that just fine. I can get through a quick trip to scope out the situation over there.'

'And what if they recognise you? You're not exactly in their good books, are you?'

'They won't recognise me.' Daisy pauses, thinking. 'I'll disguise myself. I'll wear a hat.'

'For the last time, Daisy, that spider friend of yours is not the aficionado on espionage that he makes himself out to be – hats only draw even more attention.'

'A hood, then.' Daisy folds her arms. 'I'm going, Mum. We have to. Hansel was sent a vision from the Mirror.'

Behind Daisy, Hansel gives Ethel Wicker an awkward little smile. 'Sorry again about all this, Mrs Wicker.'

'But the Mirror wants you to actually *protect* the Citadel? After what they did?'

'The Citadel's not just huntsmen,' says Hansel quietly. 'I think if I've been warned about an attack, maybe it's my duty to go.'

'Besides,' says Carpenter Fred, from the doorway, 'you can't just condemn all of the huntsmen just because they're huntsmen.'

'I can and I will, Carpenter Fred,' snaps Mrs Wicker. 'Question is, why won't you? They took the whole village! Smashed up the windmill! Separated us into work teams and – and I can't believe

I'm having to bring this up yet again – tried to murder Gretel Mudd and my Daisy!'

'Yes, I *was* there, and that was definitely going too far, but we dealt with it, and we can't have it going too far the other way.'

Mrs Wicker puts down her weaving. Daisy and Hansel instinctively take a step back.

'Our Gretel still can't come home, Freddery, and the huntsmen are still in charge. How exactly is any of that even in danger of "going too far the other way"?'

'I just don't want us going like Ashtrie did,' says Fred.

'Nobody even mentioned Ashtrie!'

'Yeah, well,' mutters Fred. 'I'm just saying. Not all huntsmen are like that.'

'Do you want this basket or not, Freddery?'

Fred pauses. 'Yes'm.'

'Do you think it might be an idea to go and wait for it somewhere quietly instead of telling us your opinions about how we should be nicer to the people who tried to kill our girls?'

'…Yes'm.'

Carpenter Fred shuffles away. Mrs Wicker shakes her head, and then takes up the weaving again. 'To be fair to him, it was horrible what happened in Ashtrie, but that don't mean the huntsmen are any better or deserve the benefit of the doubt.'

'What *did* happen in Ashtrie?' asks Daisy.

'Nothing that matters any more,' her mother tells her. 'What matters is the here and now, and the huntsmen have gone back to leaving us alone, and—'

'And that could all change again, if the Mirror's warning comes true,' argues Daisy. 'We saw how they reacted when one huntsman was killed in the Darkwood; what do you suppose would happen if a monster came and actually attacked them, in their base? Killed loads of them – killed civilians, too? How do you reckon the huntsmen would respond to *that*? What they'd do to the Darkwood, to our new friends, and Gretel, and the princess…'

30

Mrs Wicker presses her hand to her chest with a small sigh. 'Oh, that poor princess. You should have seen her, Hansel, she was so... *regal*.'

The very regal Princess Snow is busy picking a really good scab out from under her tangled hair by the time Gretel comes downstairs at dawn with her knapsack packed for the excursion north.

'Everyone ready?'

'Hang on,' says Buttercup. 'Just showing Henrietta the ropes.' She points to a series of cords bolted to the ceiling. 'And finally, Henrietta, these are the ropes. Please don't touch them, at the moment they're all that's keeping the chimney on.'

Henrietta, a pleasant piebald Centaur, frowns. 'Why's your chimney falling apart?'

'It's currently mostly Battenberg,' admits Buttercup. 'Long story. Thanks again for agreeing to Mirror-sit.'

'This is humiliating,' complains the Mirror. 'I used to be king!'

'And now you're a large, breakable household object that we can't possibly take on an expedition,' Snow tells it gently. 'You can't even show us the mountains, you get too fuzzy.'

'I think it's the altitude,' mutters the Mirror. 'But I can be useful in other ways.'

'You're no use to any of us smashed,' says Snow. She lays a hand on it. 'Especially after I only just got you back, Dad. Stop being silly.'

'I love you too, poppet.'

'Aww,' coos Buttercup.

Snow huffs at her.

'What?' Buttercup asks. 'It's sweet.' She boops Snow on the nose – a small gesture that would likely have resulted in anybody else losing their booping finger. Instead, Snow bites down a smile and boops her back.

They leave Henrietta clopping around a kitchen that was not even remotely designed with somebody of Centaur proportions in mind. As they shut the door, they hear the clatter of her accidentally knocking her haunch against a work surface and sending pans flying.

'Trousers,' comes the muffled voice from within. 'Sorry!'

'Couldn't have chosen someone with only four limbs to housesit, then, Buttercup?' asks Jack, already waiting for them outside.

'Henrietta's nice,' replies Buttercup, with a worried backward glance towards the cottage. 'I can trust her to remember to put the bins out of a Monday.'

'Besides which,' adds Trevor from Buttercup's hair, 'limb numbers are *not* a good indicator of ability, and I would thank you to avoid passing such bigoted comments on the matter in future.'

'Sorry, Trevor.'

Patience manifests next to them. 'Aren't you always making fun of that spider in the bracken with the seven legs, though, Trevor?'

'Because he's a bore,' replies Trevor, 'not because his leg's off. Can't even say how he lost it! Just wants to spin bigger webs than me. I hate that guy.'

Snow affixes the last of her many, many axes and gives the Dwarves a quick headcount.

'All accounted for. Off we go! You've got the map, New Girl.'

Gretel gets out the smelly map, and her compass. She should at least be able to plot out a route for the first few hours of the hike, before the information on the map comes to an abrupt stop. She sighs at the blank section of the map.

'Here be monsters,' she mutters.

'Everywhere be monsters, potentially,' adds Jack. 'It all just depends on who you ask.'

Gretel watches the others head off into the woods – Dwarves using their long, sharp claws to clamber through the branches, Patience simply fading through trees rather than go around them, Snow hacking at foliage with one of her axes, so that Buttercup won't get her hair or the talking spider in it tangled with twigs. 'Yeah,' she says, 'fair enough.'

4
Into the Unknown

'Didn't I tell you? Didn't I say that all we'd have to do to make Mum change her mind was mention the chance that the princess might end up in danger?'

Hansel shifts the weight of his side of the cart to the other hand again. 'I didn't ever say that that wouldn't work. Just… I wish we didn't need to.'

'As far as means to an end go, invoking our parents' weird devotion to the royals so that they'll let us potentially save thousands of lives isn't that bad, is it?'

'Hmm.' The cart's wheel hits a loose stone on the road, which Hansel has to kick away before they start lugging it onwards again. 'And why did we have to bring all these baskets, again?'

'To make us more inconspicuous.'

Hansel casts another glance at the hundred or so baskets stacked high onto the laden cart. It doesn't look particularly inconspicuous.

'We're going to look just like basket merchants, come to sell Mum's wares at the craft market.'

'Pretty sure at this point we *are* actually basket merchants, here to sell your Mum's stuff at the craft market.'

'Exactly! It's making Mum some money *and* it's a cast-iron disguise.'

'I thought your main disguise was that bonnet?'

Daisy grins at him proudly from the edge of her straw bonnet. As Mrs Wicker warned, it really does draw attention to her more than it hides her.

'They're *both* cast-iron disguises,' she says. 'Or, one's iron, one's carbon, and together they make for a steel disguise.'

They trundle the cart along some more.

'Because steel's an iron-carbon alloy,' she adds.

'Yes.'

'And it's stronger than iron. Oh, listen to me, rattling on about the relative tensile strengths of different metals and alloys, like me and Gretel used to do in the old days.'

Hansel shoots her a fond glance. 'It's fine. I like it. It's as if she's still around.'

'She'll be able to come home, some day.' Daisy's expression lights up. 'Maybe if we do manage to help the Citadel, we can get them to change their mind about witches and the Darkwood in general. It worked with the village.'

'That might be a bit of a big ask for just the two of us,' Hansel admits.

'I suppose. We had help from all witches and Ogres and so on back there. Pair of us don't even have any magical powers.'

Hansel furrows his brow. Not for the first time, he wishes he could tell her about his powers, but he doesn't speak up. Not yet. Not now. He needs the time to be right. Crucially, he needs to pluck up more courage than he currently has.

'And we need to concentrate on beating this Hydra I saw.'

'Also, selling all these baskets,' Daisy adds. 'Ideally, Mum would like us to make her a profit of a hundred silvers on this lot.'

'So we talked her from not letting you go at all into making her a load of money? And they say *you're* the clever one.'

'Oh, Mum's shrewd. I thought that was a given. But she *is* also making sure the village defences are covered, as well as your chores on the farm, so it's probably the least we can do. Anyway, these are really nice baskets. The Citadel guards will be expecting us to do well at market, so it's all part of the disguise.'

Hansel smiles again. 'As well as the bonnet.'

Daisy nods. 'As well as the bonnet. Hats are underrated disguises.'

'You really did bond with that weird little spider the other week, didn't you?'

'Oh, Trevor's great.' Daisy beams. 'Present company excepted, I think he might be one of my favourite people.'

'Somebody's talking about me.'

'Nobody's talking about you, Trevor.'

'Yes they are, I can sense it in my knees.'

'Your knees?'

'I have magically attuned legs. Probably from hanging out with you weirdos so much.'

'And you just use your magic legs for sensing when you're being talked about?' asks Jack.

'And other disturbances,' Trevor tells Jack from his comfortable perch on Buttercup's shoulder. 'My legs were able to sniff out the Mirror. And Hansel. And... ooh. Something here. We just went over a line.'

Jack looks down. 'Nope. Nothing here.'

'Actually,' says Gretel, looking at the map, 'he's right.'

Snow takes the map from her for a moment. 'We just passed the most northerly point where my birds were willing to fly.' She points at a blank section of the map. 'This is us, right?'

'Right.'

'Officially in the northern witches' territory,' mutters Buttercup warily.

Gretel looks around herself. It's still the same old Darkwood, as far as she can see. 'Not exactly the great unknown, is it?'

Snow whistles a few notes. There's a rustling from the canopy above their heads and the thicket beyond their feet. A couple of wood pigeons flutter down to a low branch, and a rat pokes its head out of a bush, to regard them with wary, beady eyes. The creatures don't seem as docile as any that Gretel's seen under

35

Snow's command before. These animals are skittish and fidgety. After a moment, the pigeons flap away again, and the rat scurries back under a root.

'They're resisting me here,' says Snow quietly. 'They're too nervous to let me in. Their fear of predators is too strong; it overpowers everything else, even me.'

'Snow.' Buttercup looks aghast. 'Your magic doesn't work here?'

Snow looks faintly embarrassed. 'Well…'

Jack's eyes widen. 'What if *none* of our magic works in other witches' territory?'

'How would that even make sense?' asks Gretel.

Shakily, Jack tries his power out, flourishing a hand and curling up his fingers as if pulling an invisible rope from the ground. A stem sprouts from the undergrowth at his command, erupts to a good three feet and then unfurls fat fern fronds.

'Oh,' says Jack.

Buttercup picks up a pebble. It instantly turns into a cherry Bakewell.

'Well, I never.'

'I did just say that it wouldn't make sense if none of your powers worked,' says Gretel, aware that at this point she's being ignored, as is usually the case when she breaks out the 'I told you so's.

A branch spins violently past everybody's feet.

'I can still do telekinesis,' announces Patience.

'Peter Piper picked a peck of pickled peppers,' says Trevor. 'Yep, still able to talk. Betty bought a bit of butter.'

'So it's only you who's been… magically neutralised, Snow,' frets Buttercup. 'Oh, Snow, you poor thing. That's not fair.'

'Betty said, "This butter's bitter."'

'I'm not "neutralised", for pity's sake! The animals are just all wrong here.'

'"If I put it in my batter, it will make my batter bitter".'

'I'm still absolutely fine,' argues Snow. 'Still got my lads.'

'Yummy…' mumbles one of the Dwarves anxiously, and Gretel notices for the first time that even those usually carefree and ferocious creatures look on edge in this part of the forest.

'So Betty bought a better bit of butter…'

'Still got my axes,' continues Snow, holding one of her many blades aloft, 'and Trevor, would you stop that now? We get it, you can talk. Kindly do so a little less, for the sake of my sanity and everyone's safety.'

Trevor pauses sulkily.

'…which made her bitter batter better,' he murmurs.

'I'm fine,' Snow tells them all. 'And it isn't so bad out here, is it? It's just another load of cursed forest, like we deal with every day. Nothing's changed, not really.' She clears her throat. 'And we're still hours away from Bear Mountain, so we should push on.' She glares at Trevor, who is now waving a foreleg aloft, and sighs. 'Yes, Trevor?'

'My knees are still tingling.'

'Well, I'm sure whoever's talking about you must have a lot to say.'

'It might not be that, though,' Trevor adds. 'It might mean… trouble.'

Snow rolls her eyes. 'Come on.'

Gretel locks gazes with Trevor as they all push ahead through the forest. 'It'll be fine.'

'You always say that,' Trevor tells her, 'and sometimes, it isn't fine.'

'Well, it will be fine this time.'

They continue heading north.

High up in the branches above where they'd been standing, something rustles amongst the leaves. Something big. Very, very big indeed. Foliage scatters to the ground, boughs creak, and a giant mass of sleek, oil-black feathers takes off into the sky, following them at a leisurely pace with great flaps of almighty, inky wings.

5
Such Big Teeth

Gretel adds to the map as they go, filling in the blank area with natural and magical landmarks. There are fewer small magical creatures in the north, she notes, but besides that, the northern woods reassuringly continue much the same as 'her' part of the forest. She is struck by the fact that, over only a couple of months, the Darkwood has gone from being a foreboding place that must be fenced off and guarded against, to being something almost normal, almost like home.

As ordinary as this part of the woods seem, still the Dwarves appear uneasy. She speeds up her pace to catch up with Snow, in the front.

'What's up with the Dwarves?' she asks.

'Same as the pigeons and rats,' Snow tells her.

'They're scared of predators, too?' Gretel asks. 'But they're not even that bothered by the Bin Men.'

'They're *used* to the Bin Men,' Snow explains. 'They know how to avoid them. This is different. They can smell something new and they don't like it. Oi!' She kicks away a Dwarf trying to cling anxiously to her leg. 'I already told you, I'm not carrying you, mate.'

The Dwarf growls.

'Oh, stop whining. People are going to think you're a cowardy-custard.'

The Dwarf snarls and spits through razor teeth.

'Pack it in. We're nowhere near Bear Mountain still, this is just more forest, it's not like anything's going to happen now…'

'Oh, don't say that,' mutters Trevor from Buttercup's hair, behind them.

'What now?' Snow groans.

'It's tempting fate, dear,' Buttercup tells her gently. 'It's never a good idea to tempt fate, especially in a cursed forest.'

'Yeah, trust someone who's done a fair amount of haunting,' Patience adds. 'If I were about to jump out and shout "boo", I'd definitely do it at the exact moment some Smart Herbert went "I'm telling you, there's no such thing as Ghosts".'

'Nothing's going to happen!'

'Stop it, Snow,' chimes in Jack.

'For crying out *loud*, guys!'

Even Gretel, for all her love of science, has to admit that in the current magical landscape, fortuity counts for a lot, and that Snow is definitely pushing it right now.

'Snow… we can't know who's listening, right now.'

Gretel also has to admit that implying to Snow that she should maybe stop doing something is a huge mistake, since it will only make her do it more. Princesses.

'You as well, New Girl? Little Miss "Everything's Probably Going to Be Fine"? I thought I could at least count on you to be rational. I'm a hunter. I'm used to being out on my own in the wilderness, I'm massively attuned to these woods, and I say…' She blinks. 'Oh, fruit. Yeah, something's definitely about to launch a stealth attack on…'

Suddenly, noise and movement burst out everywhere around them. Big things – the size of adult humans from the sounds of cracking wood and trampled leaves, but much faster – surround them, still unseen amongst the foliage, both on land and up in the branches.

'Yummy,' snarls the Dwarf that had been trying to climb Snow, its voice dripping with resentment.

'Oh, don't you start!' snaps Snow.

A large grey wolf leaps from the darkness of the trees, teeth bared, powering towards the group, all sharpness and sleek muscles. In the space of a breath, Snow drops and rolls, drawing an axe in each hand as she goes, the Dwarves scattering and grasping at their own blades at her cue.

Gretel's mind whirls. She hasn't come unarmed, but her portable propulsion device is still in her backpack, and isn't really a melee weapon, anyway. In the split second that sees the wolf still sailing in one great bound towards them, her brain presents to her another option – the dynamo-on-a-stick idea she had once crafted out of an electrical torch to rescue Jack from Swamp Mermaids. The zap from its charged wires wouldn't incapacitate a wolf as it had the smaller, slimy Mermaids, but it would give it a nasty sting, possibly enough to drive it back. Unfortunately, the dynamo-on-a-stick is also in the backpack. She tells herself that if she survives this ambush, the lesson to take from it will definitely be 'always have a melee weapon to hand when you're trudging around in wolf territory and the princess you're with keeps loudly tempting fate'.

The space of that single gasp of breath continues, the wolf still leaping, Snow and the Dwarves still rolling and sprouting axe blades, Gretel frozen with no means of self-defence to hand. There is a heavy step behind her, of someone lunging forwards. It's Jack, his hands clenched outwards. His shoulder slams into hers and she loses balance. She topples, and as she falls, she sees a line of gorse spring up between them and the airborne wolf.

The wolf hits the thorny bush. It yelps. Gretel herself cries out as she hits the ground hard on her side.

Snow spins, a throwing axe already poised over a shoulder.

'Behind you,' she shouts to Buttercup, who instinctively ducks.

Snow's throwing axe whirls gracefully over Buttercup's head, and then not quite so gracefully goes straight through Patience and wings a second wolf, emerging from the thicket.

'Fruit.' Snow reaches for a new axe at another cracking sound from the thicket. 'It's a whole pack of them.'

Cursing and winded, Gretel fumbles in her bag for her dynamo-on-a-stick. Two more wolves leap from the undergrowth simultaneously. Jack pushes a fist out again, and a poison oak erupts into sudden existence. One wolf hits its head on it, and three of the Dwarves scramble up its boughs, issuing sharp 'yummy's of pain as they go, to throw sharp flints down at the other beast.

Gretel is finally able to yank the dynamo-on-a-stick from her bag. She rolls up onto her knees, furiously winding up the dynamo. It's still only half-charged when another creature comes crashing out of the trees, practically on top of her. Still winding, she looks up at the beast looming over her. Such big eyes, such big teeth and oh *trousers*, that's not even a wolf at all.

'Bear,' Gretel manages, her voice tight.

Her half-wound dynamo still clasped in her hand, she wonders if it's worth even trying to use it against this huge brown bear, should it take a swipe at her. Thankfully, the bear doesn't try to attack. Instead it stands over her, watching her with its huge, dark eyes, muzzle curled up slightly against its massive teeth, its breath hot and stinking. Gretel shuffles back a little on her knees, feels a hand clutch at her shoulder. It's Buttercup. She helps Gretel to her feet.

'You stay away,' warns Buttercup, brandishing a curiously knife-shaped pasty at the bear.

'Really wasn't worth you packing a weapon, was it?' mutters Gretel.

Buttercup shakes her head. 'I did try to say so at the time, dear.'

'They've stopped attacking,' says Patience. 'Why have they stopped attacking?'

'Maybe,' suggests Trevor, cheerfully, 'they can see they're outnumb— oh hang on, no, wait.'

The four wolves have started circling them slowly. Out of the thicket prowls a fifth wolf, far bigger than the others, with bright red fur. It is joined by a second bear, which draws itself up to its hind legs, watching them. Above, there is something in the branches, a huge, black shape that Gretel can't make out. These animals may be just about outnumbered but they are in no way outmatched. They are, right now, the ones in charge.

'What do you suppose they want?' Jack asks the others. 'Besides, you know. Dinner.'

Still, the animals circle, and watch.

'We're the witches of the south-western territory,' Snow announces to the menacing menagerie. 'I'm the White Knight, you may have heard of me, these are my lads...'

'...yummy...'

'These guys are Buttercup of the cake cottage, Jack Trott the so-called Giant Killer, but he's been exonerated of that, before you start...'

'I mean, why did you even have to bring it up?' complains Jack softly.

'...The little scruffy one's actually the Mudd Witch, they say she's pretty powerful, and we've also got a Ghost and Trevor, who is a magical talking spider.'

'How do?' asks Trevor from the safety of Buttercup's hair.

'We've come into the northern wood to offer an allegiance. The whole of Darkwood has been put under threat recently. We believe that the forest would be stronger and safer if we worked together.' She pauses, watching the circling animals. 'What say you?'

A voice comes from somewhere in the murky undergrowth, unseen. It's thin, female, delicate and frail, and speaks using odd, old-fashioned terms.

'I say beat it, lady, if ye please.'

The animals growl and snarl. Snow scrunches up her face.

'Aww, but we came all this way. Come on, what's an invisible territory line in the forest between fellow witches?'

'Beat it, I said! This is our patch, and we don't be wanting not none of your reckless battle with the outsiders around thisaways, sure as taters ain't turnips.'

'*Our* reckless battle?' Jack calls incredulously. 'I think you'll find they started it.'

A second voice speaks up. This one is younger, and male, and, for as yet unknown reasons, coming from the high branches.

'Didn't *you* start it all, Jack Trott? With the Giants?'

'No! Turns out it was all the huntsmen, the Mirror said so, there was a whole thing!'

The wolves start circling a little closer.

'Admittedly,' adds Jack, 'you guys didn't see that, but the White Knight did just tell you about my exoneration only a couple of minutes ago. Er. Could we maybe speak with the actual people here, and not a load of creepy voices while wolves make faces at us? Feels a bit one-sided.'

'You're trespassers here, mister,' says the first voice. 'We're just asking you very sweetly to vamoose.'

'"Very sweetly?"' echoes Snow. 'You set wolves on us!'

'And you brought a whole hill of naughty axes,' says the first voice.

'What, these little things?'

'Wait,' says the second voice, from up in the trees, 'where's the Ghost?'

Gretel clutches at her dynamo-on-a-stick. Here they go, then, with Operation 'Keep Them Talking Until Patience is Able to Fade to Nothing and Then Take Them By Surprise'. It's a fairly simple plan that they hashed out during the trek, in the event that the northern witches proved violently uncooperative. Had she known just how early into the voyage north they'd need it, she wouldn't have put off coming up with a better name for it.

Patience suddenly appears out of nowhere in the middle of the wolves.

'Boo!'

The wolves yelp with alarm and all but the ginger one cringe back.

Yeah, in retrospect, as plans go, this isn't a particularly elegant one. Perhaps it never really deserved a better name after all.

Snow takes advantage of the moment of fear and confusion in the beasts. She takes a step in the direction the first voice was coming from.

'Show yourself! We just want to talk! We come in peace!'

'You're still holding two axes, lady!'

Snow looks down at the large axes in her hands. 'Oh yeah…'

'Phooey, you're all flannel. No deal!'

The bears, clearly less spooked out by Ghosts than wolves are, take lumbering steps towards the group. The group scatters out of the way of the bears. One of the bears tries chasing after the Dwarves, which, even with the Dwarves in their unusual state of high anxiety, turns out to be a bad idea. The Dwarves scrabble over one another in a snarling, spitting, toothy confusion, leaving the bear swiping at empty space near the ground.

The other bear goes for Gretel. She's able to very courageously and gracefully squeak 'nope' and duck sideways out of the way just before it's on her. She tries to turn and run, but the ginger wolf is worryingly close in the other direction. The bear raises a paw. Gretel screws her eyes shut and makes a swipe with the dynamo-on-a-stick. The exposed electrical wires push into the soft carpet of fur on the bear's belly. There are sparks, the sound of an electrical charge and the smell of burning fur. Gretel opens her eyes again. The bear is just staring down at the dynamo as it makes a small burnt patch on its belly. The bear looks across at her. It doesn't look in pain, or in any way incapacitated. What it looks to be is simply annoyed.

Ah.

So, that didn't work either, then.

Still locked into eye contact with the bear, Gretel wonders what to do next.

She starts by saying, 'Sorry.'

It doesn't have much effect.

Luckily, at that moment, an unseasonal rose bush grows between herself and the bear, and as the bear wrestles with the unexpected thorns, a cheese scone hits it on the nose.

Jack grabs Gretel's shoulder and drags her back into the tighter huddle with himself and Buttercup, away from the bear.

'Maybe if we keep them running around for a while, we can tire them out,' suggests Trevor, from Buttercup's shoulder. 'It's getting close to winter, they'll want to hibernate, won't they?'

'Not from running around a clearing for a few minutes, they won't,' replies Gretel. 'And anyway, you know what they need to do before hibernating? Eat. Loads.'

'Uh oh,' says Trevor. 'I don't want Buttercup to get eaten.'

'Why would it be eating *me*?' Buttercup protests.

'I just don't think bears really bother with spiders, mate. Lots more meat on mammals.'

'But it shouldn't be *me* in particular.'

'A man-eating animal would absolutely go for you first, Buttercup,' calls Snow as she fends off the ginger wolf with an axe. 'I'm covered in metal, Jack and Gretel are all skin and bones, Patience is incorporeal. You're all succulent; it's a no brainer.'

'Oh, well, thank you very much!'

'Don't worry.' Snow flings another axe, missing a wolf that had been creeping up behind Buttercup by inches, and sending it yelping back. 'I'll protect you.' Snow goes back to exchanging swipes with the ginger wolf, although, Gretel notes, neither of them actually makes contact with the other.

'Don't get us wrong, we don't want to hurt you,' calls the woman's voice from the undergrowth, 'but sure as heads gots skulls, we will if we have to.'

'Ditto,' shouts Snow.

'We just want you to get gone to your own bit of the forest.'

'There might not *be* a bit of the forest to call "ours" or "yours" for much longer, if we don't start working together,' replies Gretel.

'Horsefeathers,' cries the woman's voice. 'This is your fight and your worry; we've headaches of our own.'

'And we can help you with those headaches,' calls Gretel. 'That's what working together means. It's not just one-sided.'

'Help us?' replies the voice. 'Don't nobody want to help *us*.'

The bears start approaching the huddle in earnest now, the wolves circling, all of them very conspicuously leaving one path open to the group – the path south-west, back to 'their bit' of the forest.

'Leave!' cries the woman's voice.

The crackling of twigs overhead increases and down from the upper branches of the trees swoops a *thing*, black and huge, the size of a man, with a wingspan of at least ten feet. It screams at them, a terrible, throaty, rasping cry, and bears down with massive, sharp beak and claws. It could easily kill any one of them from above, yet settles for a small swat at Jack's head with its beak, pecking out a thin chunk of hair.

'Ow! Trousers! What *was* that?'

'Leave!' the woman's voice repeats.

The circle of animals tightens, their pacing speeds up; the growls increase. All of the Dwarves have joined Gretel and the witches in the huddle, now. Frightened, they cringe and cling and clamber over Snow. The thing swoops down at them again, narrowly missing Jack's head.

'Argh! Why is it picking on *me*?'

'Leave!' cries the voice again. 'Hop it, skedaddle, before things start running crimson. You got no choice but to…'

But Gretel does have other options. The circling animals are close enough now for one of the little surprises hiding in her pocket to work. She leans slightly in to Trevor. 'Operation "Ow My Eyes",' she tells him quietly. 'Next time it swoops. Pass it on.'

The animals continue to circle. She quietly touches one of the little metal balls in her pocket.

There is a crack from the branches overhead. The thing swoops down.

Gretel hurls a metal ball to the ground between herself and the creatures. A flash-bomb – designed to create a temporarily blinding light as well as disorienting smoke and noise rather than to cause any actual injury. She closes her eyes against the flash, and hopes that Trevor's had the time to warn all the others to do the same. She can hear the animals roar and whine in confusion. Just to the side of her, she hears something large land on the ground with a soft yet heavy thump.

'Ow,' comes a male voice from the forest floor, 'my eyes!'

She opens her eyes, and looks in the direction of the voice. There is a man clutching his eyes as he writhes on the ground. He's possibly in his thirties and is naked, with the exception of a single dry leaf on a bit of string around his neck. There's something else not quite right about him, too, but in this split second, Gretel doesn't have the time to really think about anything other than her surprise at seeing a fully naked adult man where she'd expected a giant crow to be.

'Got him!' Jack shouts. Ivy creepers tangle around the strange man's ankles. At the same moment, Jack himself leaps at the man, pinning down his torso. 'Argh – naked, very naked.'

'Yield,' shouts Snow, pointing an axe blade at the groaning, unclothed stranger. 'We have your… wait, this isn't a crow.'

'*Raven*,' corrects the naked man, struggling against Jack and the ivy.

Patience manifests in front of the stranger, shards of flint hovering in the air around her, all pointed at the man. 'Whoever it is, we've got him. So, you know, yield.'

The wolves and bears paw at their eyes as their vision returns to them. They don't continue circling now. Most of them look cowed and unfocused. Only the ginger wolf steps forward. It lifts itself up onto its hind legs – a disconcerting sight in a quadruped of quite such an impressive size. Gretel watches in grim fascination as the beast shifts its centre of balance further and further back, lengthening out its spine until its hips click into an upright position. More discomfiting still, the wolf then lifts its front paws up over its eyes, presses its claws into its own scalp, and pushes.

6
Fur and Feathers

Everything that has been upsetting about the display from the ginger wolf so far turns out to have been a mere warm-up for the brief but deeply disturbing concert of pure 'oh sweet trousers, oh no, please just make it stop' that comes next. The wolf's fur easily slides right off its scalp as it pushes back with its forelegs, and begins to pool, ears and all, like a soft, heavy fabric around its neck.

Only then, suddenly... it *is* soft, heavy, red fabric. The wolf's paws lengthen and warp, its face flattens, the fur on its belly peels backwards to hang from its shoulders like a cape, its chest and legs change shape. All of this takes place within only a second or so, and sounds like a side of hog being skinned and deboned at the same time.

The moment passes, the sounds of wet meat cease, and standing in front of them is no longer a large, ginger wolf, but a large, ginger human, naked limbs poking out from beneath a faded red cape.

'The Werewolf,' breathes Gretel.

'That was really cool,' gasps Trevor.

'Naked, also naked,' Jack mutters, still on top of the strange man. 'Why is everyone here so naked?'

'Oh! Because we're transmorphers,' the ginger Werewolf tells him amiably. 'Only magical garments can change with us – come on, you've been living in the magical woods for years, how do you not even know that – can none of you transmorph?'

Snow draws herself up haughtily. 'Listen, Mr Werewolf...'

'*Miss* Werewolf.' The Werewolf shakes her long red locks free from the hood.

'There are plenty of other magical powers, you know, Miss Werewolf. Better ones.'

'Like the Mudd Witch's lightning?' The ginger woman rubs her eyes once more. 'Got to admit, we weren't expecting that. Anyway, if we yield, will you let Hex go? Poor thing.'

Gretel eyes the wolves and bears warily. They still seem unfocused. They mill about, huffing at one another. One of the wolves is licking its bum.

'Oh, they won't bother you,' the ginger woman tells them. 'Even if I was lying about yielding, which I'm not, they don't usually listen to me when I'm in this form. I'll prove it. Hey!' the half-naked woman shouts to the disorientated wolves. 'Roll over.'

None of them roll over.

The woman turns back to the group cheerfully. 'See?'

'Fine.' Snow lowers her axe, and Patience allows her halo of flint shards to drop through her onto the ground. The creepers rot from the naked man's ankles, and Jack gets off him, holding out a hand to help him up.

As the naked man rises from his awkward, pinned position, Gretel is finally able to properly see what it is about him that isn't quite right. It's his left arm... or, what should have been a left arm. It isn't there. In its place is a huge, black feathered wing, folded tightly against his side, as if its owner were self-conscious about it.

The others notice the wing at the same moment as Gretel.

'Oh!' says Jack. 'So you're the...'

'The raven, yes,' says the man, and Gretel recognises his voice as the same one that had spoken to them from high up in the branches.

Jack points at the wing. 'You've, er, missed a bit.'

'Um.' The man shuffles and rustles his feathers a little, shamefaced. 'Um, no. That's permanent. Sorry.'

'Don't apologise for *that*,' Buttercup and the ginger woman say to him in unison. Buttercup gently swats at Jack's arm. 'Jack! Say sorry!'

Jack holds up his hands, adopting his most Jackish 'who, me?' expression. 'I meant no offence. Having a wing actually sounds pretty cool, wouldn't mind having one myself.'

'Yes you would,' replies the man quietly.

Snow may have lowered her axe, but she still hasn't put it away. 'There was another one,' she says. 'The olde-worlde-sounding voice from the undergrowth. I'd really prefer to talk to all of you face to face. So I can keep an eye on all of you.'

The Werewolf sighs. 'Gilde,' she shouts into the trees, 'come out of there, please.'

'Can hear you all clear as bells from here,' calls back the light, fragile voice from the thicket. 'Don't see why little ole me should leave her cosy little spot.'

'Gilde, come on, please, you've got our clothes,' replies the ginger woman. 'It's freezing out here; magic cloaks are terrible at holding heat.'

There is a grumbling and a rustling from the thicket, and out into the clearing shuffles a tiny, white-haired woman, delicate as a porcelain figurine, and carrying a large bundle of scrunched-up clothes. She shoves one set gracelessly into the ginger woman's arms, and the rest at the man, glaring furiously at them both.

'Sorry, Gilde,' mutters the man, 'the Mudd Witch had these lightning things, and…'

'I know, Sweetiebird,' interrupts the woman addressed as Gilde, 'I seen it, don't I got peepers? Looks like we'll have to hear these trouble-stirrers out, with whatever hogwash hustle they've come up with this time.'

'"Trouble-stirrers"?' Buttercup gazes at Gilde, wide-eyed. 'We're not trouble-stirrers, we're defenders. Peacekeepers.'

'Oh, of course, lady. So what's the scheme you came all this way and went to all this hardknuckle to tell us?'

'We need to dismantle the huntsmen's power over the land,' Gretel tells her.

Gilde nods at them with an over-the-top sugariness. 'A coup.'

'Not necessarily a coup,' soothes Buttercup.

'Yes, necessarily a coup,' says Patience.

Gilde simpers at them all. 'Trouble-stirrers.'

Snow takes a step towards Gilde, extending a businesslike hand. 'Gilde... is it?'

'It is,' replies Gilde. 'And I'll thank you delightfully to put away the axe in your one hand if you're asking me to shake the other.' Behind her, a bear growls softly. 'It's OK, Mamma,' Gilde tells the bear, over her shoulder. 'I got the handle on this.'

Snow sheaths the axe, and extends her hand once more. 'It's a pleasure to meet the legendary Bear Witch of the mountains, after all this time.'

Gilde's already sarcastic-looking smile deepens. Actual dimples appear in her tissue-thin face. '"Legendary", my my.' She waves a hand dismissively in the direction of the ginger woman, who is mercifully getting into an undershirt and britches. 'Missy Werewolf here's called by name of Scarlett.'

'Don't worry,' Scarlett tells them, hurriedly pulling on a pair of woollen stockings, 'I don't bite. Well... not when I'm this shape, anyway.' She gives them a grin that's a little sharper than a human's should be.

'Even if she did bite you, it's not contagious,' explains the man, shivering as he struggles with one hand to get his misshapen clothes on over the giant wing. 'Turns out, lycanthropy's all inherited.' He pauses, and gives Buttercup a grateful little smile when she darts over to free a hem caught in his feathers. 'Found that out the scary way, eh, Scarlett?'

'I didn't bite you! You collided with my mouth and then went all screechy and panicky before I could explain it to you!'

51

The man looks to the others for sympathy. 'I thought I was going to end up a raven *and* a wolf, can you imagine?'

Gretel can't help but imagine a were-raven-wolf. More specifically, she can't help but imagine what it must be like to have one fly over you after it's digested a particularly big dinner. She shudders.

'The boy one is Hex,' continues Gilde.

'He's not a boy, Gilde, he's thirty-two.'

Gilde twinkles at Scarlett, then at the whole group. Being twinkled at by Gilde is not a particularly pleasant experience. 'Kiddiewinks, the lot of you.'

'To be honest,' Buttercup tells her, continuing to help dress the thirty-two-year-old raven-man as if he were an infant, 'it's nice to meet some older witches. We were all kids when the huntsmen took over Myrsina; we couldn't help but worry that all the adult ones had been… you know…' She trails off with a bizarre mime that Gretel assumes is supposed to represent being burned at the stake.

Gilde giggles. 'Oh, those guys aren't witches. Werewolves ain't witches, they're just Werewolves.'

Scarlett just shrugs.

'And Hex is merely cursed.'

'I'm not even from Myrsina,' Hex admits, tying up his britches shyly.

'I was going to say,' replies Snow. 'Your accent… Ashtrie, right?'

Hex continues to fumble with his fly. 'Yeah, the accent always gives it away. That and the fact that I'm cursed. Lots of people from Ashtrie are cursed. That's just… what happened.'

'What *did* happen?' asks Gretel.

'And why I've been out here since I was a mere slip of a wink myself, before any of your mammas were even born,' Gilde says, cutting Gretel short. 'Long afore the huntsmen. They never bothered with little ole me, up in the mountains. So, maybe all the adult witches in Myrsina *did* get… whatever it was you were acting out with your swell mime, there.'

Buttercup slumps. 'Oh.'

'Anyhoo!' Gilde adds, with a gratingly fake brightness. 'You wanted to have a proper parlay about your trouble-stirring plans, and my poor little bones get frightful cold out in this mean ole wind, so we'll be heading back to my place now. Too far to walk, so good thing for you I've got other arrangements. Can Miss Ghost transport?'

'As long as I know where I'm going,' replies Patience. She nods at the others. 'I can latch onto these guys because they were there when I died.'

'Reckoned so,' replies Gilde. She points to Gretel, Jack and Buttercup. 'You three can ride Papa.'

Gretel exchanges concerned expressions with the others. 'Papa…?'

'Papa.' Gilde jerks a thumb at the larger of the two bears. 'He can carry three like it's nothing, 'specially since your boy one's even more skin and gristle than ours is…'

'Hey,' mutters Jack reproachfully, but without any real conviction since she is, after all, correct.

'And what are you, little girl,' continues Gilde to Gretel, 'eight?'

'Thirteen!'

'Mercy.' Gilde shakes her head. 'Barely out of nappy-rags.' Gilde turns to Snow. 'Mamma's strong enough to take you, Your White Knightship, covered in iron and Dwarves as you are, as long as the little darlings play nice.'

'You hear that?' Snow picks up a Dwarf by the scruff. 'No biting the bears.'

'Yummy,' mutters the Dwarf, eyeing the bear warily.

'And I'll ride my sweet Baby.' She looks around herself, as if only just realising that something's missing. 'Oh poot, where's he gotten to this time? Baby!'

'Aww,' coos Buttercup, 'there's a teeny bear?'

Gretel notices the troubled sideways glances between Hex and Scarlett.

'Baby!' Gilde calls again.

There is an almost familiar rumble-crack from the trees beyond, swiftly approaching.

'Wait,' says Trevor, 'did an Ogre follow us out here or something?'

Gretel realises at the same time as Snow. 'That's not an Ogre!'

The bear, astonishing in size, bounds into their clearing, scattering broken branches and uprooted saplings as it goes. He bounces right up to Gilde to huff and lick at her, like a massive, terrifying puppy.

Gilde smiles and pets the hairy colossus's snout. He bends his head obediently.

'*There* you are.' She beams.

'That's Baby?' breathes Jack.

'That's Baby,' replies Hex.

Baby grunts. The bass of his utterance rumbles up through the soles of Gretel's feet. The thing looms over the other two bears, almost twice the height of the bear Gilde had called 'Mamma'.

Gretel doesn't dare pat Mamma Bear, but manages to make eye contact with the creature and give her a small sympathetic head tilt. 'Ouch. Poor Mamma.'

Gilde rubs her hands together. 'Everyone hunky-dory? Don't worry about steering them, they'll just follow me. Miss Ghost can latch onto you and transport, Wolfie and Sweetiebird can just transform again and make their own ways.'

Hex groans.

'Gilde!' Scarlett whines. 'We only just put our clothes back on!'

7
Lodgings

Obviously, the Citadel is an impressive sight, not least to somebody such as Hansel, who's barely set foot outside his village, gets anxious around crowds of more than a hundred or so and considers three-storey buildings to be dazzling wonders of modern architecture. In the Citadel, the streets are paved with... well, with a proper paving material, such as cobbles, or stone slabs, as opposed to the gritted dirt tracks of the roads in and around the village. The buildings rise not two, not even three, but usually four or five storeys high; taller than the village's windmill, taller even than the agricultural hardware workshop in Ham. At the northern edge of the Citadel, uphill and built flush against the defensive wall, Myrsina Castle looms above the rooftops, taller and more impressive still. The numerous hard paved streets, crowded in on all sides by the towering buildings, clatter and echo with the sounds of well-cobbled boots in their thousands, as well as horseshoes, and cart wheels and barrows. Costermongers and pedlars clamour to shout their wares above the cacophony of a multitude all going about their day. Lights hang on walls to illuminate the shadows created by the impossibly tall buildings. Elsewhere, walls are plastered with notices from the huntsmen – faded old edicts and abomination lists, as well as the newer, bewilderingly similar campaign posters for several different candidates to be the new head huntsman. The whole place is overwhelmingly loud and full, too bright and too dark at the same time. The smell is an unpleasant combination of food, sweat and bad drains.

One cannot truthfully describe all of this hitting Hansel suddenly the moment he stepped out of a carriage into the big city, since he arrived on foot, dragging a cart full of baskets. What actually happened is that he very slowly became horribly aware of the sheer scale, noise and smell of the Citadel as he and Daisy walked towards it over a series of hours. There was, at least, the moment when the gate guards accepted their paperwork and duty fee as traders and allowed them to pass through the large wooden gate in the Citadel wall, and Hansel walked for the first time into the terrible magnificence of it all. That had been a pretty awful moment. He'd needed a sit down and a hot drink after that.

There's something else wrong with this place, too. Fear. Hansel has never been able to sense other people's fear before, but it's everywhere here. Perhaps he's just never been around quite such a high density of people who are all holding in quite so much fear all at the same time. It's a constant background hum of terror, from so many minds. It has no discernible voice, no words; it comes from every direction and no direction at once. It hangs thickly in the air; it's seeped into the walls like a lingering stench.

Now, he sits with his back against the basket cart and tries to take it all in as calmly as he possibly can, as Daisy bustles about their new pitch. The spot they've been allocated in the marketplace is, if it's at all possible, even noisier, smellier and more oppressive than most of the rest of the Citadel. He mustn't get upset. Above all else, he must not get upset out here.

'Three baskets already.' Daisy beams at him, handing over another pair of silver coins for the purse. 'At this rate, we'll be able to afford a hot dinner *and* lodgings tonight, and not have to sleep under the cart after all.'

He gives her a horrified glance. 'You wanted us to sleep *here*?'

'Not any more!' She turns to a well-dressed young woman inspecting the largest baskets. 'Them's three silvers, miss.' She twirls one of the pigtails that poke out from beneath her bonnet, drawing attention to the black ribbon plaited into her hair. 'My mum makes them, the poor soul.'

The woman nods, and smiles. Hansel notices that a lot of the busier stalls are run by women in widows' scarves, or else girls too young yet for marriage, wearing the same black hair ribbons as Daisy, indicating a bereavement that has left their household devoid of menfolk. Such women and girls are the only members of their gender still allowed under the huntsmen's laws to keep a trade and sell their wares, and it seems that in the Citadel there is a high demand for female-made craftwork.

The well-dressed woman notices him, peering around from behind the cart.

'That your beau?'

Hansel suddenly feels hot and cold at the same time. He ducks back behind the cart. Daisy laughs lightly, politely, like a waitress dealing with a customer who incorrectly believes themselves to be witty and charming when they're drunk.

'That's just my friend, m'm, come to help a poor widow's daughter scratch a living.'

'You'll be wanting to think about getting yourself a beau soon, though, girl,' the woman tells her. 'You won't be able to wear those ribbons much longer, and then there'll be no more selling baskets for you.' She leans in and lowers her voice. 'Made me take my ribbons out at fifteen; I used to make the loveliest lace to pay my way before that.' She hands Daisy six silver coins and takes two baskets. 'Before I met my Jaspar, of course, oh joyful day.'

'He must do well,' says Daisy, still with the same static, service-industry smile, 'if you don't mind my saying, m'm. What's his trade?'

The young woman shoots them the slyest of winks. 'He's a lace merchant.' She hefts the baskets. 'These are good. Give your poor bereaved mother my compliments.'

She walks away, leaving Daisy and Hansel blinking at one another.

'Did she just…' attempts Hansel.

'Yeah.' Daisy's smile loses its veneer of dead-eyed politeness, and grows soft and warm. 'People still manage to find a way to carry on being themselves, right under the you-know-who's noses. Good for her, I say.'

'No, I mean… did she just suggest we get married?'

'Ha! Haha!' Daisy barks out a rather nervous-sounding laugh, and plays again with her pigtail. 'Well, not right now, eh? We've got baskets to sell and a Hydra to stop.' She deliberately pulls her hand away from her hair. 'Any sign of that, by the way? Any more… special dreams?'

Hansel shakes his head. 'I'm still adjusting to this place, though. Everything feels so bad here.'

'Oh, that's just Citadel living, you'll get used to it. Yeah, it smells, but there's a coffee house on pretty much every corner… at least, there is for now, until coffee is denounced as an abomination – it's in two of the new head huntsman candidates' lists.' She nods at a nearby election poster. 'See?'

Hansel squints at the poster. He can see that there's writing on it, it's just that there's a lot of it, in very long words.

'I'm… not much of a reader…'

'Oh yes, that's right,' replies Daisy with a bright matter-of-factness, 'Gretel used to do the reading for the both of you, didn't she?'

Hansel hesitates. Before, he'd have been fine with this, but now, here, with her, it feels… childish. Or like he's some stupid illiterate farm bumpkin.

'It's fine,' continues Daisy cheerfully, 'you've got me to do that for us now.' She points to a handful of posters dotted about. 'So, these posters have lists of the key ways each candidate will run things if they're chosen. Seems to be five different candidates – three of them, besides the odd detail here and there, look like they'd be pretty much the same as the last one. "Blah blah traditional way of life, blah blah security, ask at HQ for a full manifesto, blah blah blah".' She points to a rather nicely designed poster. 'This one actually seems to want to roll back on loads of laws, get rid of most of the abominations. That would be nice, wouldn't it?' She points to a different poster. 'But this one looks like he'd be even worse.'

'Worse? It can get worse?'

'It can always get worse.'

'Does it say who's winning?'

Daisy shakes her head. 'Can't tell from the posters, but if you were on the huntsmen's side, would you really want to respond to what happened in Nearby by being nicer to us?'

'...Nearby...?' A little murmur goes up from somewhere in the throng.

Daisy shoots wide eyes at Hansel. 'Oops.'

'Yeah,' mutters Hansel, 'I think maybe we don't talk about that while we're here.'

Daisy peers off into the crowd. The murmuring voice is gone again, with no sign of who it had belonged to.

'And of course,' adds Daisy, so quietly that only Hansel can hear her, 'if there is an attack on the Citadel, well...'

'...they'll harden,' sighs Hansel. 'The worse guy will win.'

'Yes, sir!'

Hansel looks up at Daisy. Another customer has approached. He watches her turn on her waitress smile and draw attention to her black ribbons until she makes another good sale. He still can't shake the feeling of the walls and the hubbub closing in on him, of there being something bad, something very bad, some monster out here, somehow... but he's glad at least that he's here with her. Her sale made, she looks down, catches his expression and beams.

'*Another* two silvers! At this rate, we're going to have enough for a room with actual beds!'

***

The bear-back journey could never be described as 'comfortable'. The fur is soft enough, at least, and it gives Gretel and the others something to grab onto for dear life, but the bear's muscles constantly shift and flex beneath her as he runs. When Gretel was growing up on the farm, they'd almost always use their two workhorses for lugging ploughs and threshers, or pulling the cart, so she's only ever actually been on a horse one time, and even then she'd fallen off. This is very different, however. The bear is fast and heavy and sharp, and while he's magically obedient to Gilde, he is by no means a tame or domestic creature. Gretel can feel the wild beast beneath the coating of magic all the time. She spends the whole high-speed, terrifying journey with one thought foremost on her mind: you should definitely not be riding a bear.

It is, at least, considerably faster than walking. The northern mountains loom up on them with an astonishing swiftness. Just as they reach the foothills of Bear Mountain, the creatures slow down. Amongst the thinning trees and rocky outcrops stands a little wooden cottage. It's eerily similar to the cake cottage that Gretel only just left behind, except that it has several large claw marks on its walls, and none of it is accidentally made of cake.

Gilde is already at the cottage door dismounting the massive Baby when they arrive, with Mamma drawing up with Snow and seven deeply unhappy Dwarves seconds later.

'Hex?' calls Gilde.

The huge raven swoops down from the sky, lands clumsily and transforms into the naked and rather out-of-breath human form of Hex. Gilde throws his clothes at him again.

'Get a fire started, there's a Sweetiebird.'

Hex tries to get one leg into his drawers, and misses. 'One second…'

'Let's not leave our guests waiting, Hexy!'

Jack beckons forth a small, dry tree, and with a swipe of his hand collapses it into firewood. He picks up an armful and heads for the door. 'It's all right, I can see to the fire.'

Gilde gives him a too-bright smile. She tugs at a string around her neck, at the end of which is a small iron key. 'Swell, let me get the door...'

Jack turns to face the crowd and kicks backwards at the door, which gently swings open against his boot. Gretel, knowing what to look for, just about spots the glint of the lock pick disappearing back up his sleeve.

'Of course.' Gilde smiles, returning the key down the neck of her dress. 'I just invited a thief to tea, didn't I.'

Jack just winks, grins and disappears into the cottage.

'Well,' murmurs Trevor, on Gretel's shoulder, '*someone's* excited to show off in front of new people.'

There's a commotion from the trees and a panting, exhausted ginger wolf comes running up to them, lifting onto hind legs and pushing her scalp back into a cape's hood until it's the human form of Scarlett approaching at a weary jog.

She bends double, getting her breath back. 'Ooh, that's hard to do at a run. See, this is one of the reasons why we tend not to go far...' She notices the open door, and Gilde standing aside from it, key very much not in hand. 'Oh no, Gilde, did one of us leave the door unlocked?'

Gilde's smile manages to grow even more terrifying.

Patience manifests the moment they walk in through the door.

'Oh!' the Ghost exclaims, looking around. 'This is actually pretty nice. Homely. I was expecting a cave or something.'

Gilde pulls up the smallest of the three chairs in the cottage and sits in it without offering a seat to anybody else. 'Why would little ole me be living in a nasty cave?'

'Nothing wrong with living in a cave...' mutters Snow, plonking herself into the largest of the chairs.

Patience shrugs. 'You know. The mountain, the bears... living with a Werewolf and a crow guy.'

'Raven,' says Hex softly, fiddling with buttons.

'That's silly. You live with a talking spider, but I can't imagine you sleep in a web.'

'I mean, technically, I don't sleep at all. It's a Ghost thing.'

'We have a cottage too,' Buttercup tells Gilde, politely avoiding the last remaining chair along with everyone else. 'I found it, not long after I went out into the Darkwood.'

'You found it?' Scarlett plops herself down in front of the fire to pull her stockings back on. 'And it's down your end of the forest… What does it look like?'

'Mostly these days it looks like a rather eclectic gateau, I'm afraid,' Buttercup admits. 'But it's home.'

'A thief and a squatter.' Gilde folds her hands neatly. 'What larks.'

'I'm not a squatter, I'm repurposing a derelict wood lodge,' protests Buttercup quietly.

'So, you didn't find this cottage empty or take it off anyone?' Snow asks Gilde. 'Built it yourself, did you?'

'Actually I did,' Gilde tells them. 'Couple of spare beds and chairs for my two stray transmorpher friends, and my own stuff is just right. It's my sweet little cottage for sweet little me.'

'*You* built all this,' echoes Snow. 'You.'

'Me.'

'What are you… four foot nine? Six stone?'

Gilde's eyes widen. 'You don't think I could build my own nice little cottage, just because I'm wittle?'

'New Girl,' barks Snow, 'what sort of weights are we talking about here?'

Gretel casts a quick engineer's eye around the cottage. She sucks through her teeth. 'Some of these load-bearing beams have got to be a good five hundred pounds. Even with a decent pulley system, a small woman working on her own would struggle to—'

'Obviously the bears helped,' interrupts Gilde.

'Ah.' Snow adopts a victorious tone. 'So, it's made with bear labour. Not so sanctimonious now, are you?'

'The bears are my friends. They *wanted* to help poor little me, with their big strong backs. I wouldn't say such things if I were you, oh Whitest of Knights.'

Somewhere, lying not particularly deep beneath Gilde's veneer of treacle and the antiquated turns of phrase of someone who was last in human society at least sixty years ago, is an intense, angry little raisin of a witch. She's like Snow, thinks Gretel, only condensed over the extra decades of banishment and solitude. No wonder the two of them are already at each other's throats. It's like watching two hostile cats, growling, circling, sizing one another up.

Hex, finally dressed, heads to the now roaring stove and picks up a large kettle.

'I'll get tea and supper on, shall I?' He pauses apologetically. 'Um… there's not that much choice right now; we're donating most of our meat to the bears, what with hibernation season, but we did a granary raid a while back so there's plenty of porridge.'

'Porridge will be fine,' Snow tells him. 'It'll make a nice change from scones and vegetable soup, in any case.'

'You never actually *eat* my vegetable soup,' complains Jack under his breath.

'I don't want mine too hot,' announces Gilde, 'or too cold.'

'Yes,' sighs Hex. 'I know.'

8
Fighting Talk

The porridge is… OK, supposes Gretel. It isn't as nice as the porridge her step-parents would make for her back at the farm, but then the Mudds had access to creamy fresh milk. This seems to just be made with water. It's also served at a disappointingly lukewarm temperature. Gretel likes her porridge piping hot. Nevertheless, she doesn't grumble. There is at least a large honeycomb available to sweeten it, adorned with suspicious bear-claw-sized grooves. Besides, it really does make a welcome change from vegetables and accidental pastries.

Gilde takes a spoonful of tepid porridge and sighs appreciatively. 'Just right. Well done, little Sweetiebird. You wouldn't think from his cooking that he was a raven for six whole years of his young life, would you?'

'Don't,' says Hex in a quiet, pleading tone.

Gilde shrugs and takes another bite of porridge. 'Nothing to get the frowns about, Sweetiebird. Better to be an animal than a human. Given the opportunity, I'd give my left arm to be able to do it too.'

'It's probably a little bit different having to actually live with being a big raven than just imagining it,' Buttercup says carefully.

'Suddenly our guests know a lot about transmorphers,' replies Gilde brightly.

'Gilde *is* a little bit right,' says Scarlett hurriedly. 'Being a wolf's a lot freer than being a human. Nobody cares what you look like. The whole world's your dinner table, love-bed and toilet. Don't know how you lot cope with running on two legs the whole time.'

'*Some* of us run on eight,' announces Trevor proudly.

Scarlett gives him a grin. 'So, are you a transmorpher too, or…?'

'Nope,' Trevor replies happily. 'Just chatty.'

'Oh, how simply swell,' says Gilde in a tone laden with the implication that it is not simply swell at all. 'We're all becoming great pals.'

Snow scrapes the last of her porridge into her mouth, and slams the bowl down. 'Yes, lovely as all this bonding is, we came here to talk business. New Girl? The plans.'

Gretel rolls out a new map.

'And what's this pretty picture?' Gilde asks, getting up to look.

'The Citadel,' replies Gretel, with a touch of pride. 'It's quite accurate, we used Snow's birds and the Mirror to put it together.'

'Oh, I'm sure it's just super, kiddiewink, but we're seasoned raiders, we've never needed no maps. If'n we was going to do it, and I ain't saying we will, we'd be in and out before they so much as catch the onion.'

'We're not talking about a raid or a physical attack,' says Gretel. 'Not at this stage, in any case. Yes, we're talking about a coup, but it can be bloodless. And the huntsmen have actually already shown us how it can be done.' She gets a new sheet with what they've gleaned about the election and its timescale. 'The huntsmen were able to grab power all those years ago by spreading their ideas through grassroots groups, and then by infiltrating the Citadel's military and castle guards. We can use similar tactics, but for good. It's already started. News spreads. People hear stories about parts of Myrsina pushing back against the huntsmen, mere villages able to put up an effective resistance. Makes them think maybe they can do the same. Gives them permission to try. And then, they hear stories that the princess is alive and well. The huntsmen are leaderless right now, the whole Citadel's looking to see what new direction it should go in. If we can infiltrate the Citadel now, using stories and rumours instead of violence, spread the idea that maybe the tide has turned against the huntsmen, maybe enough of them can be persuaded in this moment of instability to go back to how things were, restore the crown, and…'

'What's that about the princess?' Scarlett asks. 'Wasn't she killed?'

'No,' replies Snow, 'just driven into the woods and royally trousered off.'

'But how do you know for sure?' Scarlett persists. 'Have you met h… oh wait, it's you, isn't it?'

''Fraid so.'

Scarlett nudges Hex. 'I recognised her from off the old tuppenny coins.'

Snow rolls her eyes. 'Ugh, I can't believe Mum made me sit for those.'

'A princess,' trills Gilde in a tone dripping with saccharine sarcasm, 'in my humble little shack, well I never was so thunderstruck in all my days.' She makes a show of straightening a candle and brushing dust off a shelf. 'I was going to just say "no", but considering the circumstances, and since you've come all this way and everything, I have to say, you changed my mind.'

'We have?' asks Trevor, impressed.

Gilde nods sweetly.

Snow narrows her eyes, unconvinced. 'So, what say you now?'

Gilde dips into a deep curtsey. 'I say no, *Your Majesty*.'

By the time Daisy has finished in the marketplace for the day, her money belt is heavy with silver. Hansel helps her take her cart to an inn she knows of that has a secure storage outhouse for travelling merchants' wares. As promised, there's enough money to get the two of them a room of their own instead of having to sleep in the outhouse with their goods. The room is up a dizzying four flights of stairs and is small but warm, with two beds and what Daisy refers to as 'a view', which turns out to be a view of seven different roofs. There is even enough spending money left over for something called 'local cuisine', whatever that is.

Even in this room so crazily high above the streets, the Citadel is still too loud for Hansel. As he sets his few clothes and belongings down on his side of the room, he is rattled by shouts and clops and clattering wheels and the pealing of several bells.

'Is it always like this?' he sighs.

'Pardon?'

He raises his voice. '*Is it always like this?*'

'Oh!' Daisy goes to the window. 'Um… not quite like *this*, actually. Something must be happening, there's a stage down there, and bunting and stuff.'

Hansel frowns. This sounds like the sort of thing where there's going to definitely be far too many people.

'Did you want to go and see what's going on?' asks Daisy.

No. No, he really doesn't want to. 'We probably should,' he says.

Daisy grins. 'Exciting! We might be able to find some local cuisine while we're at it.'

Hansel forces a smile. 'Yes. That sounds… yes.'

'Local cuisine' turns out to be a sort of spicy sausage in a flatbread with pickled vegetables that fall out every time Hansel tries to eat it. It comes from a tiny cart on the street with no table to sit at and no cutlery. Daisy buys one for each of them, with apparently no heed whatsoever to the fact that it costs her more than most families in Nearby would normally spend on several days' worth of food shopping.

Hansel wrestles with his local cuisine as they approach a makeshift stage that's been set up in a square not far from their inn. This stage seems to be the source of the hubbub. At seeing a temporary platform erected in a square, Hansel feels a sudden, sharp pang of panic.

'What are they going to do?'

'It's OK.' Daisy squeezes his hand and points with a hand full of half-eaten dubious sausage at the stage. 'Look. No stake, no rack, no pillories. They're not going to do anything to anyone.'

They both watch the stage, eating their local cuisine. After a moment, a huntsman wearing an orange rosette walks onto it, to a polite round of applause from the waiting crowd.

'Oh, something's happening,' says Daisy. 'Maybe he's going to sing a song?'

'Brethren,' cries the huntsman, 'loyal citizens of the Citadel, it is with great honour and solemn duty that I stand before you as a candidate to be the one to guide the huntsmen and the great land of Myrsina.'

Daisy sighs, disappointed. 'Oh. This isn't interesting, this is politics.'

'It's the debates,' says a familiar voice, from behind them. Both Hansel and Daisy turn their heads, startled. Daisy's customer from earlier, the lace merchant's wife, smiles back at them.

'Oh, hello! Enjoying your baskets, are you?'

'Very much so far, thank you. How are *you* enjoying our fine Citadel and its grand democracy?'

Hansel frowns at the huntsman on the stage. Even though Daisy was right and there are no signs that anything awful is about to happen to a suspected witch on the platform, something about it continues to fill him with panic. There's something very bad about the simple wooden stage that feels as if it relates to his Hydra nightmare; he just can't put his finger on what it is.

'So, is this how all the new head huntsmen are chosen?'

'No, it's all new.' The lace merchant's wife tucks in to some local cuisine of her own. 'I think someone must have found some old rules from when they were starting out or something.' She leans in and lowers her voice. 'They're having to do a whole load of stuff that they clearly don't want to bother with, like these "debates".'

'There's only one person speaking,' Daisy notes.

The lace maker's wife smirks. 'Yep. It was going to be all five of them together, but they decided against it. When one of them is going to eventually emerge as the head huntsman, the other four don't want to risk doing anything to upset the new boss. The question-and-answer sessions from the floor scheduled for the ends of these speeches were cancelled for similar reasons.'

'So,' reasons Daisy, 'that just leaves you with…'

'With one person talking for an hour at a time, unchallenged and unquestioned, with the occasional, scheduled, rebuff speech afterwards.' The lace maker's wife shrugs. 'It's better than nothing, I suppose. Helps people know what they're voting for.'

Daisy raises her eyebrows. 'So, all of you get to vote?'

'Yes… well, no… well, yes… sort of. The system they've worked out is really complicated, and apparently if ordinary civilians' votes were worth as much as a huntsman's, we'd swamp them, and that would be unfair.' The lace merchant's wife treats them to an expression of sarcastic faux-excitement. 'I'm just enjoying it while I can. Chances are if they ever do have another election, I won't be invited.'

She nods over to the stage, where the huntsman with the orange rosette is speaking. He seems to be the full-on fire and brimstone shouty kind of huntsman, and is getting particularly bellicose on the subject of letting women do things.

'…would change the loophole in our current rules that requires civilians of the fairer sex to put themselves through the unnatural indignity of trying to think of somebody to vote for,' he shouts. 'The current rules unfairly discriminate against the female mind by demanding all candidates identify themselves with a different colour; this leaves many females confused, wanting simply to vote for the colour they think is the prettiest.'

There is a round of applause from some of the audience near the front of the stage.

'What?' breathes Daisy.

'I even have husbands coming up to me,' continues the candidate, 'telling me that they want to vote for me, but that their wife will vote for a different candidate because my orange ribbons clash with their hair, which means that there's no point in him voting at all. A good, hard-working man's vote completely cancelled out, completely oppressed, by his own wife's foolishness! I am not making this up!'

Daisy stares, wide-eyed, at the lace merchant's wife.

'Of course he's making it up,' murmurs the lace merchant's wife, 'but who here's going to take him to task over it?'

'People are clapping it,' Daisy says. 'People are actually clapping…'

'It's out there now,' mutters Hansel. 'It's said. It's… marauding, unchecked…'

'This one's the worst of the bunch,' the lace merchant's wife tells them quietly. 'Don't worry, the other four are pretty normal, and I'm certainly not giving my vote to *him*.' She taps a green button on her dress. 'I'm with Green, she talks common sense.'

'Wait. "She"?'

The lace merchant's wife nods, with a smile. 'There was a *lot* of fuss about that, but they couldn't find anything in the rules forbidding it.' She indicates the candidate on the stage. 'He's furious about it.'

'…because how are the huntsmen supposed to lead by example,' shouts the man on the platform, 'if the leadership goes to Green? You let one female lead, they're all going to want to. Green would oversee females getting overeducated again, taking men's jobs again, spurning men's romantic proposals again, the sort of horrible division that destroys livelihoods and families. We can't let that happen!'

There is a cheer from the front of the crowd.

'And,' adds the man on the platform darkly, 'let's not forget the last time females ran Myrsina.'

'Witches,' comes a cry from the audience.

'The witch queen,' growls the huntsman on the stage. 'The terrible witch queen who turned her own husband, the king, into a mirror and snatched power for herself.'

The audience starts booing.

'Who brought another little witch-queen-in-waiting into the world,' continues the candidate on the stage. 'She must have thought the witches' reign was going to last for a thousand years, and that threat is still not over. The huntsmen are finding new witches all the time, many of which were seduced into that terrible world through overeducation and aspirations above their station. The Darkwood is still deep witch territory, even within Myrsina's own borders. And I'm sure you've all heard of the terrible witch uprising and their seizure of Nearby Village only the other week.'

The crowd roars with rage at this.

'No,' says Hansel, a little too loud.

'Kid.' The lace merchant's wife squeezes his shoulder. 'Not here. Not now. The other candidates will get their say…'

'But he's lying,' Hansel cries.

'Sshhh,' replies the lace merchant's wife. 'I know, but this isn't the way to go about it…'

'Then what is?'

For all of the woman's shushing, Hansel's voice is getting drowned out anyway, by a chant that has broken out amongst the audience.

'End the witches,' they chant. 'End the witches!'

'The threat is not over!' The candidate is practically screaming now. 'The threat is right here, right now, on our doorstep! Their invasion has already begun!'

'No!' Hansel's getting upset, he knows he is. He can feel the dark tendrils of magic thrashing and squirming through his veins. He's not even really sure what it is that's driving him to shout out – his own sense of injustice or the dark magical fury within him, demanding to be heard. Nobody even turns around at his cries; they're all too wrapped up in the roar and the rage of the chant.

'End the witches!' The candidate has joined in now. 'End the witches!'

'Stop it!'

'Hansel.' Daisy grabs his shoulders. 'Don't. I don't think this is safe. We should just go back to our room.'

'You go back.' Hansel notices that the lace merchant's wife is already making a hasty retreat through the crowds, away from them both. 'I can't just let him lie like this and get away with it. I'll be OK, Daisy.'

'No you won't!'

'But—'

'You should listen to the girl.' The new voice behind them is female, but not one that Hansel recognises. It's also slightly muffled. His arm is grasped hard and pulled behind his back.

Hansel and Daisy both turn to look behind themselves, and stare into the blank expression of a huntsman's white porcelain mask.

'Hansel Mudd, right?' says the huntsman. 'And Daisy Weaver?'

'W…Wicker,' manages Daisy. 'But what… how?'

'Oh, we've met before,' says the huntsman calmly, 'although we were all a bit distracted at the time. I was at the battle for Nearby. And I think it would be best for all of us if you were to come with me.'

9
The Cold Shoulder

'OK,' says Buttercup, 'so… what do we do now?'

Gretel's group has 'stepped outside for a private chat', a decision that almost all of them are already beginning to regret. Night has fallen, and brought with it a bitter wind, howling down from the mountains and blowing freezing droplets of rain into their eyes. Even Snow looks cold and miserable. Only Patience remains unperturbed by the wet and the cold, which simply blow straight through her. Instead, the Ghost is merely perturbed by the fact that their plan was just turned down flat and nobody's sure what to do about that.

'Well, we've still got our looks, I suppose,' mutters Patience. 'Jack, how do you fancy your chances of seducing all three of them in there to doing things our way?'

'Can't pretend it wouldn't be a challenge.' Jack manages a shivery grin. 'I'd say about fifty-fifty?'

'I'm not comfortable with using Jack as a handsome trap,' Buttercup tells everyone seriously.

'What, you think I need to bulk up first or something…?'

'Gilde's the only one who's said no,' says Trevor, buried under the neck of Buttercup's cape. 'Hex and Scarlett seem more amenable; they could still be talked into splitting away from her…'

'Come off it,' Snow replies. 'You've seen both of them around Gilde, they're terrified of her. They're never going to go against what she says.'

'But she's just a little old lady,' argues Trevor.

'She's ferocious,' Snow tells him. 'And a pain in the gooseberries.'

'She's probably just sad,' attempts Buttercup, 'and fed up. All those years shunned from human society just because she could talk to bears. Have you noticed the way she talks? She sounds like she's in an old play.'

'Buttercup,' sighs Snow.

'I'm just saying,' Buttercup continues, 'maybe if we stay, if we persist, if we show her kindness, and let her see how the plan can help her personally, as well as everyone else, I bet she's a sweetheart deep down. Crotchety witches usually are.'

'I'm not sure she wants help,' says Snow. 'Maybe she just wants to be angry.'

'Whatever we decide to do, we should do it fast,' says Gretel.

Patience nods in agreement. 'The Citadel will be voting soon.'

'And hibernation time must be any day now,' Gretel adds. 'If we're going to make use of the bears, we need Gilde right now.'

'Do we really need the bears?' Jack asks. 'If the plan is to sneak in and start a revolution through a whispering campaign, I'm not sure that bears are particularly good at any of those things.'

'The bears and wolves would be back-up,' Gretel says, 'in case anything goes wrong.'

'And how likely do you think it is that something could go wrong?'

Gretel just clears her throat.

'Oh,' says Jack.

There is a cold and miserable pause.

'Maybe this was a bad idea,' says Gretel. 'We can ask my village for back-up instead...'

'We need more witches,' replies Snow sharply.

'But we've already got an army and we've got a princess...'

'Would you *stop* with the princess thing?'

Gretel blinks at Snow's outburst. There is another chilly pause.

'So, am I still going ahead with trying to seduce all three of them, or what?' Jack asks.

The door to the cottage opens. Scarlett stands in the doorway.

'Hi,' she says cheerfully. 'So if you're going to try to seduce and split up our group in the name of this attempted revolution that you're pretty sure is going to end in bloodshed anyway, you may as well come in and start it now. Or get your things and go. If I were you, I'd just settle for a quiet night's rest in front of the fire; it's bitter out. Gilde wants to go to bed soon, though, so whatever you choose to do, could you be quiet about it?'

Gretel gapes at Scarlett. 'You heard all of that?'

'Werewolf,' she cheerfully replies by way of explanation.

'Really good sense of hearing. And smell, although that's not so relevant on this occasion.'

'Right,' mutters Gretel.

Scarlett holds the cottage door open meaningfully. Snow strides back inside, head tilted haughtily aloft, and the others shuffle and glide behind her, displaying various different levels of embarrassment.

When they get in, Gilde is dressed for bed. Hex is in a corner, his eyes cast down.

'You reckon I'm just being a stubborn ole donkey,' says Gilde gently, 'don't yer? Or that these two are only going along with my say-so because they're under my toes, and you can bring all of them round with some more 'splaining and a handsome smile?'

'You calling me handsome?' asks Jack, with his patented skin-thin cocky grin.

'She could have been talking about me,' whispers Trevor.

'Trevor, you're physically incapable of smiling.'

Trevor attempts a smile, to prove Jack wrong, and fails.

Gilde shuffles over to the smallest of the beds at the back of the cottage.

'I ain't being a meanie, babies. I'm just being practical. You ain't going to persuade the Citadel to turn around against the huntsmen and put a witch from the wood back on the throne. Miss Ghost knows that already, that's why she's sidestepping all your talk of a peaceful tide change and going straight to fighting talk.'

'Patience is an ex-huntsman,' explains Gretel. 'Violence is just sort of her natural go-to; she's not the best person to listen to when it comes to…'

Behind her, the air grows cold. Cutlery flies off the table and sticks to the ceiling. Gretel pinches the bridge of her nose.

'Patience,' warns Buttercup, 'remember your temper, we're guests here.' She pauses. 'But Gretel, that was uncalled for.'

'Wasn't "uncalled for", it was just wrong,' says Gilde, getting into bed. 'A lot of you still haven't opened the pickle jar on what a rich perspective you have in Miss Ghost, and your ignorance comes out like rudeness. Still, though, I'll thank you not to have a temper tantrum in my house, Ghostie; it's not my fault that you're right and they're wrong.'

'I know the situation, OK?' says Patience to Gretel. 'I understand the huntsmen and the Citadel.'

'A reason that the huntsman have been doing so well for so long,' adds Gilde from her bed, 'is that people – ordinary people – actually *like* what they do.'

Gretel frowns. 'No. No. What the huntsmen do is horrible. They oppress, they torture, they kill, and when they run out of witches and magical creatures to pick on, they turn on ordinary women, people's wives and mothers and daughters and—'

'And a surprising proportion of the people are hunky-dory with that,' interrupts Gilde sweetly. 'As long as the witches suffer most of all, they're even prepared to risk their own womenfolk for the cause. Even their own kiddiewinks.'

Gretel finds herself getting hot and bothered despite herself. 'No, that's not true. My village turned against them in a snap. The Mirror said more towns and villages are starting to do the same.

Most people are good at heart, they just need hope, they need a cause…'

Gilde pulls her bedspread up over her chest. 'Spoken like a newborn foal.'

'Am not,' squeaks Gretel indignantly, despite herself.

'Me and Miss Ghost ain't even the only ones to think so,' continues Gilde. 'Why try to recruit the bears and the wolves at all, unless you know there's going to be trouble, ain't that so, Majesty?'

Snow just frowns at Gilde.

'That's just our back-up plan,' soothes Buttercup, 'in case something goes wrong… right, Snow?'

Gilde locks eyes with Snow and takes a deep breath in through the nose, like a predator catching scent of something on the breeze.

'Or maybe there's something else at play here, Majesty,' adds Gilde. 'Something you're keeping secret even from your nearest and dearest.'

'Shut up,' Snow tells her.

'Maybe all this fussing is just Her Majesty's stalling technique,' says Gilde with a twinkle. 'Maybe Majesty doesn't want to take the big fight to the Citadel, because she's *fwightened*.'

Gretel doesn't dare even look at Snow's expression.

'Er, wrong,' Trevor tells Gilde. 'The White Knight isn't scared of *anything*. I've seen her pull a rotten tooth from the head of an angry Manticore and everything.'

'Snow, you're not actually worried, are you?' asks Buttercup. 'You know we can win this thing if we all pull together.'

'Maybe it's winning she's scared of,' says Gilde. 'Because what happens then, if you do beat the huntsmen, and replace them with this feral witch, on the throne? Everybody living in peace and harmony as Centaurs and Unicorns clop through the Citadel's squares?'

'It'll work,' replies Gretel, a little louder than she'd intended, 'because we just want to put things back to the way they were. It's only been thirteen years; people can remember the time before and remember that it was better. We're not talking about Wyvern in the Citadel, we're talking about people being able to go home. We all just want to go home. Don't you?'

'I *am* home,' Gilde says, snuggling down in bed.

'I mean, your home from before.' She turns to Scarlett and Hex, quiet and downcast in their corner, and tries to draw them into the conversation. 'All of you. Don't you want to go back to where you were before you were driven out here?'

'I wasn't,' says Hex in a small voice.

'What?'

'I wasn't driven anywhere. I came here of my own free will.'

'Yeah,' says Jack, 'but I bet it was because people didn't like the wing.'

'*I* don't like the wing,' Hex blurts suddenly. He darts forwards, unfurling the wing right up against Jack's face. 'A witch did this to me! There is a *reason* people hate witches! I couldn't stand their faces when they looked at me any more, so I left, I went north-west, until Gilde found me. Gilde understood. How can you have lived in the forest for thirteen years and still not understand?'

'It was my choice to come up here too,' adds Scarlett. 'Fewer people about. Safer.'

'And little ole me,' says Gilde sleepily, 'they told me to stop talking to my bears. Said it was strange and dangerous stuff. So one day I wandered into the woods and never came back, because I was a strange and dangerous girl, and I belonged in a strange and dangerous place. That's why we ain't never going to help you fight the huntsmen – the huntsmen are kinda right.'

'You can't say that,' snarls Snow. 'You don't know what they're doing.'

'I know that magical beings and humans shouldn't live together,' says Gilde, 'and I know that a witch queen is always a very, very bad idea, right, Sweetiebird?'

'Right,' says Hex quietly, moving back to his corner.

78

'I think you understand that too, deep down, Majesty,' adds Gilde, 'that's why you're kicking the rock down the road on this plan, am I right?'

Snow doesn't reply.

'Snow?' Buttercup stares at Snow incredulously.

Snow doesn't meet her gaze.

'Snow!'

'If you two are going to have a quarrel, please do it outside, it's beddie-bo's for me.' Gilde yawns daintily. 'Trott, I ain't interested in your sweet talk, but it might cheer up the others a little; Scarlett's suitors have never been big on conversation, if you know what I mean, and I don't believe my Sweetiebird's ever so much as had someone give him the eye before. It won't get you very far but it'll make a nice change for 'em. Nightie night.'

'Snow,' says Buttercup quietly, 'she is lying, isn't she? About you? You're not stalling, you know she's wrong about thinking witches and humans can't live together…?'

'What the huntsmen are doing is wrong,' says Snow levelly, 'and once we have enough allies, I will fight them to make them stop, even if it kills me. But once this is over… maybe we all belong with our own kind. Maybe that means it will be best if I stay in my cave.'

Buttercup stares at her for a second, then turns, tears in her eyes, and grabs her cape, only to have to bite down a frustrated curse word when it immediately turns into a giant flatbread. She throws the bread on the floor and hurries out into the freezing night in just her dress.

'Buttercup?' Snow folds her arms and shouts at the door. 'Buttercup!' She pauses. 'Buttercup!' Another pause. 'Butterc—'

'I'm not sure that she's talking to you right now, mate,' says Trevor, swinging down from the lintel onto Gretel's head.

Snow appears to ponder this and then shouts 'Buttercup!' again anyway.

'Keep it down, I said,' calls Gilde from her bed. 'Or take it outside. Surely you don't want one of your widdle family wandering around the scary ole mountains all on her ownsome in the pitchy black of such a gelid night? 'Specially not a cupcake as soft and squishable as poor Buttercup.'

Snow scowls, opens the door and steps out into the night. Gretel and the others hurry out behind her when Snow lets out a startled gasp.

'She's gone!'

Gretel peers around in the inky gloom. Snow is right; Buttercup is nowhere to be seen.

Scarlett and Hex follow them outside, closing the door on the chill night air at Gilde's loud and peevish request.

'Where did she go?' asks Gretel. 'How could she have got so far away? She was only out a few seconds.'

''Tis witchcraft,' Hex suggests.

''Tis not *her* witchcraft,' argues Snow. 'She just does bread and cakes; her powers don't stretch to anything like invisibility or teleportation.' Snow starts to worry her hands over one another with an irritating clatter of metal on metal. 'What could have happened to her?' She turns to Scarlett sharply. 'Wolves?'

'My pack would never,' replies Scarlett indignantly. 'Not to a guest.'

A horrible thought grabs Gretel. 'When's Bin Night round here?'

'Not till next Wednesday,' Hex tells her. 'We're fortnightly here; they don't like coming up this far.'

'See?' says Scarlett. 'She'll be fine.'

'What if she's not?' frets Snow. 'What if she's fallen into a hole in the ground somewhere out in the dark and she can't get out?'

'Come on now, mate,' says Trevor soothingly. 'Buttercup was the first of us, remember? She used to live in the woods all by herself, she put the squad together, yes she's a bit of a softie but she's a lot more capable than a lot of you bipeds give her credit for, and—'

'Help,' comes Buttercup's muffled voice from somewhere off in the darkness. 'I couldn't see where I was going and I fell into this hole and I can't get out.'

'OK,' adds Trevor, 'but she's capable of doing lots of things that not all of us round here are, like… like wearing shoes.'

'And one of my shoes has come off,' calls the voice of Buttercup.

Trevor sighs, defeated. 'Let's just rescue the big lovely, shall we?'

10
Green

Hansel tries his hardest not to panic when the mysterious huntsman grasps his and Daisy's shoulders and ushers them away from the crowd. He absolutely mustn't lose control or containment over his powers, not here, not now. The results could be catastrophic.

'It wasn't us,' attempts Daisy as the huntsman pushes them down a side street.

'We've never even been to Nearby,' adds Daisy as the huntsman drags them around a dark corner into a deserted, pitch-black alley.

'We didn't set fire to anyone,' is her last-ditch attempt as the huntsman unlocks a door and pulls them inside.

'I know you didn't,' the huntsman tells her. 'I just said – I was there. Rosier, our fallen brother, may he rest in righteousness, was a zealot who'd got himself worked up into a frenzy. He was going to get us all killed. I take it he decided to go into the Darkwood on a Monday?'

Daisy nods. 'After setting fire to his robes.'

The huntsman sighs, and in a small, quiet voice, adds, 'Idiot.'

'What?' manages Hansel, just about swallowing down the thrashing, crackling magical anxiety.

'Oh! Sorry, you missed all of that, didn't you?' says Daisy. 'A Ghost came and said she'd been killed because the forest is more dangerous than usual on a Monday and then the Head Huntsman set himself on fire and then went into the woods anyway.' She turns to the huntsman. 'Hansel wasn't even there, he was locked up the whole time, and I was tied to a bonfire; whatever you think we might have done, we're innocent, I swear.'

'What you've done,' says the huntsman, 'is you've given the huntsmen the wake-up call we all desperately needed.'

'Oh no,' mutters Hansel.

'When you stood up to us, when you said "no, no more", when you pushed back, you sparked something extraordinary that may end up changing the whole course of Myrsina's future.'

'Definitely "oh no",' Daisy agrees. 'Please believe us, Your Huntsmanship, we didn't mean to spark anything or change the whole country. It was just that...' She tries to trail off, but the huntsman simply stares at her, mutely and blankly. Daisy stumbles on, anxiously. 'Well, as you said, he was a bit of a zealot. He locked us up, and he was going to kill us, and my friend Gretel... she's not even a witch, is she, Hansel?'

Hansel shakes his head silently.

'She was just clever,' babbles Daisy helplessly. 'He didn't like clever girls, even though he forced me to invent weapons in secret, and... and... we didn't do anything wrong...'

The huntsman lays a calming hand on Daisy's arm. 'You're right, Daisy. You didn't do anything wrong. You showed many of us huntsmen that we'd lost our way. It's no wonder some of the more remote villages have started to rebel against us if this is how we treat half of the ordinary population – false witchcraft accusations, abominations, duckings... it needs to stop. All of it. You are the ones who showed us that if we don't, this wave of anger will rise and rise, and we'll lose Myrsina altogether. You're heroes. You and your poor, lost sister Gretel.'

'What?' asks Hansel. In all of his anxiety-riddled nightmares following the battle to free Nearby, the words he had imagined the huntsmen using about his friends and family had mostly been about treachery and how slowly they should all be burnt to death. They'd never included anything so much as approaching a term like 'hero'.

'Is that really true?' the huntsman asks Daisy. 'About you making the weapons in Nearby?'

Daisy nods. 'Gretel too, to protect the village from the Darkwood at first, and then of course...'

'We can use that,' mutters the huntsman thoughtfully. 'The great, untapped resource – female engineers. Could even use it for the new machines... We can show how much we've already used women's work, in secret, and how much more useful to all it would be if we got rid of all these ridiculous abomination laws, if we all worked together, as equals...'

Daisy exchanges glances with Hansel. 'Did we really make actual huntsmen start thinking all this stuff just by doing tricks with spare masks and a collapsible rack?'

'Some of us have been thinking it for a while,' admits the huntsman. 'You were the spark, but many of us have been feeling for some time now that we can't carry on like this. Something's building, can't you feel it? Something bad.'

Hansel's eyes widen. The huntsman's blank face turns on him almost instantly.

'You feel it too,' she adds, 'don't you?'

Yes, he feels it. The oppressive fear. Fear, and something behind that, too. Anger. Divisiveness. And then, that all-consuming image again. A huge beast, with a hundred heads, a thousand, more, marauding through the streets of the Citadel, breaking through the gates and galloping out into the rest of the country beyond, screaming and roaring with a thousand voices.

He nods, glad at least that the vision didn't make him black out this time.

'Something's coming,' says the huntsman. 'Unless we change our ways and stop it now, we might not be able to stop it at all.'

Daisy looks from the huntsman to Hansel and back again, the penny dropping.

'Um,' she manages, 'when you say "something"… you don't mean "monsters", do you?'

'That's a very good question,' says the huntsman. 'Who knows what still lurks in the Darkwood? And if anything did attack now, we'd be facing it divided and ill-equipped to fight back, all because men like Rosier decided to stop girls like you from reaching their full potential.'

The huntsman takes both Daisy and Hansel's hands, to Hansel's surprise.

'Do you know what I believe?' she asks. 'I believe the two of you came here for a reason. I think nature's will, or fate, or call it what you want, brought you to the Citadel at this crucial moment to help us make the whole country better. To avert disaster. What do you think?'

'Er,' says Hansel.

'Maybe we're just here to sell baskets,' adds Daisy cautiously.

The door opens again, and three more huntsmen enter. All are wearing green badges.

'Sister,' says one, 'he's finishing up; the committee have said they'll allow you to give a five-minute response to… oh!'

Hansel fills with terror at the sight of more huntsmen. He tries to pull his hand away but the female huntsman holds him fast.

'Oh indeed, Brother,' says the huntsman warmly.

'Isn't that…?'

'It is.'

'From the…'

'The village, yes.'

'The village that…'

'Roundly kicked our bottoms and sent us running, yes.'

'But what are they doing here?'

'Selling baskets,' says Daisy quickly.

'Changing the world,' says the huntsman, over her.

One of the huntsmen with the green badges walks over to them.

'Will they be changing the world right now? Because we should really get going.' He hands a green rosette to the female huntsman.

'I hope so,' replies the female huntsman earnestly, pinning the rosette to her robe. 'Will you come with me, children? Will you show the world how it can become better, by following your example?'

'Er,' says Hansel again.

'We have to go now, Sister,' says one of the other huntsmen. He grabs Hansel by the elbow and starts hauling him up.

'Richard,' snaps the female huntsman, 'stop it.'

At the utterance of the name, the huntsman apparently called Richard not only lets go of Hansel, but backs away suddenly, his hands up in shock, as if he's had a knife pulled on him.

'Woah,' he shrieks, 'woah, what are you doing?'

'Changing the way we do things,' explains the female huntsman. 'Just grabbing these children, forcing them to stand with me… that's the way John Rosier would have had us do it.'

'Stop using people's names,' whines Richard, aghast.

'Why? We already know these children's names; how can we ask them to put their trust in us if they don't even know ours? It's the least we can do. What are you so afraid of, Richard? It's only your name.'

Richard sighs, and slumps. 'Fine. But we have to go *now*. Hi, kids, I'm Richard, sorry about your village and so on.'

'Yeah, sorry about that,' adds another huntsman. 'Um, and you can call me Grey, I suppose. Just… not in public.' Grey points to a third huntsman, who is standing in a corner, trying not to be a part of this sudden spate of name sharing. 'And that's Fennel.'

Fennel just waves miserably.

'My name's Morning,' says the female huntsman with the green rosette, 'and as you may have already worked out, I'm the green candidate for the new head huntsman.'

'And you're expected to speak any moment now,' prompts Richard, 'so are you children coming up to the podium with us or not?'

'All I'm doing this time is a short response to the orange candidate's speech,' Morning tells Hansel and Daisy. 'You don't have to come, but it would help me if you could tell the people of your own experiences with how we huntsmen need to change. You heard what that other candidate was like; surely you have things to say about what he has planned.'

She gets up, and holds out both hands for Hansel and Daisy.

'Please?' she asks. 'As equals?'

Hansel looks at Daisy, still not quite able to believe that the huntsmen just freely gave up their names to them. Still cloaked and masked as they are, Morning, Richard, Fennel and Grey seem much less intimidating now that they have names. No wonder huntsmen so rarely use them.

'I think maybe,' says Daisy to Hansel, carefully, 'if either of us had any warnings to broadcast, this might be a good opportunity.'

Maybe, thinks Hansel. *Maybe* he can trust these guys. And if it all turns out to be a trap, then he should at least be able to cause enough of a magical disturbance for himself and Daisy to be able to escape and blend into the crowd. After all, he came out here to try to save the Citadel from a terrible fate, didn't he? Maybe, right now, this is the best way to do it.

'All right,' he says. 'We'll do it, just this once.'

'Excellent,' replies Morning, a smile in the voice beneath the impassive mask. She grabs both of their hands and pulls them towards the door again. 'Come on, we have to go.'

11
Buttercup and Her Big Cake Hole

'Buttercup?' calls Snow into the darkness. 'Buttercup!'

'Snow, dear, would you mind if somebody else called for me and I replied?' comes the miserable voice from somewhere out in the night. 'I'm still not really in the mood to talk to you right now.' She pauses, then adds, 'Sorry.'

'Oh for the love of—'

Gretel interrupts Snow, turning instead to Patience. 'Patience, do you think you could maybe get some sort of psychic Ghostly lock on her or something?'

The chill around Patience makes the already bitter night air so cold that she leaves a trail of frost wherever she wafts. 'Who said *I'm* in the mood to talk to *you*?'

'Perspective, Patience! Buttercup is stuck in a hole in the ground!'

Scarlett pushes her way forwards. 'Tracking people is Werewolf work; I wouldn't ask a Ghost to do it if I were you.'

'*And*,' adds Patience, spreading furling fronds of ice in pretty patterns of Ghostly rage on the rock beneath her, 'I am *not* in the market to play supernatural one-upmanship with a Werewolf.'

Scarlett gives Gretel a big, sharp, friendly grin and pulls up her hood halfway. The resulting transmogrification is even more upsetting than usual. Her body stays human-shaped, while her head elongates noisily, sprouting fur and fangs. In her horrifying wolf-headed form, she lifts her snout and gives the air a good sniff. She pauses, crouches and snuffles at the ground. She then gets up, nods her canine head and pushes the hood back once more, assuming her fully human form, along with further meaty sounds.

'Over there.' She smiles before trotting off ahead, and only slipping over a little bit on the large, intricate mandala of ice that Patience's cold fury has painted.

The crevasse in the rock isn't very far away, but by the time Gretel and the others get to it, Buttercup is extremely stuck down it. Only the top half of her head is visible.

'Buttercup!' cries Snow, running over. 'Can you breathe?'

Buttercup just looks away.

Snow growls with frustration. 'Trevor, please ask Buttercup if she can breathe.'

'If she can call for help then she can breathe,' Gretel tells her. 'Buttercup, how in Myrsina did you manage to get wedged in there like that?'

'I got into a tizzy,' Buttercup admits. 'I was only up to my waist at first, but then I grabbed at the rocks, and… and these *stupid* hands of mine! I got trapped in fudge and it just made me sink down further. And I think the cold's frozen it.'

'Sorry,' mutters Patience, looking down at the ice spreading over the already frozen fudge fissure, 'a lot of that's me. I'd better go and… haunt a tree or something, till you're out.' She vanishes, and somewhere off in the trees beyond there is the unmistakable sound of Patience practising her haunting on an unsuspecting owl.

Gretel tests the frozen cake with her heel. It feels like frosty, dense soil.

'Good news is, there's still a bit of give to it,' she says. 'Do you lot have any spades?'

'There's a couple by the cesspit,' Hex tells her. 'I can fetch them.'

'I'll help you,' offers Jack.

Hex drops his head. 'You don't have to do that, I can manage.'

'You can manage,' echoes Jack flatly. 'You can carry two big spades.'

'Yes.'

'With your one arm.'

Hex sighs. 'OK. You can come.'

'A boys' trip to the cesspit it is, then.' Jack grins his do-not-trust-me-with-your-silverware grin. 'Lucky me.'

'Careful when you pass by the cottage,' calls Scarlett. 'Best not to wake Gilde.'

Gretel sits down next to Buttercup, removes her prototype climbing winch from her belt and starts to dismantle it.

'Why do you do that?' she asks Scarlett.

'Why do I do what?' Scarlett asks in return. She watches Gretel's studious undoing of her own handiwork, her head cocked doggishly. 'And what are *you* doing?'

'Oh, she's always tinkering,' says Snow. 'Taking one thing apart and turning it into a different thing. Buttercup, are you cold? Shall I fetch you a blanket?'

'We can use the main wheel as a pulley,' explains Gretel briefly. 'Why do you let Gilde boss you about so much? She's a bitter little old lady; you're an actual Werewolf.'

'Admittedly, right now I'd only be able to put the blanket over the top of your head,' adds Snow, 'but still. Could help.'

'Wolves are pack animals,' Scarlett tells Gretel. 'We understand hierarchy. Gilde was the first of us, she took us in.' She nods down at the hapless Buttercup. 'Like that one, and I notice you're all running around after her, even though she's the weakest of your pack.'

'Hey,' whines Trevor, 'don't say that.'

'Sorry,' replies Scarlett with a friendly matter-of-factness. 'Second weakest. I keep forgetting about you, spider.' She looks across at Snow, who has taken off a badger pelt from around her waist and is trying to lay it in a way that might keep Buttercup warm. 'Would it help if I went full wolf and started digging with my claws? Break the ground a bit before the men bring the spades?'

'You're very helpful, for a Werewolf,' says Gretel, quietly working away at the winch, 'aren't you?'

'What do you mean, "for a Werewolf"?' Even while mildly affronted, Scarlett remains largely affable. 'Have you just never met a Werewolf before? We're friendly creatures, we love making ourselves useful. We have to be able to integrate into human as well as wolf societies. Apparently, manners aren't our strong point in either type of social setting; sometimes it's hard to remember what's considered rude in which form. All I'm saying is, be glad I've learned to stop sniffing people's bums while I'm this shape.' She scratches the inside of her ear, finds something in there and eats it.

'Hmm,' mutters Gretel. 'It's a pity.'

'What?'

'Well, think of how friendly and helpful you could be if you didn't have to obey Gilde constantly telling you not to be.' Gretel is finally able to pull the inner wheel mechanism out of the winch. 'I can only imagine how useful a Werewolf would be on our team. Once our Ghost had got used to not being the only supernatural any more, of course.'

Scarlett's face creases with thoughtfulness. 'Hmm.'

'Snow, stop it!' Buttercup's voice is even more muffled than before, from fully underneath Snow's badger pelt. 'Now I *can't* breathe!'

'Sorry!' Snow snatches the pelt from the top of Buttercup's head. 'Wait, does that mean you're talking to me again?'

'No!'

12

Seduction in Spades

'Not far now,' Hex tells Jack, as they stumble through the darkness.

'I can tell,' Jack replies. 'Ground's softer here.'

Hex shoots Jack a quick glance of distaste.

'Well, you're not going to be able to dig a cesspit in rock, are you?' says Jack.

'You know a lot about cesspits,' Hex replies.

'I grew up poor,' Jack tells him.

'Are you not still poor?'

'Not as poor as I was.' Jack claps Hex gently on the 'good' shoulder. 'Got bed and board in a genuine haunted house nowadays, got cleared of murder and now I'm on a bracing night walk in the mountains with a mysterious stranger; my life's just getting better and better…'

Hex shakes Jack's lightly lingering hand off his shoulder. 'Stop it.'

Jack seamlessly switches his expression to one of wounded innocence. 'Stop what?'

'You know what. I know Gilde said I'd be flattered, but she was just… teasing.'

'Does she tease you a lot, then?'

'It's just her… funny little way.'

'Oh. OK,' replies Jack. 'We all have our quirks, I suppose.'

'Such as deliberately singling out the most useless and isolated member of a group and following him out to the privy to try to sweet-talk him into leaving his people and joining yours, like he's some desperate, needy child? Quirks like that?'

'Woah!' Jack tries another winsome smile, still with emphasis on the innocence. 'Where did that outburst come from? I'm just helping you fetch spades. I'm not doing what you think I'm doing, and I certainly don't think any of those things about you. Why would I think you were useless? You turn into a bird!'

Hex turns his face away from Jack. 'No I don't. I *got* turned into a bird by a witch, along with all my brothers. My sister Septa was a witch too, and she almost died bringing us back. Only she ran out of time with me, hence the wing. None of this is my power. This is the magic of two witches, at war with one another over what shape my body should be. And the more powerful of those two witches is the malevolent one who wanted me to stay a bird forever, just to hurt my sister.' Hex snorts a small laugh. 'None of this is even about me. I was just… there. So, yes, I'm the useless one. I wouldn't expect someone who can summon hundred-foot vegetables to understand.' He stops beside a small wooden shack that smells strongly and distinctly of poor drainage. A couple of spades rest against its wall. Hex snatches one up and shoves it into Jack's hands. 'You should have sent your spider to try to talk me round; at least he'd have seen eye to eye with me, rubbish one to rubbish one.'

'You are *not* "the rubbish one"…' Jack pauses, wincing, as Hex drops the second spade and swears. 'And Trevor definitely wouldn't thank you for calling him that either. We have no "rubbish one". Everybody's valued at Buttercup's house for their different skills. Trevor's actually an excellent little spy.'

Hex picks the second spade up, frowning. 'He's not spying on me right now, is he?'

'Oh, no,' Jack reassures him, 'he worries about Buttercup when she gets herself into her cake-related scrapes; he's staying with her for emotional support.'

Hex pushes past Jack. 'Then he's a rubbish spy.'

Jack persists, following Hex with his spade. 'But why would he even want to spy on you – you're not the enemy, are you? We're all friends here.'

'Are we, now?'

'I'd certainly like us to be.' Jack attempts a playful nudge on Hex's wing.

Hex winces away from him. 'I asked you to stop that.'

'Just being friendly…'

'No. You're not, Jack Trott. I get it. You're handsome and charming and flirty. I can see what you're trying to do and it isn't going to work. You're not seducing anybody into anything, so please stop embarrassing us both.'

'Oh. OK.' Jack falls silent for a moment, before adding, 'Still, people on this trip keep calling me handsome, so that's something, right?'

Hex actually manages a small smile. 'If you want to be a master seducer, you're going to really need to work on that craving for constant validation, you know.'

'Yeah, I'll admit I haven't had much practice at this seduction lark.'

'You live in a house full of women.'

'No, I live in a house with a little girl, a Ghost, a spider and Buttercup and Snow, who are… Buttercup and Snow. It's a whole world of people not to flirt with. And if we're going by that, *you* live in a house full of women, too. Should I be worried about your masterful flirting, Hex of Ashtrie?'

'Me?' Hex barks a bitter laugh. He unfurls his great, black wing. '*Look* at me.'

'I *am* looking at you. I wonder when the last time is that *you* really looked at yourself, and saw something other than an old witch's pet Sweetiebird.'

Hex meets Jack's gaze for a second, then snorts, shaking his head and casting his eyes back down to the ground. 'You're still trying it on.'

'What?'

'And you're still terrible at it.'

'What??'

The group around Buttercup starts to become visible through the night-time gloom as Hex and Jack approach.

'The menfolk have returnéd,' calls Jack, 'with spades!' He pauses, squinting at the group in the dark. 'Why does Buttercup have a tea cosy on her head?'

'She's cold,' snaps Snow, snatching the spade from Hex.

'*She's* overcompensating,' adds Buttercup, from her hole. 'Trevor, tell Snow to stop overcompensating.'

'Gretel, do something,' Trevor pleads. 'I can't stand being stuck in the middle of all this, and' – here, the spider lowers his voice – 'it's making us look bad in front of the Werewolf and the birdman.'

Scarlett and Hex exchange glances. Trevor turns to them, voice raised again as if they both hadn't just heard his previous comment perfectly well over the sound of Snow's furious digging.

'Sorry about this, guys,' Trevor tells them, 'we're not usually like this, I think it's the new territory, it's put everyone on edge. Normally we make a lovely team, we saved a village and everything.'

'Yes.' With a slightly too friendly smile, Scarlett takes Jack's spade out of his hands. 'We heard.'

Scarlett joins Snow in digging around Buttercup. She easily surpasses Snow's pace, combining the strength and digging skills of the wolf within, with all the benefits of her human shape, such as thumbs.

'Have you out in no time, mate,' Trevor calls to Buttercup by means of encouragement. 'Tell me we'll get her out soon,' he says desperately to Gretel in another horribly audible stage whisper.

'Don't worry,' replies Gretel. 'Jack? A tree here, please.' She points to a spot a few feet away from Buttercup.

Jack grins. 'My pleasure. Any requests? Oak? Ash? Spruce? I can do you a cheeky little cherry blossom, complete with unseasonal flowers, if anyone's feeling romantic…?'

Snow scoffs, mid-dig. Hex looks down at his feet.

'I quite like flowers,' says Trevor.

'Me too,' adds Scarlett, not even out of puff.

'They attract all sorts of tasty insects,' says Trevor wistfully.

'Sometimes I just like to eat a whole load of flowers,' continues Scarlett, just as wistfully. 'Don't know why.'

'Anything's fine, as long as it's strong, and has a thick horizontal branch this high,' Gretel tells him, getting onto tiptoe to indicate a point as high up as she can reach.

Jack obliges with a sturdy pear tree, complete with a branch of exactly the dimensions and height Gretel requested, laden with perfect fruit.

'Can Werewolves eat flowers, then?' Trevor asks Scarlett.

'No, they make me really sick; as I say, I don't know why I do it. Hex says he had a dog used to do the same thing.'

'That was a cat,' says Hex quietly. 'Back before I got... feathered. He used to eat grass, not flowers.'

'Really?' replies Scarlett, with amiable inattentiveness. 'Should have got a dog, dogs are better. A dog wouldn't have tried to eat you when you got turned into a raven.'

'I'll need a good, strong creeper, too,' Gretel tells Jack over the burgeoning cats versus dogs debate. 'Needs to be able to fit this pulley, and still be alive, so Buttercup won't accidentally cakeify it.'

'Anyone like pears?' calls Jack, summoning a set of twisted vines. 'Perfectly ripe straight off the tree and all, would you believe.'

'You don't know a dog wouldn't have tried to eat me too,' Hex tells Scarlett.

'Rude,' replies Scarlett. '*I've* never tried to eat you.' She holds up her spade. 'Oh. My spade just turned into an apple turnover.'

'Sorry,' says Buttercup, her head and hands now above ground. 'It knocked my fingers. I'm a bit stressed.'

'It's OK.' Gretel passes the vines to Buttercup. 'I think that's enough digging now anyway. Buttercup, hold tight; the rest of you need to help me pull.'

'It's actually really hard to catch a pear at the moment when it's neither too hard nor too squishy,' continues Jack, taking hold of a section of vine beneath the pulley, and wondering whether anyone is even listening to him. 'You should all try one.'

'You did bite me that one time, though,' continues Hex to Scarlett as they take their own places grabbing hold of the vine behind Jack.

'For the last time, Hex, that was an accident.'

'You see?' says Trevor, scuttling onto Jack's shoulder to address the Werewolf and the magical raven. 'Who bit who, cats versus dogs, this is the sort of prime banter we could be having all the time, if you joined us. What about you, Jack? Cats or dogs? Let's get a scintillating group conversation happening. For my part, I'm terrified of both. What about you, Snow? Cats or dogs?'

Snow barges in front of Gretel, and grabs the vine.

'Hold on tight, Buttercup,' she says, 'we're getting you out of there.'

Buttercup turns her head away from Snow as best as she is able, still up to her chest in a combination of densely packed soil, rock and fudge. 'Humph,' she humphs.

On Snow's command, they all heave on the vine. After considerable heaving and ho-ing and Trevor trying to engage everyone in some light-hearted cats versus dogs chat, Buttercup is dislodged and is able to haul herself up, miserable and covered in caramel, above ground. She sniffs, cold and humiliated, and tries in vain to wipe off some of her thick, sticky coating of confectionary, which only serves to spread it all the more.

'Sorry about that, everyone,' she murmurs.

'It's all right, Buttercup,' Trevor tells her cheerfully, 'happens to everyone.'

Buttercup glances down. 'No it doesn't.' She gets to her feet, stickily. 'Well, I think I've singlehandedly managed to prove to poor Scarlett and Hex here that we definitely need them more than they need us, haven't I? We may as well just go.'

The group look over to Scarlett and Hex. It's the sort of expectant pause that calls for a reply such as, 'Ah, but no, because you see, you just proved how well we all work as a team, so of course we'll join you.' Scarlett and Hex seem to be unaware of this fact, because they don't make any reply at all.

Buttercup sighs. 'Right.'

'So what now?' Jack asks. He feels weirdly sad. Defeated. Hex and Scarlett don't want to join the gang. People *always* want to join the gang, the gang's great. Has he... has he somehow not been charming enough? Surely, that's impossible.

'We could go east.'

The suggestion is made in a low tone of voice that Snow only ever uses when she's feeling particularly thoughtful, usually about something really very dangerous. Jack has spent thirteen years learning to be deeply wary of that tone of voice.

'...yummy.' Even the Dwarf by Snow's ankle seems perturbed by this suggestion.

'You can't go east,' Hex tells her, in a quiet, quavering voice.

'I thought our whole reason for coming here was it's too dangerous to go east,' argues Jack.

'You *can't* go east,' repeats Hex, louder.

'It is riskier,' Snow admits, 'but less so than trying to take on the Citadel without decent back-up. And since this lot here have made up their minds...'

'You can't go east,' says Hex again, his voice strained. 'You don't understand what's out there.'

'Well, you're kind of giving us no choice here, Bird Boy, if you won't help us.'

'Gilde!' Hex shouts. 'Gilde, you were right!'

'What are you doing?' Jack cries, appalled.

'What are *you* doing?' Buttercup asks Snow. 'Suddenly you want to go east and put yourself in danger? What are you trying to prove this time?'

'We don't want a situation here,' Scarlett warns them nervously. Hex continues to cry out for Gilde's help.

'I'm not trying to prove anything,' Snow replies, exasperated.

'Ain't you, though?'

Gilde steps towards them, not from the cottage after all but from the dark trees, treading softly and silently in bearskin-wrapped nightclothes. She could have slipped out of the house at any point when they were digging Buttercup out, and none of them would have noticed.

'Is this why you cause much trouble, Majesty? To please your Cupcake? Impress her a bit? Make her all a-flutter about you bein' such a big hero?' Gilde giggles a little. 'Her face, when you suggested it might be an idea fer us all to know our place and live a quiet life. That's when I knew you were going to go all out to prove yourself to her, and rain all kinds of calamity down on the rest of us in doing so.'

Snow glares at her, stony-faced. The Dwarves around her huddle, fidgeting nervously. Jack becomes aware that he's being watched by a multitude of eyes in the dark trees and rocky outcrops beyond.

'I thought you were going to bed,' says Snow.

'Oh, I'd hoped to, Majesty,' simpers Gilde. 'Early to bed, early to rise and so on, but I just couldn't rest, knowing that you were fixing on causing more trouble. Maybe even trying to poach my lovely Wolfie and Sweetiebird off of me, loyal though they are. So, I stayed up past my bedtime. Snuck out, listened to all of you yammering from the trees.'

'A spy!' Trevor sounds excited. 'She's a spy; sorry, I should probably have picked up on that, but in my defence I never claimed to be a *counter*-spy.'

Gilde smiles. 'Oh, the honey you poured on my friends, to try to get them to leave a poor little ole lady all alone in the mountains.' She twinkles at Jack. Jack does not enjoy the experience. 'Jack the lad, I gotta commend you 'specially, I don't think Hexy's ever had such attention. I'm so sorry nobody wanted none of your fruit, perfectly ripe as it may be. And Buttercup, my sugarwitch, I will give you this – of all the expectations I had about what you all would get up to while guesting with me, even I never imagined any of you just plain falling in a hole in the ground, so kudos to you for managing that.'

'Are you quite finished?' Snow asks coldly. 'I take it that we are no longer welcome here, with immediate effect.'

'Oh, no,' Gilde coos. 'Quite the opposite. You had your opportunity to leave earlier, and you chose not to take it. Now you're talkin' about upsetting the balance with the Citadel *and* the eastern woods, I'm afraid we simply cannot let that slide.'

The many eyes that have been watching them start creeping forwards now, taking shape as great, hulking animals. There seem to be more wolves about than before, and amongst them are Mamma, Papa and the giant, shadowy form of Baby.

'What do you think you're doing?' asks Snow. She automatically reaches her hand to the strap on her back where she keeps her axes. Jack suddenly remembers, with a sick sensation, that Snow, Gretel and the Dwarves had, in the name of being polite houseguests, removed their weapons when they'd gone into Gilde's cottage. From Snow's expression as her hand hits empty leather, she's only just realised this detail too.

'Stopping you, Majesty,' Gilde replies. She nods meaningfully at Hex and Scarlett, who – begrudgingly, considering the cold – begin to get undressed. 'Saving you. Saving us all. Like my Sweetiebird said, you *mustn't* go east. It's simply too dangerous.'

'So you'd sooner have another battle? On your doorstep, this time? Considering how the last one went for you?'

Gilde giggles. 'You ain't got no weaponry, Majesty.'

'We've got our magic and our wits.'

Snow nods to Jack, who summons forth a patch of nettles to prove her point. He's a little taken aback by Hex's expression. The man stops struggling out of his underwear and stares at the nettles. From his hurt expression, it's as if Jack has just sent Hex a deeply personal and offensive insult. Before Jack can so much as react to Hex's sudden and mysterious umbrage, the other man's face warps. Black feathers sprout, his nose lengthens and hardens to a jagged beak. His eyes move to the sides of his head, but otherwise remain the same, which is frankly upsetting to look at. Jack winces away from the sight, and turns his attention back to the standoff between Gilde and Snow.

'You also ain't got all your people with you,' says Gilde. She cocks her head. 'What happen – you forget about your Ghost, or just think we might not count her again?'

This is a terrible moment for Jack to realise he hasn't seen Patience in ages.

'Uh oh,' he says. To himself, obviously.

Gilde pulls a small glass bell jar out of her furs. Trapped inside it is a tiny little translucent monochrome figure, which would look like Patience if Patience were only five inches tall.

'Just picked this up in the trees. You don't get to live in a cursed forest as long as I have without learning how to make your own Ghost traps.' Gilde smiles.

'What have you done?' barks Snow.

'Just a lil casual hostage situation, Majesty,' Gilde replies. 'Same as you did with our poor Hexy when you demanded we hear you out. Well, we heard you out enough to know your plan's too risky to all of us. Kind of backfired on you there, huh?'

Inside the bell jar, Patience is so furious that she's fast becoming invisible behind swirling fronds of frost on the glass. Snow lunges forwards, makes a grab for the icy jar. Gilde pulls it out of range of her grasp swiftly. Close by in the gloom, a giant bear lollops and softly growls.

'Nuh-uh, Majesty,' Gilde trills. 'You also don't get to live in a cursed forest this long without learning to perform an exorcism or two.'

'Don't, Snow,' Buttercup warns.

It's not Snow who raises her hands in surrender first, but Gretel. This means, reasons Jack, that either Gretel's completely out of ideas as to how to get all of them out of this latest situation, or she's already come up with a plan to get them out of it, but it depends on them being made prisoner by this horrible old woman first. Either way, it suggests to Jack that he should probably go along with her.

He also raises his hands, closely followed by Buttercup and Trevor, who lifts up four legs in a show of willing. Snow and her Dwarves don't raise a thing, but Snow sighs dejectedly, and makes no attempt to fight back when Scarlett corrals her back towards Gilde's cottage, with apologetic, doggish eyes.

Jack tries to meet Hex's gaze, to try to gauge exactly how happy or otherwise he might be about this new development of actual hostage-taking. Hex, still in full bird form, won't even look at him. Buttercup notices, and shoots him a sad, sympathetic little smile, which doesn't exactly make matters better. When a young man tries to flirt, the last reaction he wants is one of pity from somebody who's just spent most of the night up to her eyebrows in a hole in the ground.

All in all, he thinks to himself, it's hard to imagine anyone having a worse night tonight than they are.

13

In Which Hansel Is Having a Worse Night Than Jack

Hansel knows that he said yes to going with Morning. He knows that it meant 'yes, right now'. He knows. He understands. He wants to help, really he does... only the hand on his wrist is so tight, and Morning moves so fast with her huntsman team, through the twisted, dark, narrow side streets of the Citadel, nothing but continuous looming walls and clattering cobbles to Hansel. He feels the magical terror rise up in him again. It seems so much louder, here in this place, with so little sky, so little air, so very many people. He swallows the thrashing magical power back inside him with such a force that it makes him feel dizzy for a moment.

Morning has been talking almost nonstop since they started hurrying through the alleys. Hansel is able to catch only snippets of it through the crackling haze of his own anxiety.

'I don't want you children to worry about your safety; I think you'll find a lot more sympathy here for your village than you're probably expecting...'

He tunes out again, the scream in his head temporarily drowning out her words. When the swell of magic ebbs down enough for him to take in what she's saying again, the scaffold is in sight.

'…of even the huntsmen don't see Nearby's rebellion as part of any kind of aggressive act,' Morning is saying, 'rather, an example of how the current system is failing to live up to our initial expectations.'

They're at the scaffold. Morning pauses briefly, and gives both of them a quick, tight hug. The sensation of being hugged by a huntsman is a singular one for Hansel – no huntsman he's ever crossed paths with before has been the particularly huggy type – and with the figure hugging him still swathed from head to toe in robes, her face totally masked in serene porcelain, it has a decidedly off-putting element to it. It's like being hugged by an idea, and somebody else's idea, at that.

Without another word, she climbs the scaffold. Her cohorts – Hansel can't tell, in the darkened confusion of bodies, which is Richard, which is Grey and which is Fennel – nudge Hansel and Daisy onto the steps to follow her.

Hansel is surprised by the level of applause that greets Morning when she steps to the front to address the crowd. The banners around the stage are still orange – this is just her rebuff statement at the end of the other candidate's big speech, he recalls. He notes that there are quite a few green handheld flags being waved in the audience. There's something else, as well. The atmosphere shifts when she steps forward. It feels as though thousands of people in the dark just had a window onto bright sunlight opened for them. There's a sense of relief, of warmth, a brief spark of elation, even. Other feelings break through, too. Sharp flashes of anger and hatred are suddenly illuminated by the light she seems to cast over the crowd. There really are a lot of orange flags out there too, Hansel notes.

Morning casts her arms wide, as if trying to embrace the air around the crowd.

'Friends,' she calls cordially, 'and brethren.'

There are a handful of boos from the crowd.

'And' – here she pauses, for dramatic effect – 'those of you who will not call me "friend".' Another pause. 'Yet.'

104

The boos are drowned out by amiable laughter.

'You've heard what my brother the orange candidate has to say, and I know that many of you will be as concerned by his plans as I. Creating yet more abominations to hold our fellow human citizens in fear is not the way forward. That was our fallen head huntsman's way, and we all know where that led us.'

Hansel feels the whisper rippling through the crowd. 'Nearby.'

'It led us to Nearby,' says Morning.

An uneasy murmur issues from the crowd. Hansel spots that some of the huntsman masks at the front of the crowd have turned towards himself and Daisy. It's sometimes hard to tell with a huntsman whether they're looking directly at you from behind their mask or not; that's part of the point of the masks in the first place.

'Where we were defeated,' continues Morning.

The disquieted murmur swells. Some of the masked figures near the front are nudging one another, and pointing at Hansel and Daisy.

Morning opens her arms again. 'It's all right,' she says. 'It's OK to admit it. In fact, it's crucial that we do. We were defeated, because the people of Nearby no longer welcomed huntsmen.'

The murmur grows again. Hansel can pick out individual voices heckling from the crowd.

'Bewitched by the cursed forest,' calls one voice.

'Lost my spectacles,' cries another, 'never did get that money back.'

'And it wasn't due to their proximity to the Darkwood,' continues Morning, raising her voice, 'but because of the heavy-handed way the huntsmen treated their community.' She pauses again. 'Hansel Mudd and Daisy Wicker, isn't that right?'

All eyes, masked and unmasked, now turn to them. Hansel feels as though his stomach has just dropped through the floor. Daisy takes his hand and leads him to make his way slowly, shakily, towards the front of the stage.

'It's *them*,' comes one voice from the crowd.

'Collaborators,' shouts another voice.

'Should have burned you,' cries a third.

'Shush,' says a fourth.

'Let them speak,' says a fifth.

'They're just kids,' comes a sixth voice, sounding genuinely surprised.

And then, the applause starts. It begins with a smattering so small that Hansel initially assumes it to be sarcastic, but it grows quickly into something loud and real and warm. He blinks across at Daisy. She seems as surprised by it as he is.

They reach Morning at the front of the stage, a tower of calm confidence in her placid mask. She holds hands with both of them, so that she stands between them. Hansel understands it as a supportive gesture, but still, he feels bereft of Daisy's hand.

'It's all right,' she tells them quietly. 'Speak. They want to hear your story. They *need* to hear your story.'

'Um,' says Hansel. He feels, helplessly, as if he is speaking too loudly and too quietly at the same time. There is a cacophony of voices, and of voiceless feelings, tumbling through his mind. There are too many people here, and they're all frightened or angry or both, and they're all looking to him, waiting for *him*. And there's a monster coming. And when the monster came for Nearby – not an Ogre or a Wyvern but the *real* monster, the monster of rage and hate and spite – when it had come for his friends and his family, he had failed, he'd let them down. It had taken Daisy and his sister and the Darkwood to fix it. What was his story? His story was that he'd allowed the monster to banish his sister, and take his village and threaten his friend, while he'd gone to pieces, locked up in a cage, useless.

'Um,' he says again, 'they took… *you* took my… well, not all of you, I suppose. One of you. And you didn't take her, I suppose, but not for want of trying, and…'

'Can't hear the boy,' says somebody a few rows back.

'Speak up, lad,' shouts somebody else.

'Might be the accent,' adds a well-to-do-sounding woman. 'Boy, could you try to sound a little less east-country rural? There's a good chap.'

'Um…' He panics.

'It all started when a huntsman came for his sister,' says Daisy, loudly and clearly. 'My friend. Gretel Mudd.'

'The Mudd Witch,' growls a voice from the crowd.

'She's not a witch,' Daisy protests. 'She never did any witchcraft. Just maths.'

'She did do witchcraft,' comes another voice. 'All that stuff in the battle.'

'Escaping the rack as if it were made of paper,' cries somebody else.

'That was all science trickery; sleight of hand,' Daisy explains.

'But the ground, the shadows…' comes another voice.

'You will recall that Gretel Mudd was aided and abetted by real witches, powerful witches, with whom she would never have come into contact had she not been wrongfully accused of witchcraft by this preposterous system,' adds Morning. 'Such is the legacy of these ridiculous "abominations". They do nothing but turn our own people against us. Do they hold back the witches? A normal human girl cannot become a witch simply through learning, or keeping a trade, or speaking out, or living as a valued member of our society. That's not a witch. That is a woman, and we're turning our own womenfolk over to the Darkwood with these rules! And with them, their communities give up on the Citadel and turn their own faces towards the Darkwood. Nearby might have been the first, but you all must have heard about the other villages who have turned huntsmen away in the past week.'

Hansel frowns, and wishes that Morning weren't standing between Daisy and him. Other villages have rebelled?

'Miggleham,' lists Morning, 'Lesser Spun, Turney and Yon, *and* there have been reports this evening of trouble stirring up in Slate.'

A new, worried mumble starts up in the crowd. The villages she's listed are all similar to Nearby: small farming villages near the Darkwood's border, but Slate's up near the mountains, and a full-sized mining town.

'And what started all this?' Morning asks. 'A human girl being falsely accused of witchcraft. By us, the very people who were supposed to protect her. Is it any wonder the people are angry? Is it any wonder they're beginning to rebel? And my fellow candidate believes that the way to counter this is to double down on the abominations? I say no!'

The applause starts up again, and spreads through the crowd like an unchecked fire. Morning has to shout in order to be heard above the white noise of their approval.

'I say the old ways are not working,' she continues at the top of her voice. 'I say we must no longer dictate to the people how they should live their lives, as we stand apart from them, aloof in this Citadel, with no comeback, no consequences.'

The applause becomes even louder. Morning is practically screaming in order to remain audible.

'When I met these children tonight,' she continues, 'they were scared of me. Scared. They didn't know who I was. I was just another mask and robe. We huntsmen must search our consciences and truly ask ourselves why it is we never share our names or faces. Those of you who were at Nearby will remember the words of our poor fallen sister, Patience.'

The applause dies down a little. Hansel can make out a disquieted muttering amongst the huntsmen near the front.

'I know that those words rang true for a lot of us, even coming from a wretched shadow of death as they were. They certainly rang true for me. To lead the people fairly, we must have accountability, and in order to have accountability, we huntsmen must make a sacrifice. But I believe that in doing so, we can gain something far more valuable. And that sacrifice is this.'

She reaches up to her mask, and removes it.

The crowd goes wild. The gasps of horror and cries of outrage from the huntsmen are barely audible amidst the screams of shocked delight and approval from the rest of the audience.

She throws the mask down onto the wooden slats of the platform. The nose chips a little on impact, but the mask stays relatively intact. The noise of the crowd grows even louder. Hansel can hardly bear it. As loud as the roar in his ears is, it's surpassed by the overwhelming cacophony flooding his mind. So many of them. So many screams, from so many mouths and minds. A thousand heads and a thousand voices. The monster. The monster is still coming. He feels dizzy and distant, as if he's watching himself from far away. He tries to look to Daisy, but Morning is still standing between them, clutching his hand. Morning smiles at him. He realises that this is the first time he's really seen her. She's fortyish, with a pleasant, slightly creased face and prominent front teeth shining brightly from within a warmly lopsided smile. Her blonde hair sticks up wildly in parts, like a dandelion. She looks sweet, comical even, like an overworked mum who's forgotten to brush her hair.

She says something to him, but he can't hear.

'What?' He can't even hear himself speak.

She repeats herself. At least with the mask off, he's able to read her lips to help make her out.

'Smash it,' she shouts, grinning wonkily. 'It's OK. Stamp on it. I want you to.'

'Er…' His head feels too full to even so much as process her simple request. The monster is coming. He agreed to do this so he could warn them about the monster. He needs to warn them about the monster. He needs to…

Daisy steps forward, hitches up her skirt to the knee and stamps down hard on Morning's mask. The porcelain shatters under the heel of her boot. The crowd reaches a frenzied volume. Morning, the hood of her cowl pushed back, framed by a halo of messy hair, flings her arms wide once more.

'My name,' she screams, surely still inaudible to all but the first few rows, 'is Morning Quarry. I was born and raised in Slate. I joined the huntsmen to make a positive difference. This is what I look like. I'm the green candidate for the position of head huntsman, and if you think that the system needs changing, then I believe I'm the candidate for you.'

She steps back towards Hansel and Daisy again, the broken mask crunching under her feet. Once more, she takes their hands in hers. She lifts their hands together triumphantly.

The monster, thinks Hansel, the monster. He has to warn them. He fights to hold back the squirming magical terror within him as the image fills his mind. He can see it. A Hydra. So many heads, so many mouths, so many teeth, filling the streets, destroying buildings, destroying homes, destroying lives. So many voices, filling the whole land with a thousand screams.

'Muh…' he manages. He tries to pull his hand away from Morning's, but her grip is too tight.

'Almost done,' Morning tells him through the gritted teeth of a winsome grin.

The platform, the crowd and the Citadel beyond seem to melt away. There is nothing except Hansel and the Hydra. There is no Daisy, and no Morning. The Hydra fills everything.

'Please leave them alone,' he whispers to it, inside his head. 'Please don't come here. You'll hurt them.'

The Hydra whispers back to him in countless voices. 'Stupid little farm boy,' it tells him, 'I am already here.'

No.

The magic crackles through him. It wants to shake the ground and suck out the stars and create shadows thick as lard. He can't do it here, not here… desperately, he holds it in, but in doing so manages to push the contents of his stomach out. He's vaguely aware of the front row reacting in revulsion as vomit surges up, stinging his throat, landing with a disgusting splatter on the platform, as well as several huntsmen's masks and robes. The last dribble of it runs miserably down his chin and soaks into his shirt.

How embarrassing, one small, painfully alert and rational part of his mind tells him, as blackness descends over his eyes, his head spins and his knees buckle. *Eurgh, I hope we don't land in the sick*, adds the last part of his brain to make any sense, before that too switches off, and he is left in a cold, hard oblivion.

14
Something in the Woodshed

'I *am* charming though, aren't I?' Jack asks, for the fourth time. 'Like, I know there's better-looking fellas and all that, but I *do* have the gift of charm…?'

'Is that a euphemism or something?' asks Trevor. His voice is muffled, coming as it is from beneath an upturned tin cup on a shelf.

'For what?' Jack asks.

'For being able to do magic,' replies the Trevory cup. 'You know, how you charm the vine and so on.'

Jack contemplates this. 'That is quite an impressive way of describing what I do,' he says. '"Charm the vine". I'm going to start using that in the future. Cheers, Trevor.'

'You're welcome,' comes the muffled reply.

Quietness falls throughout the group again. Gretel gently exhales in relief. It isn't that Jack's not great and all, it's just not ideal to be tied up next to him in a locked woodshed when he's just had his ego mildly bruised.

'Although that wasn't what I meant,' adds Jack. At the other side of the shed, Snow rolls her eyes wearily. 'None of you would have suggested I try charming Hex if you didn't think I was already good at being charming, right?'

'Well, Hex is a bit quiet, isn't he?' Trevor replies. 'Bit of a frosty reception there. You should try charming Scarlett instead; I like Scarlett.'

'It was Scarlett who put you in that cup,' Snow reminds him.

'Yeah, but only because she was told to. And she was lovely and gentle with me, poked a little air hole in the side, made sure not to hurt my legs.'

'You like her because she didn't deliberately try to maim you?' asks Gretel.

'When you're a little spider, the pool of people who haven't tried to maim or kill you is surprisingly small. Even Patience tried to kill me before she died, and we're mates now, aren't we, Patience?' Trevor pauses. 'Is she agreeing with me? I can't see.'

On the shelf next to Trevor's crockery prison is Patience, still tiny and translucent beneath the glass jar, a circle of salt and sage ash around the rim. She sits slumped in the middle of the jar, tired and defeated, so diminished by the Ghost trap that she's rendered mute behind the glass.

'Ironic, innit, Patience,' adds Trevor, conversationally and without malice, 'how the first time we met, you identified me as a weak target and took me hostage to make the others do as you said, and this time… well. Just goes to show, what goes around comes around, as my old mum used to say.'

Behind the glass jar, Patience pulls a face at the tin cup.

'Wait, not my mum,' continues Trevor, 'I never knew my mum, I just sort of hatched. Who do I mean…? Buttercup! Like Buttercup used to say. And still does say, in fact, just not this time because she doesn't have to say it this time, because I'm the one saying it.'

In her corner of the shed, Buttercup, her hands tightly wrapped in cloth and tied together, still hasn't said a word. Gretel glances over in concern. Buttercup gives her a small, tight smile. Gretel gets the feeling that this is less for her sake and more so that Buttercup can carry on steadfastly refusing to meet Snow's ongoing, searching gaze.

'It's just that none of you lot are very charmable, so I don't get much practice in,' says Jack, his lament falling into every awkward silence in the shed like spilled tomato sauce rushing to find new bits of white clothing.

'Well,' says Gretel. 'This isn't ideal.'

'Agreed,' replies Snow. 'I mean, sitting us on log piles. Not very comfortable.' She lowers her voice. 'So, when are we escaping? Because I don't know about the rest of you, but I could break us all out of here incredibly easily.'

Even with hands tied behind his back, Jack is able to beckon a couple of thin creepers through the crack beneath the shed door. 'Door would be a piece of cake. Mind you, if we get Buttercup untied, it could be a literal piece of cake.'

The cloths and ropes around Buttercup's hands turn to thin pastry that comes apart at her slightest tug. 'I don't need untying, thank you,' she says quietly, picking pie crust from her fingernails, and shaking the life back into her limbs. 'I was waiting for Gretel.'

'And I was waiting for one of them to come in and stand guard over us,' Gretel admits in a low whisper, in case of keen Werewolf ears, 'but it's been about an hour now. Somebody must have decided to guard the shed from outside, instead. I wasn't expecting that.'

'Maybe they all fancied some peace and quiet,' murmurs Snow meaningfully.

'What,' asks Jack, clocking Snow's expression, 'is Trevor talking too much, again?'

'Hey,' Trevor replies resentfully, just as Buttercup reaches up to his shelf and releases him from the cup. 'Oh! Thanks, mate.'

Buttercup carefully lifts the glass jar off Patience next, and sweeps the ring of salt and sage away. The jar turns to marzipan and most of the salt becomes hundreds and thousands. Patience's tiny, diaphanous form flickers, fizzles and is suddenly full size again, hovering gently in a seated position above the shelf.

She stretches, relieved, then snaps her focus back on the rest of the group.

'Jack, will you shut up; Birdbrain didn't fancy you – it's not the end of the world.'

'Hey.'

'I've been wanting to say that for *ages*,' adds Patience.

Buttercup squats down between Gretel and Jack, and starts seeing to their ropes.

'Um,' says Gretel. 'While we're on the subject of things we've been wanting to say for a while… Sorry, for lumping you in with the huntsmen.'

Patience shrugs. 'I *was* a huntsman; I'm not asking anyone to ignore that. It does also mean I understand them in ways you don't, you know.'

'OK.' Gretel starts munching on the bonds around her wrists, which have turned into some sort of delicious pretzel. 'I still don't think trying to kill people is the answer, you know,' she adds, her mouth full.

'You could at least consult me a little more,' Patience tells her.

'Hmm.' Gretel swallows another mouthful of pretzel-rope. 'No more advocating for killing, though.'

'No promises.' Patience nods at Buttercup, who has turned her attention to trying to free the Dwarves – not an easy task, with them all fast asleep in a hairy huddle. 'Besides, it looks like I'm not the only one whose feelings and opinions have gone ignored lately.'

Buttercup doesn't say anything. Clearly convinced that she's done enough to untangle the Dwarves, she looks across at Snow. Snow, for her part, has very nearly finished sawing through her own wrist ties, using the beak of one of the bird skulls decorating her armour as a handy blade. Buttercup sighs faintly.

Gretel breaks free of the last of her bready bonds and gets up for a stretch. 'Well, that's more comfortable, at least.' She cracks her knuckles. 'So I take it from the fact nobody's heard what we're doing and come in that Scarlett isn't on guard out there; we're probably just being guarded by Hex right now, which is a pain because he'd be quite easy to overpower.' She gazes around at the witches in the woodshed. 'Could you all try only overpowering him a *little*?'

Jack raises a questioning hand.

'No attempting to charm him, Jack. We just need to do a sufficiently bad job of escaping so that they catch us and tie us up again with a bit more care.'

'Oh, *what* now?' huffs Patience. 'I'm not going back in that jar!'

'Just for a little while,' Gretel reassures her, 'to buy us a bit more persuasion time. I reckon we'll be done by morning. We were starting to win them over.'

Jack raises his eyebrows at her. 'Really?'

'Oh… maybe not on your part, sorry, Jack, and Gilde's a lost cause, but I seemed to be making some headway with Scarlett at least.'

Jack frowns down at his feet. 'Oh.'

'If we escape now… well, we just escape,' Gretel reasons.

Somewhere out in the mountains, a bear roars.

'Or,' adds Trevor, 'get mauled by bears.'

Gretel nods thoughtfully. 'Or get mauled by bears, yes.'

Patience still looks unconvinced. 'Those elections will be soon, you know. Time's running out.'

'They'll still be in disarray after the elections,' mutters Snow. 'Cementing power takes time. Growing our army needs to be the priority for us right now. We mustn't be hamstrung by their deadlines.'

Patience frowns at Snow. '*Are* you stalling?'

Snow snaps the last few strands of rope fibre, gets up and marches towards the locked door. 'Don't worry about the door, Buttercup, I'll get it.'

Buttercup, one hand already extended towards the door, has to swiftly flinch out of the way when Snow pushes past her and kicks the door down.

116

'Snow! Will you *stop* kicking doors to open them? I have asked you politely a *hundred* times!'

'There'll be time for that later,' says Gretel, nudging the still-sleeping Dwarves with her boot to try to get them up. 'Come on, Hex will be here any second; we need this escape to look convincing.'

Snow drags a complaining Dwarf up by the scruff of its neck. 'Look lively, lads.'

Gretel tries to help by grabbing two Dwarves herself. Both of them react by making themselves go floppy, like cats that don't want to move. It manages to make the already fairly heavy creatures feel even heavier, like hairy sacks of wet sand.

Buttercup, Jack and Patience, for their part, do their best job of 'escaping', even though that's limited to just going through the splintered doorway into the cold night outside, and then loitering about a bit.

'Oh no,' cries Trevor loudly from his perch on top of Buttercup's head, 'the prisoners are escaping!'

'Um,' says Patience.

'Gretel?' calls Jack. 'Snow? There's no one here.'

Gretel stumbles out past the kicked-down door, panting under the weight of two uncooperative Dwarves. 'What?'

She looks about. There is a chair outside the woodshed, but it's empty. The boughs of the trees above are empty. There is, indeed, nobody watching the building. Nobody has been guarding them, all this time. Not even Hex. Not even a little bit.

'I think they all went to bed, dear,' says Buttercup.

Snow arrives in the doorway, lugging the rest of the Dwarves. 'Huh. They don't think much of our capabilities, do they?'

A wolf howl goes up nearby. Gretel is aware of canine eyes watching her once more.

'Well, at least they've got the perimeter alarmed,' notes Trevor cheerfully.

The back door of the nearby cottage opens, and Scarlett appears, halfway through a huge, toothsome, dog-like yawn.

'M'coming,' she mutters sleepily, 'what's the…' She stops, and takes in the scene at the doorway of the woodshed. 'Oh for *pity's* sake,' she whines. She indicates the broken door. 'Who did that?'

Jack, Patience and even Buttercup all point Snow out as the culprit.

The Werewolf shakes her head. 'Princesses.'

15
The Hydra

Hansel becomes aware of daylight, and the stale smell of the city. He also becomes aware of terrible pain throughout his body.

'Oh no,' he says, before he so much as opens his eyes.

'Yep,' comes Daisy's voice, from his side. 'Still in the Citadel, I'm afraid.'

He finally persuades his eyes to open, and instantly regrets the decision. The room is too bright, the décor too starkly white; the sun is in entirely the wrong place. He realises that this hotel room is the highest up he's ever slept, and neither his mental state nor the magical energy inside him is particularly happy about having spent most of the night so far away from the ground.

Other realisations start coming to him in lumps, blaring through the pain.

He'd gone up on that platform with Morning, in front of all those people. They'd been told who he was, who Daisy was, where they were from... they'd been told about Gretel. And... and they'd *sympathised*. Even here, in the Citadel. They'd sympathised.

And yet, there'd been all that anger in the crowd, all that fear, still.

And the Hydra... the Hydra...

Oh. Wait.

He closes his eyes again. 'Did... I...?'

'Throw up on the front row and yourself, with everybody watching?' Daisy pats his hand softly. 'Yeah. Sorry.'

'And… did I…?'

'Land in the sick when you fainted? Also yeah, but we cleaned you up best as we could.'

Hansel groans, and brings his hands up to his face. His left eye is tender and bruised, along with his cheekbone. He must have ended up face first in it. He's fairly certain that the unmistakable acrid, carroty whiff of old vomit is coming from his hair.

'The innkeeper said once you were awake he'd bring up plenty of hot water for a bath,' adds Daisy. 'Morning paid him extra. *And* we get something called a "continental breakfast" now. Mostly, it's tea and croissants.'

Hansel opens his eyes again. They find Daisy, a beacon of soothing warmth in a sea of cold, harsh daylight, stuffing pastry into her mouth.

'I asked them what a continental even is, and apparently Myrsina's a part of one. Who knew? Also it means we get jam in really, really, really tiny pots. Look.'

The jam pot she shows him is, to be fair, ridiculously small.

He prods at his sore face, trying to summon up some more memories of the night before, preferably ones not involving vomit.

'What time is it?' he mumbles after a while.

''Bout ten?'

He sits up suddenly, and hurts so much he has to lie back down again. 'Your baskets…'

'Oh, don't worry about that, we can get back to selling them tomorrow. Market's closed today anyway, for voting.'

Hansel tries sitting up slower this time. 'That's today?'

Daisy nods, popping open another minuscule pot of jam. 'They were setting up for it in the inn's front lobby first thing. Tiny little wooden cubicles.'

'What, like privies?'

'Exactly like privies.'

'Eurgh.'

'I know.' Daisy struggles to get an adequate serving of jam out of a pot so tiny that she can barely fit her knife inside. 'Morning said last night went really well. Not counting – you know. Your incident.'

'Hmm.' Hansel frowns, and picks at his smelly hair.

'She says it's going to be a close call, but between what we said and what she did, it might have been enough to tip the votes in her favour. All in all, it's a good job that those visions of yours had us turn up when we did.'

The visions... suddenly, Hansel remembers. The Hydra. It was already there. All that fear. All that anger...

'Oh no,' he breathes, trying to get up off the bed. 'The monster. We might be too late.'

Daisy pushes him down again gently. 'Nothing's happened, there's been no monster, not even sightings of one elsewhere.'

'But I saw it, Daisy. It spoke to me. I finally understand what it is. The monster isn't what we thought; it isn't going to attack the huntsmen. The monster *is* the huntsmen.'

'What?' asks Daisy, spitting pastry flakes.

'It's always been here because it's always been the huntsmen, all our lives,' Hansel tells her. 'I could feel it when they took the village, but it's been getting stronger since. It's everywhere, here. All around, closing in, like the walls, and last night I felt it on top of me, crushing me... A monster, made out of fear and anger and hatred, and if you cut off its head then even more grow back, more dangerous than before...'

'The other candidate,' Daisy breathes. 'The one who just wants to make everything worse. Those were his supporters in the front row, closest to you. You know, the ones you were sick on? Those ones.'

'Yes, Daisy.'

'Do you think,' Daisy continues, 'maybe the Mirror's messages were warning you about him?'

Oh yes, Hansel reminds himself, Daisy still thinks that all of this is coming from the Mirror. He feels his usual pang of guilt at keeping the truth from her, followed as always by the gut-wrench of fear at the danger he'd put her in if he were to tell her the truth, especially here. As usual, he tries to ignore the accompanying sickly, slimy selfish worry – namely, that he simply doesn't know for certain she would still like him if she knew that he was a witch. He doesn't know if she would smile at a witch the way she's smiling at him right now, fond and trusting, cheering the room like a wildflower on a windowsill. Right now, he doesn't think he's strong enough to bear her finding out the truth. He never has been.

'Maybe,' Hansel concedes. 'Maybe it was all about helping Morning.'

'Well, if it was, and it worked, then the visions and the horrible feeling should have left you by now,' Daisy reasons. 'Have they…?'

Hansel shakes his head. 'The feeling's still here. It's a sort of a thick dread, seeping through the walls like treacle.'

Daisy frowns. 'Does treacle "seep through walls"?'

'I don't know. But that's what it feels like.'

Daisy ponders this. 'Maybe if there were cracks in the walls. And a *lot* of treacle…'

'Maybe there's something else we still have to do. Maybe… ugh, do we have to do another speech?'

'Not allowed,' Daisy tells him. 'Not once voting's started. Even the town criers and madrigal men have to swear off political topics until the polls close. The one in the street below's mostly been singing about particularly cute dogs he's seen outside the voting cubicles.'

'Hmm.' Hansel tries to think.

'Apparently, one of the dogs was wearing a little bow,' Daisy adds.

'D'awww,' concedes Hansel.

'Maybe Morning will know.'

'Hmm?'

'If there's anything else we can do to help her, I mean,' says Daisy. She shrugs cheerfully. 'It's that or sit around waiting for madrigals with updates about the dogs.'

Hansel smiles at her. 'Good idea. Although I really would quite like to hear more about the dogs.'

The sudden shift in mood at Morning's HQ just from the night before is palpable at first sight. The building, which only hours ago had been a dark and anonymous warehouse, is now festooned with green bunting. There is even a hastily sketched portrait of Morning in the front window, with the simple caption 'MORNING!' written above it in large, green letters. Unlike last night, the front door is open, with people milling in and out, a few in huntsman's masks, but most without.

Hansel follows Daisy inside. Despite the burst of optimism in the HQ, the sense of general dread still pervades, nagging at his senses like a bad smell.

Morning is sitting on the floor, surrounded by campaigners. One is reading a series of numbers and percentages out to her from a clipboard. It sounds like gibberish to Hansel, but Morning nods in understanding. She seems relaxed and upbeat. She is eating toast and fussing over a dog. Somebody notices Hansel and Daisy and nudges Morning. She looks up, dandelion hair wild, eyes twinkling.

'*Here* they are!' Morning cries in delight.

She leaps to her feet, runs over and hugs them both. The dog, being a dog, immediately wants to be an integral part of this exciting hug session and bounds over to join in, a whirlwind of scrabbly paws, thwacking tail and uncontained woofing.

'Here are the heroes of the eleventh hour,' continues Morning. 'How are you both? Oh, Hansel, you were so ill last night; has a rest done you some good at least?'

Hansel can't answer for a moment, as he's attacked with an onslaught of meaty doggy kisses.

'Is that your dog?' he manages after a moment.

'Sausages, get *down*!' Morning grabs the dog and pulls it off Hansel. 'Yes. Sorry. This is Sausages… before you ask, I let my little nephew name her; never again. She's very excited, she's not used to all this attention. She's already had a madrigal man write a song about her.'

'Ahh.' Hansel pets the dog. 'Hello, Sausages.' Sausages goes wild with excitement at hearing a new human speak her frankly absurd name.

'I never pictured huntsmen having pets,' Daisy admits.

'Of course we have pets. We're ordinary people, just like you,' says Morning. 'Honestly, we really have so many of Rosier's false narratives to dismantle. He was the one who wanted us to be seen as above the normal folk, somehow – an elite tier.'

'Did… *he* have pets?' Daisy asks.

'Oh goodness no, Rosier hated animals,' Morning tells them, leaning in and dropping her voice as if in confidence, which only serves to excite Sausages all the more. 'So does the orange candidate. I tell you, you just can't trust someone that doesn't like animals.'

Hansel ruffles the dog's fur. The claustrophobic sense of fear and rage persists, but Sausages radiates so much joy and trust, she's like a balm. He has to remember to talk to her as any normal human boy would talk to a dog, and not to actually converse with her as he sometimes does with the animals at the farm when he's alone with them, but he can still understand that Sausages' love and devotion for Morning is absolute, with plenty of affection overspill for any other human that she happens to see. The farm boy in him can tell that this is a very well-cared-for dog as much as the animal-sensitive witch can.

Morning bends to scratch Sausages' ear. The dog beams wetly at being fussed over by two people at the same time. 'Look at all this,' she says gently, and it takes Hansel a moment to realise she's talking to him and Daisy, rather than the dog. 'Look what you did, in a single night.'

'It wasn't us,' replies Hansel nervously. 'All that stuff you said, your name, the thing with the mask… those were your ideas, we just sort of stood there.'

'You were the spark. You were my inspiration. You still are.' With Sausages' ear thoroughly scratched, Morning stands again and takes Daisy's hand. 'Whether we win or lose today, we started something last night. Something important.'

Daisy meets eyes with Hansel, troubled. Sausages paws her thigh. 'You still might not win?'

'Oh, I'm still very much the underdog in this race.'

'But how?' Daisy asks. 'That crowd last night loved you. Everywhere I go I see people with green ribbons and buttons.'

Morning nods. 'Civilians,' she tells them. 'My support amongst fellow huntsmen is much lower. Tried winning them over by donating to commission a whole raft of inventions to further the cause. Massively backfired. A woman, showing initiative and an interest in new technology? Far too modern.'

'Does it really make much difference whether it's civilians or huntsmen voting for you?' Daisy asks, as Sausages smacks her repeatedly in the legs with her tail.

'Oh, yes,' Morning replies lightly, with a jocular roll of the eyes as if recounting the exploits of a potty old uncle. 'All citizens of the Citadel must have a vote, it's in the huntsmen's original statute, but the statute didn't say that all votes have to count the same, so they moved things about a bit. Votes are actually cast for a precinct representative to pass a ballot on which candidate has the majority backing of the area, and then *those* ballots are counted.'

'What?'

'I know – needlessly complicated. The precincts are ordered to ensure the huntsmen have much more say than civilians. Civilians outnumber huntsmen twenty to one even in the Citadel, but huntsmen have half the precincts.'

'Ouch.'

'Mm, and that's a simplified explanation of it. So yes, I have a lot of support with certain demographics, but from the way the huntsmen have organised things, they're generally the ones whose votes mean the least. Obviously I'd love to change that, but to do so I'd need to be in power, and that's going to be an uphill struggle even now.'

'But it *is* possible?'

'It's possible. I'd need to win over a lot of civilians, though, as well as a fair few huntsmen. I do think a lot of my brethren know we need reform, but…'

'But when it comes to the crunch, maybe asking them to lose their anonymity and power is a bit much for them to stomach?' Hansel hazards.

Morning's face crumples into another warm and wonky smile. 'You are a deeply perceptive boy, Hansel Mudd.'

She doesn't know the half of it, thinks Hansel, and for a horrible moment, the claustrophobic dread in the atmosphere swells, pushing through the happy bubble of innocent adoration stemming from Sausages. He fights off the wave of crackling magic that automatically rises inside of him, and then has to shake off the resulting aftershock of giddiness and nausea.

'Are there any other factors?' asks Daisy. Hansel can see from her expression that she's noticed he's struggling again.

'Well, yes,' Morning tells them. 'We're not allowed to canvass, give any speeches and so on, but a lot of the other candidates will have a few potential little tricks up their sleeve to help the last few voters get off the fence.'

'Such as?'

'Whispering campaigns.'

'Against you?'

'Yes. But also against you, I'm afraid.'

'What?' Hansel panics, fights back the magic and almost throws up again, all within a couple of seconds. Sausages, sensing his distress, nudges him gently with her head.

'Oh! Oh no, Hansel, I shouldn't have said that, not with you feeling so poorly.' Morning puts her arms around his shoulders supportively. 'It's nothing that they'd come for you over or anything, you're safe, I promise. It's just that the defeat at Nearby is a flashpoint. I say it shows we've overreached our authority over the people; other candidates will say it showed we were too soft, and that the residents of Nearby were too permissive over abominations. It'll play especially well for the orange candidate to paint you unfavourably, because it suits his agenda, and because he was so close to both of you during the occupation. People will see him as having special insight.'

'What do you mean, "he was close to us"?'

'Oh! He was one of Rosier's right-hand men,' Morning explains. 'He was with you the whole time you were locked up in that town hall. He was one of your guards.'

'He was?' Hansel finds himself shaking. He'd had no idea. He hadn't recognised the voice when the orange candidate had spoken, but then most of the guards at the town hall had menaced them in silence. Only Rosier had talked, really. And now, this person who'd locked him in a cage, who'd watched him fret and sob and struggle, and had done nothing to alleviate his suffering… this person was going to use that to spread malicious lies about them, in order to try to grab power? It feels like a violation. No wonder the sense of horror hasn't subsided. A candidate wanting to carry on where the last head huntsman left off, making things even worse, *that's* the Hydra, stamping about the streets. They cut the monster's head off at the battle for Nearby, but more heads have grown back in its place. How dare this masked bully use his own cruelty against Hansel and his family and friends? Against the people? How *dare* he?

'He'll be making up accounts of all sorts of things from when he was guarding you,' Morning tells them, 'trying to cast you as amoral, or liars, or even in league with the monsters of Darkwood. Anything to make you look bad, so that I'll look bad through association. They don't even need to stand up to much scrutiny, he just needs to convince enough huntsmen by the end of the day. Pathetic, really. It's only a worry because he was there, Rosier's gone and who else is there to dispute what he says happened in that prison?'

'There's us,' replies Daisy sharply. 'And he really isn't in a good position at *all* to go around whispering about the lies and dirty tricks and abuse of magic that went on in the town hall.'

Morning's eyebrows almost hit her dishevelled fringe. 'Oh?' Her lips curl in that way so many lips do when a hot bit of gossip is about to go down. 'Did you two see something? Was John Rosier being a naughty boy as well as a stuck-up bully?'

'Every weapon that was built for you in occupied Nearby was designed by Daisy.' The words pour out of Hansel in a torrent of rage. 'That's why he locked us up; I was the hostage to make her comply. He told people he was putting her to work in the laundry, but he lied! He lied to all of you! He broke his own abomination rules, all the time! *And* he had that Mirror with him constantly; he used it several times a day, sometimes in private. Spying on everyone. Using *magic*. He was a no-good dirty hypocrite.'

Morning looks impressed. 'And his henchmen,' she says. 'Our friend, the orange candidate. He'd have known about all this?'

If he were calmer, Hansel would have taken a breath, and wondered whether Rosier's henchmen *had* been in on his secret plots, plans and obsessions any more than any other senior huntsmen had been. Right now, however, Hansel is not calm. Right now, all he can think about is that barred cell, and the fear, and the pain, and the infuriatingly placid faces watching over him, and who was to say back then whether it had been Rosier himself or a henchman at any given moment; how was he supposed to know? They'd been wearing masks, that had been their choice, so any confusion over who was where at what time was down to them, not him, and this former henchman, this firebrand candidate, this Hydra *must* be stopped, and… and…

'Yes,' Hansel tells Morning confidently. 'He was there. He knew.'

Morning nods, her eyes gleaming. 'And would the two of you feel confident about taking a walk around the Citadel with me today, and repeating the conversation we've just had? Discreetly, of course? In whispers, if need be?'

He looks across at Daisy. She squeezes his hand in support. Sausages leaps up in between them, in the hope that another group hug might be in the offing.

Sausages believes in him, thinks Hansel. Sausages believes in all of them.

'No,' he says. 'I wouldn't feel confident doing that at all. But I'll do it anyway.'

16
That's a Suspiciously Large Oven

The oven is, if anything, even less comfortable than the woodshed. It's hard and cold and cramped. There are also other, more glaringly unpleasant ramifications to being barricaded inside an oven, even if it is currently, mercifully not in use. Gretel is trying her best not to think about this, or about just how many creatures in the thrall of the people she's just massively annoyed are carnivorous and low on meat supplies. She tries to tell herself that Gilde and the others have only put her in the oven because they're running out of places to hold everybody. There are a lot of worrying noises in the kitchen beyond the close iron walls of her new prison before she makes out Snow's raised voice.

'Leave them be!'

'Cool your boots, Majesty,' replies Gilde. 'They're only Dwarves.'

'How dare you! They're my lads! They're no threat to you!'

'I know, Princess. But you see, the bears and wolves need meat...'

'No!'

'Let me finish, Princess! I know the Dwarves need meat too, and we ain't got none to spare, this corner of the year.'

'What are you doing?' Snow demands.

Gretel hears the cottage door being unlocked and opened.

'It was a lousy idea bringing dumb Dwarves with you in the first place, Majesty, I'm just rectifying that.'

'Yummy?' mutters a confused Dwarf, muffled beyond the oven.

'Scram,' Gilde tells them.

'No!' Snow sounds furious. 'You can't do that!'

'They'll be fine,' Gilde tells them. 'I'll see to it they make it to your neck of the woods, and don't come back.'

'They wouldn't leave me,' Snow announces, but she's cut off by a low growl from beyond the cottage door, and the sound of Dwarves scrabbling to escape.

'Oi!' calls Snow. 'Oi! Lads! Come back!'

'They really are just feral creatures I'm afraid, Majesty,' trills Gilde as a series of startled 'yummy's fade off into the distance. 'You really oughtn't a come round here testing the loyalty of my little family, when your own was so weak. I wonder who the next of your lot to split from you will be. Probably the Ghost. Reckon she should only need another day or two in the jar to sharpen her mind right.'

Days? thinks Gretel. She might be stuck in this oven for days? She's starting to seriously second-guess how well she's thought this latest plan through. She can't think of much worse than being trapped in an unused oven for days on end.

'Well then,' adds Gilde. 'If everybody is sitting nice and tight now, I would surely like a little cup of sweet tea.'

Gretel can suddenly think of something much worse than being trapped in an unused oven for days: being trapped in a used oven for a few minutes. She bangs on the oven door.

'Oh, rats,' says Gilde, beyond. 'I s'pose we'd better let girlie out of there, then.'

The chair holding the oven door shut is scraped aside, and the large, freckled arms of Scarlett push through the opened door to pull Gretel out, shaking slightly and heaving to catch her breath.

'Don't fret, girlie,' twinkles Gilde. 'The oven was only a temporary measure while we got the others settled. I wasn't going to cook yer. Ever *smelled* charred people-flesh?'

'No,' chorus Gretel and her Werewolf captor together. Hex, crouching to light the now vacated stove for Gilde, casts his eyes down, troubled.

'Stinks to high whoseits,' Gilde sighs. 'Can't shift the stench for weeks, neither. Not worth it.'

Gretel takes the moment to look around the cottage for her friends. Oh. Gilde and the others *have* been busy while she was in the oven.

All of the furniture has been shifted away from the centre of the cottage's interior, to make room for a cage of living tree branches, snaking in from an ajar window and completely trapping both Buttercup and Snow inside. Snow, Gretel notes, has been relieved even of her armour and instead wears a simple faded yellow and blue dress – one of Scarlett's cast-offs, from the size of it.

Gilde spots what Gretel's staring at.

'A nice dress is much more appropriate for a princess, wouldn't you say? She'll thank me in time. No more of this "White Knight" nonsense.'

'Give me back my armour. My lads hand-beat that stuff for me themselves, didn't y…' Snow falters. The cottage door is locked fast once more. The only trace left of the Dwarves is a few scraps of moulted tatty hair on the floor.

'And very shiny and, um, skully your pretty armour was too, Majesty,' simpers Gilde, 'but it also had a lot of sharp bits and I wouldn't want anything scary happening while you're in your time-out cage. Specially since you and your sugarwitch seem to be going through a little quarrel right now.'

Snow's eyes are bright with fury. 'Are you implying that I'd ever, *ever* hurt one of my own? Especially Buttercup?'

'Well,' mutters Buttercup miserably, from her side of the cramped wooden cage, 'maybe not physically.'

'You just don't want me to be able to cut these branches,' continues Snow.

'That too,' trills Gilde merrily.

Branches, thinks Gretel. She looks for Jack and finds him tied to a wooden chair, looking as drained as he did that awful night when his magical strength had failed under the strain to save them all from the Bin Men. Gretel frowns. They must have made him grow the cage, but something like that shouldn't have taxed his powers as much as his worn-out expression suggests it has.

'What have you done to Jack?'

'I'm fine, Gretel,' Jack tells her dully. 'I'm not hurt, at least. Well. Not badly hurt.'

'Why, Jack the Lad, I'd 'spect you to be cock-a-hoop,' says Gilde through her sugary smile. 'Flirty boy like you getting a precious token off your newest sweetie.'

'Please don't,' breathes Hex, so quietly that Gretel suspects it wasn't actually intended for anyone else to hear.

If Gilde has indeed heard him, his plea hasn't even slowed her down. She steps over to where Jack's tied up and indicates a tiny scrap of what looks like brown paper sitting below his collarbone, just above the neck of his shirt. No… not paper. It looks more organic than that. Gretel squints at it again. It's a scrap of leaf. Nettle leaf. Right on his skin, ouch. *Right* on his skin, indeed. Sticking to it in a way that seems wrong. She gasps in outrage. The scrap of leaf is brown with blood.

'You *sewed* a leaf to him?'

Gilde shrugs. 'Just to keep it good and close to his heart. One teeny ickle stitch, swip, swap, snip, nice and neat. Brave boy barely even flinched, and it's such a special leaf, after all.'

'You said they hadn't hurt you, Jack.' Gretel tries to put a hand on Jack's shoulder, but Gilde bats her hand away.

'Not *badly*, I said.' Jack lifts his chin at Gilde cockily. 'I've had worse.'

'Our Sweetiebird,' Gilde tells Gretel in self-satisfied tones, 'has given young Jack a scrap of his special lucky leaf, ain't that the cutest?'

'It isn't a "lucky leaf",' mutters Hex. 'It's a charm, or what's left of it.' His human hand moves up to the tattered nettle leaf around his neck instinctively. 'It subdues magic.'

'You took Jack's magic away?' Gretel asks accusingly.

'Just froze his spells for a bit,' Gilde replies. 'Don't fret, nothing's going to rot, we don't want another of *those* disasters on our hands, do we, Jack?'

'It's like my magic's a word on the tip of my tongue,' Jack tells Gretel. 'It's there, but it's buried, and won't come out. Not going to lie, it doesn't feel great.' Jack looks across at Hex. 'And you go around wearing this stuff all the time? Voluntarily?'

'Please don't talk about my nettle charm like that when you don't understand it,' Hex replies sharply. 'It saved me from my curse.'

'Well, mostly it did,' chatters Gilde cheerily. 'A pity Septa never got the chance to finish it, wasn't it?'

Hex's hand moves from the nettle to cradle his wing self-consciously. 'Well, there's only one leaf left now anyway, so I can't spare any more of it.'

'Aww.' Gilde brushes her hand down Hex's wing playfully. 'Now, don't you flap about having so little to give, my Sweetiebird. The princess don't have her weapons or Dwarves, the sugarwitch can't do a little thing inside a living cage, we've put a stop to Jack the Lad's nonsense and I'm sure the others are going to behave, ain't you?'

Gilde makes a wide gesture around the interior of the cottage. Gretel follows Gilde's hand with her gaze, at last taking in what's been done with the rest of the group. On a high shelf is a new salted jar, with Patience sulking inside once more, tiny and mute. Next to it is the upturned cup they'd been keeping Trevor in before. Gretel guesses that he's been put back under it again, especially since this time, the cup has a paperweight on top of it. In the distance, a bear roars again, continuing to force the Dwarves away from the mountains.

All Gretel had meant to achieve in their deliberately failed attempt to escape was to force either Hex or Scarlett into guarding them in the woodshed, so that they could talk them around to joining their cause. Not this. The woodshed had been a vast underestimation of their abilities, but this is just overkill now. Would it hurt the northern witches to come up with some sort of happy medium, prisoner-taking wise?

'Yes,' Gretel admits. 'We're going to behave.'

'So.' Gilde takes a step towards Gretel. 'The one question we have left is, what do we do with you, Mudd Witch?'

Gretel gives a nervous glance towards the oven. She swallows.

'I'm not a witch.'

Inside the cage, Snow groans. Gilde blinks several times at Gretel, a hostile smile frozen on her face.

'What was that again, cutie? My old ears must be deceiving me, because I'm sure you just said something that simply cannot be true.'

'Why can't it be true? I'm not a witch. Neither are Trevor or Patience. Neither are Scarlett or Hex, for that matter.'

'So, you've been a mendacious Mary over what kind of magic you got.'

'I'm not magical at all.'

In the cage, Snow groans again, louder this time.

Gretel shrugs at Gilde, as casually as she can. 'You just assumed I was. It's OK, so did these guys at first. So did the huntsmen who drove me from my home.'

'You're a human,' says Gilde. 'In a gang of witches that looks to be starting a war with humans. Why'd they keep yer?'

'Not against humans,' argues Gretel, 'against huntsmen. There's a huge difference, that's what we're trying to—'

'She's useful,' interrupts Snow. 'That's why we kept her.'

'Hey...' begins Gretel, but she notices Snow's meaningful glare, and remembers what just happened with the Dwarves. She changes tack. 'Yep,' she tells Gilde. 'I'm useful. I make inventions. Modify the cottage. Improve the defences. Like... design some booby traps for the perimeter, or self-heating soundproof nightcaps for people who go to bed earlier than everyone else. That sort of thing.'

Gilde raises an eyebrow. 'Heated nightcaps, you say?'

Scarlett looks up. 'We've got a perimeter?'

'How's about I do you a deal?' Gretel asks. 'How's about, if I make myself useful to *you*, do lots of nice new modifications around the cottage, really beef up your defences so that nobody will dare bother you even in hibernation season... do you think maybe you could let my friends go?'

'Don't let them go east,' mutters Hex.

Gilde holds up a hand. 'You going to work properly? No dilly-dallying, plenty of elbow grease?'

'My elbows will be lubricated as anything, I promise.'

Gilde considers this. 'You all stay.'

There is an exasperated tut from underneath Trevor's cup.

'For now,' continues Gilde. 'But if girlie here makes nicey-nice, and if we like what she makes us and it keeps trouble from our door... then we'll think about letting you go.'

Gretel sighs with relief. 'Thank you. I can get started straight away. Um.' She looks around at the cottage again. 'I'm probably going to need some sort of forge. Somewhere hot enough to do metalwork, at least. Do you have anything like...' Everybody's eyes go back to rest on the detested oven. 'Oh, no.'

''Fraid so, girlie. Hey ho. At least you get to be on the outside of it this time.' Gilde clicks her fingers. 'One of youse, tie her to the oven. Close enough to work, not close enough to burn although I'm afraid, girlie, it does get frightful hot, so stay hydrated.'

As Hex pulls Gretel towards the oven, Scarlett gets to her feet. 'Gilde, listen, now they're all secure, I had the worst night, and you know the lycanthropy takes it out of me, wolves need so much sleep, so…'

'You want to go to your bed?' asks Gilde kindly.

Scarlett nods wearily.

'Certainly not,' continues Gilde in the same kind tones. 'The prisoners need watching. Properly, this time.' She walks past Scarlett to her own bed. 'And keep it down. I need my beauty rest.'

17
Do Not Disturb

The cottage has taken on that particular quietness that descends when somebody is having a nap. Gilde snoozes comfortably at the far end of the cottage's one room. For some time, the only sounds are those of her soft snores, the prisoners and captors alike shifting uncomfortably, and the metallic sounds of Gretel working on contraptions from her spot, tied next to the oven. The room is warm and dozy; Gretel can feel it trying to tug her towards sleep. It's clear that Scarlett in particular is having difficulty staying awake.

'I've never seen such a sleepy Werewolf before,' mutters Jack.

'You ever seen any kind of Werewolf before?' Scarlett asks, nodding awake with a start for the fourth time.

'Well… no.'

'Exactly,' says Scarlett. 'Werewolves need loads of sleep as it is, without troublesome houseguests keeping us up at all hours.'

There is a pause. Scarlett closes her eyes again.

'And Gilde doesn't let you rest?' Gretel asks Scarlett, unfortunately at exactly the same moment that Jack asks, 'What about Vampires?'

'Hmm?'

'What about Vampires? Do they get tired too? Because Ghosts don't need sleep at all, do you, Patience?'

Inside the jar, Patience is still sulking.

'I was just wondering how it worked for Vampires, and other… you know. Night-time people.'

Scarlett rubs her eyes. '"Night-time people"? Really? Besides, I've never even met a Vampire; I don't think they come this far west. Do you think we just hang out with them all the time or something?'

Jack looks a little shamefaced. 'Is that not how it works, then?'

'No! Werewolves aren't even undead, why do I have to keep telling people this? We're just born lycanthropic, same as you witches. Passed down through the family, in our case. Closest thing in here to some poor beggar half-dead of Vampirism is your Miss Ghost, but I bet you never asked *her* if she's met one.'

'She wouldn't have had the chance, she only died a few weeks ago.'

'Oh.' Scarlett gives an embarrassed, toothy grimace. It reminds Gretel of the expression the sheepdog back at the farm would pull whenever it was mildly rebuked. 'Sorry for your loss, Miss Ghost.'

Patience shrugs grumpily.

There's another awkward pause. Gretel draws breath to ask Scarlett again about Gilde's treatment of her.

'Zombies, on the other hand, are constantly knackered,' announces Scarlett. 'We've had a few of them come out of the caves higher up in the mountains over the years. Gilde said there was a mining accident about fifty years ago; they're only just digging their way out now. They actually seem like a nice bunch. Generally pretty depressed but then, wouldn't you be?'

'You really should be given more chance to rest, you know,' Gretel tells her, hoping to get the conversation back on track, but also finding that she has no helpful or appropriate response to that really sad stuff about the Zombies.

'You do look very tired, dear,' adds Buttercup from the cage. 'Why don't you take forty winks? It's not like we can do much right now.'

Scarlett gazes at her, exhausted longing in her expression.

'It's a trick,' Hex reminds her, looking sleepy himself, perched in the gap between the top of the branch cage and the ceiling. 'Gilde wants us alert.'

Scarlett yawns ruefully. 'I know.'

Outside the cottage comes the by now familiar, ponderous sound of Baby the bear shambling past. It's the bear's third approach so far of the day – a reminder to the prisoners not to try to run again, and a reminder to Scarlett and Hex that the Bear Witch remains in charge, even in her sleep. The unseen bear sounds sluggish, as if he too resents being kept up by this unexpected hostage situation.

'Must be almost time for hibernation by now,' notes Snow, listening as the heavy footfall fades away. She nods over at Gilde's bed. 'Is that why she needs to sleep so much? Or is it just because she's getting on a bit?'

'Wouldn't you like to know?' asks Hex.

'Yes, I would, actually. That's why I'm asking.' Snow pauses. 'What's this place even like, come hibernation season? Does she lose all her powers? Go to sleep for months on end? Is that why she needs the two of you around? To protect her through the winter?'

'Stop it,' replies Scarlett, a frustrated, doggish whine to her tone.

'Is that her plan with us, ultimately?' continues Snow, unabashed. 'Get a whole gang of bodyguards and nursemaids?'

'We're keeping you from making trouble,' whispers Scarlett. 'There've been anti-huntsman movements springing up all along the border, the past week. Even as far up as Slate. What if the Citadel blames us for that? Me and Hex came here for a simpler life, to get away from all this turbulence that keeps sparking up whenever the magical and the human collide.' Her tone softens again. 'Sorry. But that's the truth. We're all in agreement, Gilde, Hex and me.'

'What does she do to you when you're *not* in agreement with her?' Gretel asks gently.

The change in Scarlett is terrifyingly swift. Her ears point, her eyes narrow, her face elongates and fills with thick hair and sharp fangs.

'Shut up,' she just about manages to snarl before her mouth becomes too animalistic to form words. She tries to say something else, but it comes out as muted growls.

'Scarlett?' Hex scrambles down from the cage and faces her, his hand and wing raised, his voice and expression deliberately neutral. 'Scarlett. It's OK. You know changing without using your hood muddles you.'

Gretel stares back at her, as calmly and unflinchingly as she can, although she does notice Jack and Buttercup wince slightly at the sight of those colossal, pointed teeth.

'I know. You're tired and upset.' Hex makes no attempt to touch the snarling Werewolf. 'Relax. Breathe. Focus.'

Scarlett pulls back from her wolf form as quickly as she went into it. Her hands don't even get the chance to fully become paws before the human fingers lengthen out of them again. As her snout and fur recede back, Scarlett's expression is a curious combination of doggy and human embarrassment.

'I'm sorry,' she says, tripping over a still slightly canine tongue. 'I've got to stop slipping into the wolf when I'm overwhelmed. I'm just not used to keeping prisoners; I don't know how to go about it but it's *exhausting*, and… and…'

Scarlett tries to discreetly wipe away a couple of tired, frustrated tears, but more take their place. She begins to quietly sob a little, in strange, high-pitched, doglike whines.

'We're sorry you're tired,' says Buttercup gently.

'No you're not,' whimpers Scarlett.

Fair enough, Gretel thinks to herself, she really isn't that sorry that their jailer is a bit tired and emotional, in the grand scheme of things. Perhaps it means she'll be more susceptible to somebody capable of laying on the charm rather thicker than Gretel can.

With Hex and Scarlett temporarily distracted, Gretel hurls a spare screw at Jack's head. Jack shoots her a silent expression of indignation. His attention grabbed, Gretel nods towards the whining Werewolf. Jack shrugs, confused. Gretel nods across at Scarlett again, as meaningfully as she can. Jack thinks for a moment, and then nods at Gretel with a cautious air of understanding.

'Hey.' Jack leans forward a little, a familiar, fake, sparkle to his eyes. 'Hey, Hex.'

Gretel sighs.

'Oh, for goodness' sake.' Hex clambers back up the cage. 'This, still? I know what you're doing. Buttering me up for when your princess has questions about hibernation. I know how good witch, bad witch works, you know!'

'I'm not a "bad witch",' huffs Snow.

'Bad communicator though,' mutters Buttercup.

'Not now, Buttercup.'

'Just saying, dear.'

'Will you two *please* pack it in?' moans Trevor from under the cup. 'Honestly, I've never known the pair of you carry on like this for so long before, and in front of company, too! Sorry about this, new guys, between one thing and the other, you are *not* seeing us at our best right now.'

'Yes, well.' Hex crouches on the top of the cage again, watching the exhausted Werewolf rub her eyes. 'We could say the same of us.'

Gretel looks up from her metalworking, sensing another opportunity. 'I expect you know what it can get like. When you've done something wrong and they won't tell you what it was…'

'*Thank* you,' says Snow. 'See, Buttercup? If you won't tell me…'

'*I* won't tell *you*?' hisses Buttercup, in spite of the fact that trapped in a cage in the middle of a packed cottage while trying not to wake one of your captors is not exactly the time or place to have this sort of conversation. '*You* never told me about how you

142

think we should all have to stay in these rotten woods forever! You let me think that someday... someday...'

'What, that someday we could go riding triumphantly back to my old castle, past the scaffold where I watched them kill my mother and take up residence in the throne room where they tortured my father for thirteen years?'

'You're their queen! You're their beacon of hope...'

'They killed my mum, Buttercup! Would you think humans and witches could still live happily together if they'd killed your mum?'

'Well, they didn't kill *my* mum,' retorts Buttercup. 'They *rewarded* my mum, when she reported me.'

'Oh,' breathes Snow.

'Oh,' gasp Gretel and the others in a sad echo.

'I didn't know that,' Snow says softly. 'I'm so sorry, Buttercup.'

'They hated me, in my old town.' Buttercup catches a couple of errant tears. They hit her hand and turn into tiny droplets of custard. 'They knew my magic wasn't malicious, it wasn't on purpose, but they still hated me and my... little accidents. But that doesn't mean I've given up on ever trying to live in human civilisation again. Maybe in a place like Nearby. Or, you know... actually in Nearby. It's nice there.'

'It *is* nice there,' agrees Gretel, almost inaudibly.

'But to hear you say that you wouldn't even try... that you don't believe witches *should* try to live in human territory... how could I make a home for myself without you, Snow?' Buttercup tries to wipe the custard tear on her sleeve, but just ends up with a handful of wet filo pastry. 'You're my family. You're my Snow.'

'Oh, you soppy apeth,' sighs Snow fondly. She shuffles over to Buttercup in the cramped cage and wipes the glutinous goop from the Cake Witch's hands.

'Is... this all part of the good witch, bad witch thing?' asks Hex, warily.

Snow glares at him. 'There *is* no "good witch, bad witch"! Why would this be about you?'

Hex looks sheepish. 'I thought maybe you were drawing on how important family always was to me? And how Septa and us brothers were always so close after we lost our mother? And…'

'I never knew my mother,' comes Trevor's sad voice from under the cup. 'She could have been eaten by a hedgehog before I could so much as hatch, for all I know.'

'My mum sent me off to live with my granny in the woods,' adds Scarlett. 'On account of the lycanthropy skipping a generation.' She pulls the elderly magical cape around her large arms self-consciously. 'Amongst other things.'

'I don't know what happened to mine, after I ran away,' says Jack, 'but we were very, very poor, and I took all the gold I'd nicked with me, so… probably didn't end well.'

Gretel holds her tongue, a sense of gratitude for her comparatively comfortable upbringing on the farm colliding with a desperate yearning to return there.

'I assumed you felt the same as me,' Snow admits to Buttercup. 'I never imagined you might ever want to leave your cottage.' She finishes cleaning up Buttercup's hands and smiles at her. 'It's such a nice cottage. Really cosy and welcoming, and that's all been down to you.'

Buttercup sniffs again. 'It's down to me that it's mostly cake.'

'I like that it's mostly cake.'

'No you don't.'

'Course I do. Because it makes it yours.'

Buttercup smiles, despite herself. 'Aww.'

'I like the cake element too,' comes Trevor's muffled voice. 'Great at attracting flies.'

'Your house sounds so weird,' says Hex.

'Has to be seen to be believed,' Trevor tells them. 'You should come and take a look. You're always welcome.'

Hex stares at the cup, then around at the room, and for the briefest moment, Gretel notes an expression of hesitation on the bird-man's face. He shakes his head swiftly, as if trying to shake the very thoughts out of it.

'You're troublemakers.'

'They *are* troublemakers,' agrees Scarlett.

'We're not,' sighs Buttercup wearily.

'You'll go east…'

'We won't if we don't have to,' Snow tells them. 'We'd rather form alliances right here.'

'Gilde will have none of it!'

'Yeah, we gathered that,' says Trevor, under the cup. 'But, as far as I see it, she's a permanently tired little old lady, and you're a fully grown man… bird… thing. What can she do to stop you if you want to go and see the cake house?'

'I *don't* want to see the cake house.'

'Course you do, it's a house made of cake. And if you came with us, you'd be a part of the team, so you'd have a say on what we did next.'

This seems to get Hex's attention. He clambers across to reach his giant wing out to the cup on the shelf.

'Hex…' warns Scarlett.

Hex hesitates again, then pushes the cup with the tip of his wing so that it tilts onto its side. Trevor pokes his head out cheerfully.

'So…' Hex mutters, 'so if I agreed to go with you, then I could tell you not to go east, and you'd do as I said?'

'Hex,' frets Scarlett again. 'No.'

Hex persists. 'I could tell you not to start a war with the humans, and…'

'Well, it doesn't quite work like that,' says Trevor gently. 'There's no "telling", as such. Down our neck of the woods, it's not just one person giving orders and the rest of us following them.'

Hex casts a sceptical sideways look in Snow's direction.

'OK,' Trevor admits, '*most* of the time we listen to what others have to say instead of just giving orders.'

'In my defence, I'm getting better at the whole "listening" thing,' adds Snow. 'Literally just resolved a massive argument with Buttercup. By listening.'

'You didn't resolve it, dear, just defused it; the underlying issues are still there.'

'Still, though, I was pretty good. Better than usual, right?'

Buttercup rolls her eyes. 'Yes, dear.'

'But you'd listen to me and Scarlett?' asks Hex.

'Don't bring me into this please.' The Werewolf cringes.

'I could get you to keep the peace with the humans? Stop this war before it overtakes the whole forest?'

'Well…' attempts Snow.

'It really isn't a "war", you know,' says Gretel. 'It's a lot more one-sided than that, and—'

'And,' interjects Trevor, 'we're certainly all ears as to ways we can put an end to the situation.' He pauses. 'Well. Not me. I don't have ears. But I can listen to you with my leg hairs.' He waggles a leg at a thoughtful-looking Hex.

Scarlett is pacing anxiously. 'Gilde isn't going to like this, Hex.'

'Has Gilde liked anything you've done?' Trevor asks. 'Besides following her orders?'

Hex shakes his head, and meets eyes with Scarlett, a new spark of resoluteness in his expression.

'Hex, no,' Scarlett pleads. 'There'll be a fuss.'

'You can come with us too,' Gretel attempts, but Scarlett is nowhere near as convinced as Hex. The hardwired loyalty in her part-canine brain must run deep.

'Can't we sleep on it, Hex?' Scarlett whines. 'We're all tired, we aren't thinking straight. This isn't like you; you're usually such a good bird!'

Gretel notices that Hex is trembling, but she can tell from his face that he's made up his mind. He gestures with his wing for Trevor to climb onto the feathers. The spider does so, scuttling swiftly up to Hex's shoulder.

'Thank you, Trevor,' murmurs Hex.

'Wait,' says Jack indignantly, 'Trevor? Nothing I said or did could sway you, but you've been won over by *Trevor*?'

Gretel grins to herself. Hex hadn't expected a charm offensive from a guileless little spider. Nobody *ever* suspects much from a little spider, which is *exactly* why anybody living in a magic forest should really consider befriending a little spider. Well. That and the fly control.

Hex shoots Jack a troubled look, and whispers something to Trevor.

'I really don't think he *is* making fun, mate.'

Hex frowns, bewildered.

'What?' asks Jack, just as perplexed. 'What did I do wrong? Oh no, I didn't lay it on too thick, did I?'

'But then what would I know?' Trevor continues, ignoring Jack. 'I'm hardly an expert in human mating rituals.' He nods over at Buttercup and Snow. 'For about three months, I thought those two were just feeding one another straight from the gullet.'

Gretel has to stuff her fist into her mouth to stop herself barking out a laugh.

'Trevor!' Snow exclaims through gritted teeth, her eyes wide with horror.

'We agreed not to talk about that,' Buttercup adds.

Gretel forces herself to stop giggling. Inside the salt-rimmed glass jar, Patience has gone foetal in silent hysterics of schadenfreude. The others all seem too distracted to have even noticed. Scarlett is still anxious, Jack is still indignant and Hex still seems surprised both by his own courage and by Trevor's suggestion that Jack might not have been making fun of him after all.

'We should get out now,' Hex tells them, 'while she's asleep.'

'Hex, *no*.' Scarlett is as skittish as a puppy left tied outside a butcher's shop. 'What about me? What about when she wakes up? If you do this, I'll… I'll *howl*.'

'Scarlett,' says Gretel, 'how is locking us up in here going to stop a fight between huntsmen and witches, or keep it from your doorstep? What if a gang of huntsmen are out in the mountains looking for us "troublemakers" right now, and they find us here, with a witch and two transmorphers?'

'You think we hadn't already thought of that?' Scarlett asks.

'Frankly,' replies Gretel, 'yes.'

Scarlett sniffles. 'Well, you're right, I hadn't considered that at all; oh trousers, what if you're right? My pack and three sleepy bears can't fight off a whole army, we're dead, what have you done?'

'No no no,' Hex frets quietly, 'don't cry, Scarlett. You'll wake her up.'

'What I mean,' adds Gretel quickly, 'is that, while it doesn't really matter whose fault it is—'

'*Your* fault.'

'While that doesn't matter, there's nowhere in the Darkwood that can be said to be truly safe for magical beings. Not any more. Dividing us won't help that, neither will locking us away where we can't fight back. The one thing that *will* help is listening to those of us who've already faced the huntsmen, so we can end all of this together. As a team.' Gretel pauses, and decides to rephrase. 'As a pack.'

'I've already got a pack. And I've already got a team.' Scarlett gazes sadly at Hex. 'Or, at least I thought I did.'

'We're not a team if we just do everything Gilde says,' argues Hex in hushed tones. 'We're just... henchmen.'

Scarlett starts her high-pitched whining again. 'Don't say that. Not in front of the proper witches...'

Hex lays his wing on her shoulder, and Trevor clambers over to her.

'Hey, now,' soothes the spider. 'We're not perfect either. It's us who came to you for help, remember? But we'd help you in return. You and your wolf pack, I know you're worried about them. Plenty of good hunting to be had in the southern woods, right, Snow?'

'Rabbits galore,' confirms Snow.

'But who'd look after *her*?' Scarlett worries, nodding at Gilde's sleeping form. 'Yes, she can be grumpy, but she's still a little old lady who's been alone for too long, and took us in out of the kindness of her heart, and her powers are on the wane as winter draws in, and… and…'

'She has her bears for company,' Hex replies, 'and she'll probably be asleep most of the time we're away anyway.'

'Besides,' adds Trevor, into her ear, 'once we get out of here, we'll be helping to keep trouble far away from the mountains. *And* Gretel's making some self-defence inventions for her right now, aren't you, Gretel?'

Gretel covers her latest invention with her hands defensively. This particular contraption isn't intended to be for Gilde at all. She's been quietly making an easily hidden device containing a multitude of secretive tools and blades for her own personal use come their escape. 'Yes,' Gretel lies.

The expression on Scarlett's face changes subtly. It loses some of its anxiety, and takes on a hint of hopefulness. Gretel wonders if Trevor might be some sort of persuasive genius.

'You'll give my pack safe passage to your territory?'

Snow nods. 'If you help us escape, then yes.'

Scarlett takes a deep breath, her eyes darting once more to the sleeping figure. 'I'll go out and give them the howl.' She starts moving towards the door. 'How quickly can you have them all freed?' she asks Hex.

Hex pulls a pair of scissors from a drawer. 'Jack should be able to undo the cage almost as soon as the nettle's off. Couple of minutes?'

'OK.' She opens the door quietly. 'I'll meet you at the southwards path in… oh no.'

Directly beyond the cottage door that Scarlett has just opened is a wall. A wall not of wood or stone, but of heaving brown fur.

Yeah, thinks Gretel, seconded on the 'oh no'.

The wall of fur moves heavily, until a huge, toothsome face looms into view beneath the head of the doorframe.

Baby.

Hex drops the scissors with a clatter. 'We weren't doing anything!'

'Yeah,' agrees Scarlett. 'I was just... going for a wee.' She brushes the incriminating spider off her shoulder quickly. Gretel doesn't see where he lands.

Scarlett spins on her heel to face Gilde, who is now sitting up in bed, rubbing her eyes like a sleepy toddler.

'What is it, Baby?' asks the Bear Witch.

'I was just going for a wee, Gilde,' repeats Scarlett, her voice loud with hysteria.

Gilde wafts her hands dismissively. 'Permission granted. Go and do your business.'

Baby stands aside a little, so that Scarlett, mortified, can squeeze past.

'Mamma will make sure you don't get lost out there, little Wolfie,' calls Gilde after her. 'We all know tired lil doggies sometimes take wrong turns, out in the mountains.'

She stretches, and smiles at the rest of the cottage. 'Hex, sweetie, looks like you dropped your scissors. Best to put those back away where you found 'em, nice and neat. We don't want you hurting yourself again now, do we?'

Hex shakes his head, eyes down at the floor. He quickly picks the scissors up and puts them back in the drawer.

'So swell to see you're all finally behaving yourselves,' she tells her captives. 'Just one teeny thing. Girlie?'

Gretel meets her gaze.

'Is that thing you're making there my self-heating nightcap? Because it sure as chalk ain't cheese doesn't look like one.'

Gretel's heart sinks. She pulls her hands away from her badly hidden 'secret' weapon.

'Not quite,' she admits. 'It's just a prototype defensive device for you.'

Gilde nods brightly. 'Well, after that, I'd like you to get on with them other things you promised me, girlie, because I'm keeping you safe here for one thing only, and it's not for you to dilly-dally. You don't mind me saying, do you? You'd rather I'd be honest, I can tell.' Gilde steps daintily out of bed and straightens out her silver hair. 'Ooh, I feel refreshed.'

Gretel wonders how many times Gilde has flaunted her restedness to an exhausted Scarlett, or casually humiliated Hex. She tries to get on with her work. She tries to ignore the cage, and the thought of the banished Dwarves, and Patience despairing in the jar, and a bloodstained Jack watching Hex with an expression she's never seen Jack wear ever before. She tries to ignore her nagging worry over the fact that she currently has no idea where Trevor is. Most of all, as she concentrates on her inventions, she tries to ignore the fact that she's really, really starting to dislike that horrible old woman.

18
Et Tu, Sausages?

Stopping a Hydra was never going to be easy, or clean. Even though the monster his magical senses warned him about has turned out to be a metaphorical one, still Hansel understands that to put an end to its damage, he will have to be prepared to do things he wouldn't usually dream of. In the grand scheme of things, walking around the Citadel on polling day, spreading rumours that he isn't sure, thinking back, are completely true, isn't remotely in the same league as skewering a monster's heart, or burying it under the earth, or whatever it is one has to do to slay an actual Hydra. However, his day spent walking around with Morning and Daisy still leaves him feeling uneasy. It's one thing telling yourself you'd definitely push the boat out for the greater good, but it's an altogether different thing actually having to do it, especially when you're a rather quiet and anxious farm boy whose boat has, for thirteen years, been very securely tethered to the shore.

Perhaps it's the way they go about it that makes Hansel feel so uncomfortable. There's no running to the town criers or madrigal men, who are still under strict orders not to deliver any news any more politically contentious than that of an unusual polling station that also sells chips. Instead, Hansel and Daisy trail Morning as she strides about, mask off, beaming her big, crooked, toothy grin at everybody she sees, her flyaway dandelion hair and noisily excited dog creating a beacon of attention everywhere she goes. Then, while people turn to note the dog, the hair, the uncovered face, Hansel and Daisy just… talk, amongst themselves, in a tone calculated to sound as if it's not meant for the ears of others, while remaining loud enough to hear. If they've learned one thing from growing up in a small rural village, it's that people don't always listen, but they *love* to 'overhear'. He's not spreading misinformation; he's just talking with his friend, about things that are mostly true anyway, about the way John Rosier broke his own laws during the occupation of Nearby, and his closest henchmen aided and abetted this. There's no blood, no guts, no shrieking of a terrible monster through the streets. This is so much easier than facing down what he saw in the visions.

It's too easy, in fact. Maybe that's why Hansel feels so wrong all day.

By the evening, Hansel's sense of unease has turned into an anxious, sick feeling. The high walls of the Citadel loom down on him more than ever, and the thrashing magical panic within him is getting difficult to contain again. Both Daisy and Morning notice his increasingly troubled air.

'It's not enough,' he explains, as Sausages tries to jump up on him and lick him at the same time. 'All of this, it won't be enough, we should have done more, and now it's too late. What good can a load of last-minute rumours do?'

'Hansel, the whole of Myrsina runs on rumours,' Daisy reminds him. 'Rumours can be life-or-death stuff, especially under the huntsmen.'

'There's an hour still to go,' Morning adds, 'and look.' She points to the nearest polling station. 'Look at that queue.'

'But people have been queuing at those things all day,' replies Hansel.

'Exactly,' Morning tells them. 'The turnout must be really high.'

'But we don't know who they're voting for.'

'Lots of citizens,' Daisy points out. 'Lots of women, did you notice? That's good, isn't it?'

'Honestly?' Morning lays a hand on each teen's shoulder. 'I can't tell for sure. Hansel could be right; it could be too little, too late. The system might mean that getting lots of ordinary civilians to show up may still not make up for the huntsmen's say. Maybe they're all turning out in these numbers to vote for a different candidate after all. What matters is that you two little wonders showed up, and helped. You did your best, and that's what matters.'

'No, it's *not* what matters! What matters is stopping all of this; lives are at stake!'

'Hansel,' Morning soothes him, 'I know it feels like life or death at the moment, but it's all just politics. If one of the other candidates gets in, life won't be as nice as it could be, but we'll all muddle through. I'll probably get kicked out of the huntsmen for taking off my mask, but I'll be OK, I'll get by. I tried, and so did you.'

The magical panic begins to thrum; he can feel the tendrils of shadow trying to escape.

'So, if you lose tonight, that's it? It's over, we've lost? You won't help us fight any more?'

'I said I'd get by, not that I wouldn't do what I could. We'll think of other ways, Hansel.' She smiles again, that bright, sunny grin. 'But for now, everything's still there for the taking.' She pats his shoulder in a manner that cheerfully suggests that the conversation is over and it's time to move on. 'One more hour. Do you want to go and have a rest? It'll be a long night while they do the count.'

Hansel shakes his head. 'What if it comes to one or two votes? No, let's squeeze every second out of this that we can.'

Daisy grasps his hand in silent agreement.

Morning nods approvingly. 'Good lad.' She stoops and ruffles her dog's ears. 'Come along, Sausages. More walkies.'

Sausages pricks up her ears at the magical W word and runs in an excited circle, despite the fact that she's been walking all day long, on tiny little legs. The happy warmth of the dog is enough to temporarily subdue the rising terror in Hansel, even though the sick feeling persists. Not for the first time in his life, he really wishes that he were a dog.

After another hour, the bells toll out, marking the end of the voting day. The clanging vibrates through Hansel's whole body, renewing the mournful sense of imminent doom. With every baritone chime, every part of his magic that's been warning him of the Hydra for weeks tells him, *It wasn't enough. You failed. The monster is still here. It's still going to tear this whole land down.*

The evening turns into a strange, hushed, pregnant night. He and Daisy don't go back to the inn; instead they return to Morning's HQ to await the results with the others. They feel like a part of the team now, and waiting out the count amongst them seems more comforting than doing it in that tiny room above the rooftops. Neither of them were going to get any sleep this night, anyway.

'I feel like we're about to go into battle again,' Daisy tells him softly at one point in that interminable, endless, restless night. Hansel doesn't reply. It feels worse than that, to him.

The sky is still dark when Morning's aide, Richard, walks over to them. 'Fennel's back,' he tells them. Hansel and Daisy get to their feet quickly. Fennel has spent the past few hours at a major counting station. Everybody crowds Fennel the moment she steps through the door. All Hansel is able to see of her is a scrap of hair from behind Richard's head.

'What news, Sister?'

'It's... close,' Fennel tells them. 'Too close to call, between Morning, and our brother in orange.'

'Well, I'm in with a good shot, at least,' Morning tells them cheerfully.

'Except...' Fennel shifts to one side slightly, and Hansel is finally able to see how worried her expression is. 'The counting stations are by district. I was at Upper West, it's almost all civilian votes there.'

Morning's smile remains as sunny as ever, but the hope drains out of her eyes. 'Oh.'

'You needed a huge amount of civilians to vote for you, to make up for the system and to overcome all the huntsmen voting for Brother Orange…'

'Yes,' replies Morning, as cheerfully as possible, 'I do know that, thank you.'

'And,' continues Fennel, seemingly incapable of stopping, now, 'if even the civilians are split over you and Brother Orange, then…'

'Yes!' Morning's smile looks tight. 'Thank you! Well. I suppose we won't know for certain for a few hours yet, and we won't get a fuller picture until Grey reports back from Upper West, so—'

'No,' Fennel interrupts, confused. '*I* went to Upper West. Grey went to Higher West to see how the huntsman-heavy counts were going.'

Richard frowns down at a sheet. 'Says here "Grey Upper W, Fennel Higher W".'

Fennel pushes towards Richard, takes the sheet from him, squints at it, then at a sheet of her own, then gently hands Richard's paper back to him. 'OK, so, in my defence, these districts are very confusing. If I go to somewhere that's literally up a hill, I'd call it "Upper", because, you know, I've walked upwards.'

'No, I think they meant it's more towards the north.'

'Well then, why didn't they say "north-west"?'

'I don't know, Fennel, I didn't name the counting stations!'

'So,' says Morning, 'which count have you actually just come from, Fennel?'

'Higher West.'

'But that one's counting lots of huntsman votes.'

'Yes,' replies Fennel, weary and embarrassed.

Daisy's eyes light up. 'So…'

Fennel catches on to the new wave of optimism. 'Oh! Wait! Yes!'

'It's a close call between you and Brother Orange *amongst the huntsmen*,' says Richard, his voice low and shaky with shocked delight, holding his sheet of paper like it's a treasure map they've just decoded. 'So unless something very strange has happened, and Grey comes back with terrible news…'

And something very strange *has* just happened in Higher West, Hansel reminds himself, so there's no telling for certain how the count will end. Even as the others are starting to seem cautiously optimistic, the sick feeling thrumming through him persists. Something is still wrong.

Grey bursts through the door. 'Guys! OK, first of all, the distinction between Upper West and Higher West is really confusing, Richard, I almost went to the wrong one…'

'*Thank* you,' exclaims Fennel.

'Secondly, Upper West loves you, Morning, you're absolutely storming the count over there. I know, I know, it doesn't count for as much against the huntsman votes, but…' He trails off, noticing the sharp intakes of breath and tear-pricked eyes around him. 'What?'

'I think…' Momentary shades of surprise, bewilderment and joy pass across Morning's face, like iridescent bubbles in a dazzling sky. 'I think we might have just won.'

'Yes!' It's Daisy who cheers first, punching the air. Morning's team fast follow suit, hugging one another. Daisy pulls Hansel tight in celebration, but stops suddenly, stepping back and watching his face with concern. He gives her a small smile, the best he can muster. In spite of the news, in spite of all the celebrations, the terrible sensation remains, and his magical warning system, or whatever this is, has never steered him wrong before.

'Speech,' calls Richard, 'speech!'

Morning waves her hands modestly. 'I haven't definitely won yet, I don't want to jinx it.'

'"Jinx"?' Fennel laughs. 'That sounds like witch talk!'

'Ooh, Fennel, you rotter.' Morning laughs too. 'OK, fine. Let's leave the main speech till after the announcement. However, I will say this, to all of you. Thank you. From the bottom of my heart. There is a very good chance that we have made a major change in Myrsina tonight, making it a better, safer and freer land for all humans.' Everybody claps and cheers again. Morning continues. 'We may be able to finally put an end to these ridiculous "abominations", as if learning and developing skills and trades could possibly turn our own normal human girls and women into witches or other magical beasties.' More clapping. Daisy stops after a moment, still watching Hansel. He feels faint again. Like that moment on the platform, he feels as if the Hydra's right on top of them all. He can practically sense its heavy feet pacing around the warehouse.

'If we have indeed won,' Morning continues, 'then we can look forward to a Myrsina with no more masks. No more anonymity. No more edicts. No more ducking stools for minor transgressions. Under Rosier, we huntsmen turned our quarrel against our own kind! No wonder people are rising up! Even in Slate, my own hometown, humans are finding more sympathy with the inhuman brutes and animalistic thieves of the Darkwood than with their own governing body, because we acted like *we* were their enemy. We're going to put a stop to that. Huntsmen and civilians alike will join in peace and freedom once more against our true common foe. The Darkwood is a growing threat, and we ignore its hypnotic spell over our own people at our peril. We must defeat it. We must stand shoulder to shoulder with our fellow men and women as equals, to eradicate those enchanters, those mind controllers, those dangerous beasts and witches. Then and only then will the menace be stopped once and for all.'

Oh no.

The magic thrashes. The Hydra is here. The Hydra was always right here. It always had so very many heads, he hadn't realised that some of those heads would whisper sweet things at him, pretend to be on his side. And he just helped it. He just let it win.

'Oh Hansel, my dear, sweet boy.' Hansel notices that tears are streaming down his face. Morning wipes her eyes emotionally as well. 'I know exactly how you feel. We'll save your sister, I promise, and free your poor village from the Darkwood's spell. I swear to you, Hansel, nothing like what happened to Gretel will ever happen to one of our kind again. No more innocent girls will be chased out into that cursed forest to become infected and rot. The true witches will be weeded out using logic and reason, not outmoded bigoted ideology, and they will be ended efficiently, using modern technology. I have special machines all ready; I commissioned them years ago, even made sure some of the designers on the payroll were secretly women. I'll be able to unveil them as soon as I'm officially elected. We'll scoop your sister out of there and then, before you know it, there'll no more witches to worry about. They'll simply be scary stories from the past, once they have been completely – humanely – eliminated.'

Morning's aides cheer gleefully. Morning herself tries to give Hansel a wide, happy smile, but she, like Daisy, notes him with concern.

'Daisy, my dear girl, is Hansel OK? He looks poorly, like the other night.'

The Hydra head, still saying such sweet words. Hansel realises with horror that it was never pretending to be on his side. Part of it always genuinely believed that Hansel was one of its own, and still does, still entreats him to join forces in its rampage of death and destruction.

Daisy gazes into his distant eyes. 'I think he just needs some air, Morning. He gets lightheaded, ever since our village's invasion.'

Morning's face crumples with sympathy. 'Oh yes, the poor boy. And you two are only kids; it's been such a long day. Go and have a rest, that's an order from the new boss.'

A warm chuckle breaks out around the room. It isn't mocking or mean spirited; it includes them in its camaraderie, and that just makes it all the worse.

Daisy puts her arm around his shoulder and starts leading him towards the back door. 'Come on.'

'Let's hear it for Hansel and Daisy, my little last-minute wonders,' calls Morning after them. 'Hip hip...'

'Hooray,' cheer her aides.

Sausages the dog bounds over to see them off, wagging and licking and still overflowing with adoration and trust.

Oh, Sausages, thinks Hansel, your love is a lie. You're only a dog, you love your human because she's kind to you, you don't understand... The magic throbs in him again. For a moment he almost blacks out trying to hold it in. In fact, he doesn't manage to contain it quite enough to evade Sausages' canine sensitivity. She whines, aware that something's wrong.

He should have understood. He should have seen beyond her superficial and selective kindness. He should have been able to comprehend the situation a little better than a trousering *dog*; what a stupid hick he's been.

'Hip hip...'

'Hooray!'

Their cheers, the dog's confused whine at the innate wrongness of the magic he's struggling to keep swallowed down, the very fact that a dog's wholehearted affection for Morning had deceived him as to her nature... it's all too much for him.

'Hip hip...'

He doesn't faint, this time. He wishes he had. He wishes even that he'd thrown up on himself as opposed to what actually happens next.

He loses control. Completely. Only for a moment, less than a second, but the power he expels in that instant is alarmingly forceful and impossible to ignore. It's akin to a particularly loud magical sneeze. Dark, crackling tendrils of magic shoot from his

160

head and fingers, desperate to earth themselves. The shadows in the already gloomy warehouse briefly solidify and, deep beneath his toes, the ground complains like a severely upset stomach. It all stops again as suddenly as it started, but by then it's too late.

19
Witching Hour

Sausages yelps and runs to Morning, cringing and barking. All of Morning's aides stop and stare, mid 'Hooray'. Morning locks eyes with him. He can't look away, can't move, in spite of Daisy tugging at his arm.

When Morning speaks, it's with a surprising tenderness. 'It was *you*.'

'Come on, Hansel,' begs Daisy. She tugs at his frame, but all he manages are a few faltering steps towards the door. After all this time, managing to keep it secret. After everything Gretel went through to keep it hidden. He's just ruined everything.

Quite calmly, Morning approaches him with even steps.

'Rosier had it almost right after all, didn't he? Just sent his men after the wrong twin.'

'Hansel, come *on*!'

'And that was your same magic in the village square when we lost Nearby, wasn't it?' asks Morning, in the sort of tone she would use if asking where he'd got his shirt. 'I recognise it.'

'Hansel!'

Morning shifts her attention to Daisy, and says with the same casual airiness, 'And did *you* know about this, Miss Wicker?'

Daisy.

Daisy witnessed it, too.

Daisy doesn't respond to Morning. Instead she puts all of her weight against Hansel's hulky, farm-thickened frame, and shoves.

'Hansel! We need to go!'

Hansel just about manages to shake himself out of his torpor enough to run. He allows Daisy to take his hand and lead him at a sprint out of the warehouse, down the narrow alleyways and out into the main streets.

The streets are still full of people, even at such an hour, straddling that strange time between 'too late' and 'too early'. It reminds Hansel of the village square, when the huntsmen had first come for Gretel in the small hours. The odd atmosphere is the same – the disquiet, the fear. As he runs through the crowd, hand in hand with Daisy, a realisation hits him. The sick, claustrophobic sensation he's had ever since coming to the Citadel hasn't ever simply been down to the high walls and noisy, narrow streets. The fear Hansel has been feeling all this time hasn't been his fear alone. There are witches here, hundreds of them. People like him, right here in the Citadel, hiding out of self-preservation just as he has always done, and terrified of being found out. Cramped densely in with them, their alarm ratcheting up as the head huntsman candidates tried to outdo one another over anti-witch rhetoric, Hansel must have magically sensed their anxiety in the same way he'd heard all those footsteps and cart rattles and shouted conversations in the packed marketplace. There's so much magical terror here that it's become a part of the urban ambience.

'Stupid, stupid, stupid,' mutters Daisy as they run. 'Should have known!'

'Sorry,' breathes Hansel. This is all his fault! He never even told Daisy about his powers; she's just had to find out about them in a warehouse full of zealous huntsmen, and all because Hansel got upset about a dog's judge of character.

'It's as much my fault as yours,' Daisy puffs. 'She said such nice things about girls like me and Gretel, she had such a friendly face, but at the end of the day she was still a huntsman, and huntsmen hunt down magicals, it's the whole point of them. I should have read her full manifesto or something before agreeing to help. I tell you what blindsided me – that dog. I think I must just automatically trust people who are nice to dogs.'

'I know, right?' Hansel manages. 'It was a really good dog, too.'

'*Such* a cute dog, I honestly can't believe it.'

Daisy pulls him down a side street, away from their inn.

'What are you doing?' he pants.

'The East Gate's pretty small,' she explains. 'It'll only be barred from the inside, and not guarded this time of night.'

'But... your stuff.'

'What?'

'Your cart, all the baskets...'

Daisy stops briefly, to edge around some inconsiderately placed bins.

'We made some silvers the first day,' Daisy tells him, stepping carefully over a pool of assorted food slop. 'The rest of the baskets can be the innkeeper's fee for our room.'

'But your mum...'

Daisy looks at him seriously. 'Mum wants us to come home. Yes, she'd rather us come home with the work cart and a tidy profit – Mum's still Mum, after all – but she'd rather I bring you home safe. She does love you, you know.' She pauses for just a breath, then turns and carries on dragging him towards the East Gate. 'We all do.'

'But, Daisy...'

'It's fine.'

'But it's not.' Hansel stops, keeping hold of her hand so that she turns to look back at him again. 'Daisy, I'm so sorry.'

'It's just a few baskets and an old cart, Hansel.'

'No. I'm sorry about... all this time, I never told you about what I am. I wasn't doing it because I didn't trust you, I wanted to tell you, but...'

'But you weren't ready yet.' Daisy gives him a small smile. 'It's OK. It's a big thing, especially with all our huntsman troubles. I knew you'd tell me when you were ready.'

She turns to go again, but Hansel takes another step forward and stops her. His gallant gesture is marred slightly by him putting his foot in something warm, wet and acrid in the dark. He winces a little, but carries on.

'You knew?'

Daisy nods. 'I worked it out.'

'How long ago?'

'Not that long. Had my suspicions for a while, but I properly put it all together on Liberation Day. I could certainly tell you were struggling with it here.' She taps the side of her head. 'Not just a very pretty face.'

'But you never said anything.'

She shrugs. 'As I say, it wasn't my place; it was yours. I think a few people in Nearby might have an inkling, you know. It really doesn't change anything. You're still our farm boy who brings us milk and grains, and talks to animals, and feels everything so keenly, and knows how to work all of his sister's inventions, and rallies us together in the many, many times we're under attack. You're still our Hansel. Still *my* Hansel.'

'Oh.' Hansel feels quite overcome.

'You are aware,' adds Daisy solemnly, 'that you're standing in an open sewer right now?'

'Yes, I wondered what that was,' Hansel admits. He shakes his foot out of it. 'It's really filthy down this end of the Citadel, isn't it?'

'It's one of the reasons why they often don't have a guard on duty at the gate,' Daisy tells him. She pulls at his hand again. 'Come on. The imminent head huntsman knows exactly what you are, and exactly what she wants to do to you. That means we have to get out of here. Now.'

20
Bear with Us

In Gilde's cottage, a frustrating, uncomfortable day passes by with all the speed of marmalade sliding down a very slight incline. Gretel is at least able to keep busy by carrying on with her semi-secret weapon while Gilde's not looking, and by making home improvements when Gilde *is* looking, in an attempt to win over their captor's favour. The former turns out to be a much easier task than the latter. Gretel has met drystone walls easier to impress than Gilde.

'And what's this doohickey, girlie?' Gilde asks at one point, holding up a half-built dynamo.

'That's for generating electrical charge,' Gretel explains.

'Lemon trickle what now?'

'It's a sort of energy; you get it in lightning bolts and static and some magic.'

'You want me to keep lightning in this thing?'

'No.' Gretel sighs, taking the unfinished gadget from her to fit on a new part. 'It creates its own charge when you wind it.' She demonstrates. The incomplete machine sparks as she briefly cranks the handle.

Gilde steps back, regarding it with distrust. 'Goodness to Betsy! Seems to me like you're looking to kill me more than help me, girlie.'

'It really is no different to harnessing fire for everyday uses, you know,' Gretel tells her in soothing tones. She gives a pointed look to the massive oven she's still tied to.

'But I know what fire is *for*,' argues Gilde.

'Electricity can be used for lighting, or as a weapon,' Gretel attempts.

'So can fire!'

'OK, but this particular generator is going to be used to run an electrical charge through a perimeter fence,' Gretel tells her. 'You can switch it off easily to let your bears come and go, and the rest of the time it'll provide a non-lethal deterrent for any trouble trying to make its way to your home. All you'll have to do is wind the crank up three times a day.'

'Jumpin' Jiminies, so now you not only want me to keep lightning in my home, but I've got to mill it myself from the sweat of my little old brow? Three times a day?' She turns, with a dismissive wave of her hand. 'Some help you're turning out to be.'

Gretel glares at the back of the old woman's head. 'If you don't like my inventions, you could always let us go.'

'Oh, you'd like that, wouldn't you?'

Yes and no, admits Gretel silently to herself. As uncomfortable as she is at the oven, and as much time as they're currently wasting, there's no point in them being freed yet if they can't also take Hex and Scarlett with them. Besides which, she still hasn't seen any sign of Trevor yet.

The day turns, painfully slowly, into night. After sharing an unpleasant meal of lukewarm porridge with her henchmen and captors, Gilde returns to bed for another early night, leaving Scarlett, by now tearful with exhaustion, as well as a particularly browbeaten Hex to guard the prisoners. The sensation of desperately needing to sleep swells unpleasantly in Gretel, scratching at her eyes and scrambling her brain. She feels as if she could sleep all

167

winter. She can tell from the expressions of the others that they're faring no better.

'Does anybody else,' says Buttercup after a while, 'really need to use the privy?'

'Yes,' admit Gretel and Jack in chorus.

In her jar, Patience shakes her head and performs a mime, vaguely indicating that the dead have no toilet needs.

'I've just been using a corner of this cage,' Snow tells everyone.

'Yes,' says Buttercup, 'we know.'

'Sorry again about splashing you.'

'I'd escort you down there one by one,' frets Scarlett, 'but, you know.' She opens the cottage door by way of demonstration. A few feet outside the door, Baby looks up at them sharply, just as he has done every time anybody has opened the cottage door since the morning. The one guard that Gilde definitely knows she can rely on, and the hardest to circumvent. The possibility of Scarlett using her pack to fend him off has already been quietly raised and quickly dismissed, due to the likelihood of wolves being killed in the resulting battle, and the inevitable ire of Gilde if she found out for certain that Scarlett and Hex were no longer on her side.

'Would the bears seriously not even let us be taken to the privy?' Jack groans.

Hex shakes his head. 'I don't think Gilde trusts any of us enough for that right now.'

'Well,' adds Scarlett, 'that at least is justifiable right now.'

'She's just punishing us all, isn't she,' says Gretel glumly. 'That's what all of this is really about.' She's hot, and tired, and dispirited. She's never met a genuinely nasty witch before, and she is not enjoying the new perspective on what it can be like when one uses their magic for no reason other than spite. An unpleasant little voice in the back of her head tells her that, well, the human hatred of witches has to have come from *somewhere*, so maybe…

She banishes the thought before it has a chance to finish. Gilde was out on her own in the wilderness for who knows how long;

it's bound to turn anyone all insular and mean. And it's still no excuse for the way witches are treated. It's certainly no excuse for casually contemplating how easy it might be to shove Gilde into that big oven.

It's not like she'd light it, or anything, just lock her in while they escaped. See how *she* liked it…

No. What is she thinking? This place is making her as bitter and mean as her captor. She chides herself silently for even entertaining the notion, and tries to put it down to the tiredness.

Even if Gilde is horrible. And she *is* horrible.

And Gretel *still* can't find Trevor. She can see Buttercup quietly scanning the room for him from time to time, too. Gretel wonders if Trevor's taken himself off on some espionage mission to find a way to free them. Still, she wishes he'd show up again.

'I'll see if I can get you guys a bucket or something,' offers Scarlett.

Buttercup sighs. 'State I'm in right now, I'll probably turn it into an oatcake as soon as I touch the thing.'

Gretel blinks, a porridgey memory hitting her. 'Those honeycombs Gilde has…'

'One thing I am really grateful to the bears for,' Hex sighs. 'Only food we have that actually tastes of anything.'

'So, the bears fetch it.'

'Of course. They always know where to find it. They love that stuff. Runs low this time of year, of course, along with everything else.'

Buttercup gasps excitedly, meeting eyes with Gretel as the realisation hits her. 'You're thinking flapjacks, aren't you?'

Gretel nods.

'Flapjacks?' asks Hex.

'I generally can't control my powers very well or choose what form my cakes are going to take,' Buttercup explains, 'but the one thing I can reliably get right, provided I'm able to concentrate, is flapjacks.'

Jack nods in agreement. 'Nobody knows why.'

'And flapjacks have loads of honey,' Gretel reminds Hex and Scarlett. 'Maybe if you two could pass Buttercup a load of things into the cage that she can change, she can make enough to distract Baby long enough for us all to sneak past, and we can get away.'

'And use the privy.'

'And use the privy, yes, thank you, Jack, I'm a bit bursting too.'

Scarlett and Hex look at one another.

'I'll get a load of plates,' Scarlett tells her.

'I'll get cloths,' adds Hex.

'Great. Thank you.'

'Um,' adds Buttercup, 'while you're fetching them, would you mind keeping an eye out for a little spider? He might have decided to put on a false moustache.'

21
Flapjacks

Within five minutes, the inside of the cramped and dirty cage is stacked with about two dozen, honey-and-oat-scented flapjacks the size of dinner plates and dishcloths. Snow and Buttercup do their best to keep the flapjacks away from Snow's toilet corner while Hex carefully snips the nettle fragment off Jack's skin.

'Sorry again about this,' murmurs Hex, with every tiny, painful snip to the stitches.

'It's OK,' Jack replies, grinning through gritted teeth. 'So, can you not… stick that bit of nettle back onto your bit now it's been used on me?'

'No, I've tried that with bits that got torn off the shirt,' Hex whispers. 'At best, it would just fall off again; often it would take more bits with it, hence having so little left of it now.'

'It used to be a whole shirt?' Jack asks, eyeing the single piece of nettle Hex has left.

'No.' Hex manages to snip the last fragment of nettle from Jack. 'It used to be three quarters of a shirt.' He throws the bloodied scrap away. 'It's a really long story.'

'Well,' Jack reasons, as Hex unties him, 'if this plan works, we'll have lots of time for you to tell it to me.'

'Hmm!' Hex contemplates this. 'It's not a very happy story.'

Jack flexes his newly freed hands. 'Well, thank trousers for that; it'll fit right in with the rest of our stories.'

With the unmistakable gait of somebody whose buttocks have gone to sleep from too much sitting in one position, Jack moves quietly over to the open window from which the cage of branches sprouts. He gestures, as if unwinding something out of the cottage. The branches shrink down to slender shoots and silently retreat back into a nearby tree beyond the window.

'Oh, thank goodness.' Buttercup gets gratefully to her feet, and stretches her spine. Snow tries windmilling the life back into her arms, but is quickly persuaded by Buttercup that even though she's not currently wearing armour, it's still not the best thing to do when trying not to wake a sleeping captor in the same cluttered room, especially not while carrying several large flapjacks.

As Scarlett unties Gretel, Buttercup takes herself on a very quiet and limited Trevor-finding mission, which mostly consists of peering into corners and cracks, and whispering 'Trevor?' to no reply.

'Where is he?' Buttercup frets quietly. 'Gretel, do you have some sort of spider-finding device?'

'Sorry, no.'

'We can't leave without him, we've got the whole gang now but not Trevor...'

Behind Buttercup, Patience rattles the inside of her jar irritably.

'Oh! Sorry, Patience!' Buttercup takes the jar off the Ghost, who expands to full size with a sigh of relief.

'Finally, thank you.'

'Oh, Patience, I should have freed you earlier.'

'It's OK...'

'Do *you* have any sort of spider-location ability?'

Patience rolls her eyes. 'Witch, please. I'm a Ghost, not a cat.'

'Ghosts are a lot like cats, I suppose,' says Snow. 'Largely nocturnal, come and go as they please... jump up and scare people... kind of haughty.'

'*I'm* haughty?' Patience gasps haughtily. 'You're literally heir to the throne!'

'Guys, this isn't helping,' whispers Gretel. 'We need to get out of here as soon as possible, but not without Trevor.' She pauses awkwardly. 'Um. Hex, Scarlett? I don't suppose if you were in animal form you might have better senses for spotting him?'

Hex frowns. 'Are you telling us to change?'

'Not like that, it's not an order, we're not like Gilde. See it as... a request. An appeal, even. We just can't leave without...'

Suddenly, Gretel feels the faint but unmistakable sensation of a house spider dropping onto her shoulder. Trevor is looking particularly pleased with himself, and appears to be wearing a tiny wig.

'Question for you all,' says Trevor. 'Who's got eight legs, no thumbs and an absolutely cracking plan to get you all out of here?' He points to himself with four of his legs. 'This guy. First, I infiltrate the bears as one of them, using this incredible disguise I managed to knock together out of webbing and Dwarf hair. Second, the seduction commences. This stage may take a while. Then—'

'We were just going to distract them with these flapjacks,' Buttercup tells him.

Trevor nods stoically. 'Yep, that'll work too, and I still get a bear disguise to keep in case of emergencies. Everyone's a winner. Good use of your cake powers, Buttercup.'

Gretel quietly slips the sort-of-secret weapon invention up her sleeve and undoes the latch of the front door, while Patience wafts straight through the wood, translucent as a raindrop, to scout the situation outside.

'Don't congratulate me yet,' whispers Buttercup, 'it still might not work.'

'It will,' Snow tells her.

Patience floats back in, concern etched all over her dead face. 'I don't think this will work,' she whispers. 'We're looking at all three bears patrolling the perimeter now.'

'But we've got all these flapjacks,' says the increasingly sticky Werewolf.

'Where's the best place to put them so we can sneak past the bears?' Gretel asks Patience. 'And can you telekinesis them all where we need them to go, or should some of us help carry them?'

'Um,' says Patience. 'Let me think.'

'You used to do recon and campaign strategy all the time when you were alive,' Gretel reminds her.

'Give me a minute, I've been in a jar all day!'

'Quick as you can,' Gretel urges, her hand still on the latch. 'We do really need to escape before—'

'What in the Sam Hill is it *this* time?'

Gilde is sitting blearily up in bed yet again. Gretel groans inwardly, and wishes that instead of a functioning electrical border fence and an as-yet-unused secret escape weapon, she'd just invented Gilde that noise-cancelling nightcap after all.

22

A Spot of Bother

'Can't a little old lady catch her beauty sleep around here any more?' The Bear Witch rubs her eyes and takes in the frozen, guilt-ridden scene at the front door.

'Wolfie? Sweetiebird? What is all this? The prisoners are looking mighty escapey.'

'Gilde…'

'And you two are seeming mighty backslidey, might I add.'

'Gilde.'

'Why all the biscuits?'

'They're flapjacks, Gilde.'

'Oh, neato. That makes much more sense.'

Scarlett squares her shoulders resolutely. 'Gilde, we're leaving.'

'No, you're not,' Gilde replies sweetly.

'We are. All of us. Hex and me aren't your servants; you always made it very clear we were staying here on your mercy, and, well, now we're going with these guys.' She pauses, a doggish cringe creeping in to undermine her display of fortitude. 'Sorry.'

'No, you're not,' says Gilde again in the same sugary tones. 'We need you here for the winter, and our guests will be released once they've cooled their heels and girlie over here has made us some home improvements like she promised…'

'I have actually finished the electric fence I was telling you about,' Gretel tells her. 'It's just spooled up on the floor there, you can nail it up around the perimeter tomorrow.'

'Oh, you couldn't actually put the dang thing together yourself?'

'Not really, on the grounds that you've been keeping me tied to an oven.'

Gilde shrugs. 'Maybe Wolfie can take you out on a leash tomorrow or something.'

'No, because we're leaving.'

'No, you're *not*.' Gilde giggles a little. 'How many times've you fixed to go, now? Feels like every time I've so much as closed my eyes. You people make your little plan, me and my bears stop you, I take another nap, you make another bad plan and round and round the garden we go.' She gets out of bed, smoothing her blankets. 'It's for the best; soon you'll realise you got no hope of taking on either the huntsmen or the witch of the east if you can't even get past a half-hibernating old lady and a few... Baby, *no!*'

Gilde's exclamation is due to the fact that the doorway is suddenly full of bear. Baby's giant head pulls back and makes another attempt to force its way into the cottage, but his huge shoulders remain too wide to get through the doorway. Behind him, there are more grunts. Mamma and Papa are at the door as well, behind Baby's hulking frame. Baby roars, snuffles and snaps his giant mouth at the magical cakes.

Gilde slaps her own forehead. 'Flapjacks! Those things must be full of honey, you dunderheads.'

'Yes,' says Buttercup. 'That was the idea. And don't call us dunderheads, please.'

'Dunderheads,' repeats Gilde angrily. 'Codfish, ninnyhammers!'

'I am finding out so many olde worlde insults on this outing,' mutters Trevor. 'Remind me to use "ninnyhammer" in the future.'

'What did you think would happen next,' rails Gilde, 'once you'd got all my bears honey-happy?'

'Easy,' Gretel tells her.

176

She takes a few plate-sized flapjacks from Scarlett, shoves the window open and throws the treats outside, along with half the latch that came away with her push.

'My window!' cries Gilde.

Outside, Mamma and Papa roar excitedly. Both older bears swiftly appear on the other side of the ruined window, squabbling over the flapjacks, no longer showing any interest in stopping an escape.

Scarlett follows suit, breaking open a second window to throw her remaining flapjacks outside.

'Scarlett!' Gilde's tone is sharp and shocked at the Werewolf's display of rebellion. Even Scarlett seems surprised, if a little thrilled, by her own breakage. Behind her, a third window is smashed by a poker-wielding Snow, although this is probably just because Snow likes breaking stuff and doesn't want to miss out on an opportunity.

Gretel frowns at the doorway. Even though Mamma and Papa are joyfully feasting on the flapjacks that have been hurled outside, Baby is still blocking the whole of the doorway, massive razor teeth snapping. Either the giant bear is very stuck or very stupid. Possibly both.

'What are you *doing*?' Gilde demands, marching right up to Scarlett.

'Getting out of here,' Scarlett tells her, 'like we said.'

Gilde's face pinches bitterly, and a hand lashes out as if on impulse, to slap the Werewolf's face. Gilde's so much shorter than Scarlett that her papery little hand only really catches Scarlett across the chin.

'Hey,' cries Snow. 'No need for that!'

Out of the corner of her eye, Gretel notices Hex cringing back in response to the slap, but Scarlett doesn't even wince. The cottage would be leaden with a tense silence were it not for Baby continuing to wriggle and snap, rammed halfway through the doorframe.

'I'm sorry,' Gilde tells her, after a moment of being stared down, 'but sometimes, the pair of you just make me hopping mad, and—'

Scarlett growls at her, drawing her lips right back to reveal rows of needle teeth.

'Don't you talk back to me like that,' gasps Gilde, affronted. 'Hexy, what are *you* going to do about all of this, if your head hasn't been too turned by a young flirt who's only making fun of you...'

'That's enough,' mumbles Hex, almost inaudible under the competing noises of the bears outside and Baby's cacophony in the creaking doorway.

'Pardon?' asks Gilde.

Carefully watching Baby's struggles and the faint splintering of wood, Gretel shuffles forward a little to try to manoeuvre Buttercup away from her spot close to the doorway.

'I said,' repeats Hex, slightly louder, 'that's...'

'Baby, I said *no!*' shrieks Gilde suddenly, but it's too late.

With one last grunt of effort, the bear pushes through into the cottage like a large dog desperate to get in through a cat flap. Unlike a large dog, Baby manages to take the doorframe and chunks of the surrounding wall with him. Gretel makes a lunge to pull Buttercup to safety at the same time as Snow does, resulting in all three of them clumsily colliding with one another as well as an awful lot of hungry, honey-maddened bear. For a moment, everything is a jumble of fur, heavy flesh, limbs, claws and teeth, then Gretel's pressed breathlessly against the floor along with Snow and Buttercup. Somewhere beyond the mass of bear flesh, people are screaming. She spots Trevor valiantly clamber from Buttercup's squashed head onto the bear's fur and try to burrow in for a painful bite. She can't call out, can't try to dissuade Trevor from what's probably quite a bad idea; she can't breathe. She realises with annoyance that the secret weapon she spent ages making and cleverly hiding up her sleeve would come in really handy right now, but that she's dropped it. She hopes that this won't be the last thought she ever has. That would be a pain.

'Baby!' comes Gilde's muffled voice from beyond. 'Over here, sugar-pie! Over here!'

The bear shifts again, and Gretel can breathe and move once more. She gets to her elbows as Snow pulls up a winded but unhurt Buttercup. Gilde is pressed against the far wall of the cottage, hurling the remaining flapjacks at the corner furthest from the broken door.

'C'mon, cutie, get off those naughty witches, there's good eating over here,' Gilde continues. Gretel notices that her face is still bitterly twisted up. There are tears in the old woman's eyes.

'Did you just save our lives?' Snow asks, helping Buttercup and Gretel to their feet.

The bear lumbers over to the flapjacks in the corner, smashing chairs and beds as he goes, until his huge frame stands completely between Gilde and the rest of them. Gilde regards them all furiously from between the bear's legs.

'I didn't never want to kill any of youse,' she croaks. 'I just wanted to be left lonesome; all of you demanded to come to my little cottage, every one! And then all I did was try to keep you safe from your own hare-brained selves. And how am I repaid? You turn against me, and break everything. Well, if that's the way you want to play it, you can all just scram. Go on, scat!'

'Gilde, please don't end things like this,' Hex begs.

'Too late, birdbrain!' Gilde winces a little as Baby shifts and smashes his haunch into the oven. 'You want out, well then get out! Go and get cursed again out east, or get killed by those huntsmen, see if I care, just don't you dare ever set a feather my way again!'

'You can come with us. Together we can—'

'Phooey. Ain't no "us"; seems now like there never was! Leave me alone!'

Jack tugs at Hex's shoulder. 'Let's do as she says.'

'Sure, Hex.' Gilde's expression hardens. 'Do as I says. Or else. I still don't want to hurt you, but I am so het up right now, I can't guarantee a thing.'

'Gilde…?'

'*Out!*' Gilde's voice becomes a roar, the roar of a multitude of bears. At the door, Gretel notices that Mamma and Papa have stopped eating and are flanking the cottage, snarling. Even Baby looks across from his pile of honeyed treats and bares his fangs.

Scarlett grabs Gretel's shoulders, the top half of her body already halfway between human and wolf, her hackles raised. 'Gotta go. Now,' she manages through a barely human mouth.

'OUT!' roars Gilde again, and this time the three bears roar too. Baby makes a warning lunge at Hex, further splintering a bedframe in the process.

Jack grabs Hex and drags him from the cottage. For her part, Gretel needs no further encouragement to run, and nor do the rest of the group. Snow is still in the borrowed dress, without her usual armour or axes, the poker now somewhere on the cottage floor along with Gretel's secret weapon. The sight of Snow hitching up skirts to run looks horribly wrong to Gretel. Buttercup, startled by a too-close swipe of Mamma's great paw, has lost a chunk of her own skirt to accidental cakeification. Scarlett, too distressed to use her hood, can't seem to decide on a shape to take, and is escaping the bears in a bizarre, panicked gait, a few steps on human feet, transforming into a wolf for a few more strides before getting tangled up in clothes that no longer fit her canine form but which she doesn't have time to remove, straightening back up into something more human again, only for the cycle to repeat. Patience has vanished; running from a sleuth of enraged bears is very much an activity that only concerns the living, and any attempts to spook them in this state would be extremely ill-advised. A quick check over Gretel's shoulder reveals that Jack and Hex are still with the group, taking up the rear, with Jack throwing trees up to slow the path of Mamma and Papa as they pursue the fleeing group at a steady pace.

Mamma and Papa continue to follow them after they have stumbled and slithered down the foothills, out of sight of the smashed-up cottage. The forest around them thickens, and more animal footsteps join the chase. It takes a moment for Gretel to realise that it isn't more pursuers on their tail, rather the rest of Scarlett's wolf pack, joining them in their exodus from the bears' territory. The whining wolf pack does nothing to deter the bears; in fact, it only seems to make them even more aggressive in chasing everybody away. The chase continues for what feels like miles. By the time the bears finally slow to a walk, give one final roar of warning and turn to lollop back towards the mountains, Gretel's legs and lungs are in exhausted agony. Trembling, with limbs that feel simultaneously as weak as wet paper and as heavy as clay, she drops down onto something soft and warm, which turns out to be a collapsed wolf. Both panting as hard as the other, she and the wolf share a glance of mutual apology, without either of them actually moving from the spot where they've both dropped. In fact, Gretel leans the back of her head down momentarily onto the exhausted wolf's furry flank. It makes no complaint.

Snow too has sunk to a crouch. It would look almost princessly, with her skirts pooled about her, were it not for the profuse sweating and breathless swearing.

'My armour,' she complains. 'That was my best armour! And all my best axes!'

Hex is looking considerably more panicked. 'I can't believe we did that! Trousers, she was really angry; what have we done? That was my home!'

'It wasn't a home,' replies a mostly human-shaped Scarlett. 'It was a cage and she was the key-master.'

'But what will become of us…?'

'You'll stay with us, of course,' Buttercup tells them. 'We can make room in the cottage, right, everyone…? Buttercup frowns around herself, with the expression of somebody who's sure she's forgotten something but has also temporarily forgotten what it is she may have forgotten.

Patience manifests in front of an unsuspecting wolf, making it yelp.

'I'm here,' she announces. 'Everyone OK?'

'I lost my best suit of armour,' complains Snow. 'It took the lads ages to make me that.'

'Well,' Patience tells her, 'I did find something that might cheer you up a bit.'

'More armour?' asks Snow hopefully.

Patience shakes her head. From out of the thickets, seven grubby faces appear and stare at them sheepishly.

'Lads!' Snow cries, with a genuine relief.

'They must have been waiting for you at the territory border all this time,' Patience says.

Snow throws her arms wide to them. They scurry over to her for grateful hugs.

'Did *you* manage to grab me some more armour?' she asks them.

One Dwarf looks down, shamefaced. 'Yummy.'

'Oi. Joking.' She pulls all seven of the creatures tight to her. 'We're all together again!'

'Oh no,' cries Buttercup suddenly. She pats down her long black hair frantically, then pats her sleeves, turning the cuffs into bagels.

'Oh no,' echoes Gretel. Her eyes widen as the realisation hits her.

'What?' asks Jack.

Gretel and Buttercup turn to him, as one. 'Trevor!'

182

23
Taking Flight

The road back from the Citadel to Nearby feels even longer than the journey there, in spite of the fact that Hansel and Daisy no longer have a cart to push. Time feels much more of the essence now, and nothing makes a destination feel quite so far away as when you know you need to reach it as quickly as possible. Behind a heavy sheet of cloud, a dull, grey dawn breaks over the thin line of Darkwood on the eastern horizon. Will they have finished the counting by now? wonders Hansel. Is Morning the official head huntsman already? Is she standing on a platform outside the castle and making that same speech about wiping out all magicals right at this moment? Is she really going to start right away? And where would she start it? How would she start it? Another march on Darkwood? And what about those machines she mentioned? Hansel wishes he'd given himself the time to find out, but for now all he can really do is get some distance between himself and the huntsmen, and try to warn the residents of Darkwood.

He tries to reach a message out to Gretel again, as he has been doing since he and Daisy escaped the Citadel hours ago, but yet again he finds his sister's mind closed off, too filled with swirling, unreadable problems of her own to be receptive to any psychic warning from Hansel.

'This is bad,' he says for probably the tenth time so far.

'Yes,' Daisy concedes. 'But things have been bad before. Remember that time you were locked in a cage and I was tied to a stake?'

'Course I do, that was two weeks last Monday.'

'Feels like forever ago, though, doesn't it? And we're different people now. Older.'

'Two weeks older.'

'And wiser.'

'We just got tricked by a huntsman with funny hair and a dog.'

'Plus, you're a big, powerful witch.'

'I've always been a witch, though. And, according to you, you've known about it for ages.'

'Yeah, but we're being open about it now, aren't we?' Daisy pauses, watching him carefully as they speed-walk. 'Also, we have the power of love behind us.'

'We do?'

'Because we're stepping out together.'

Hansel blinks. He does so several times. 'We are?'

'I mean, literally yes, we are right now, we're stepping and we're out and we're together.'

'Oh.'

'But, if you wanted to, we could also…'

'Yes…?'

'You know. Hold hands.'

In spite of the severity of the situation, Hansel can't help but smile a little.

'Yes. I'd like to step out and hold hands.'

Daisy matches his smile, and reaches her hand out for him to take. Just as he takes hold of her hand, however, there is a strange rumbling from behind them.

'What is that?'

They both turn. The road out of the Citadel remains empty at this early hour. There are no marching huntsmen, no trundling machines, no masked horseback posse galloping their way. Still,

Hansel can't shake the sensation of trouble following them. The image of the Hydra flashes again across his mind's eye, bright and loud and racing on many feet right up to him. Just as it's about to collide with Hansel, its back opens up into a kaleidoscope of wings. It leaps, and flaps, and for a moment Hansel feels as if the only beings in the whole world are himself and the Hydra soaring over his head, crushing him in its downdraught. For a moment, he feels alone, and the solitude feels oddly soothing.

He isn't alone, he reminds himself. It's not him versus a monster; it's a monstrous idea versus a whole people. And that's worse, that's scarier – it always is, when there are others to protect. The Hydra passes over him, flying east towards the forest, leaving him unscathed. The vision winks out of existence.

'What is it?' Daisy asks. She's still holding onto him tightly.

'It's in the air,' manages Hansel.

'What?'

The rumbling is louder now, and yes, Hansel realises, it really is coming from the sky, above the thick grey cloud.

'What in the world *is* that?' Daisy asks.

'Huntsmen,' breathes Hansel, searching the noisy clouds for some sight of the contraption above.

'They sent out one of their machines to find us,' says Daisy, eyes wide. 'What do we do? Can we get off the road, before it's too late? Where can we hide?'

Hansel shakes his head. 'It's not about us. Not about me, anyway.'

Daisy watches the sky, realising. 'Oh, trousers. She's starting it already. That thing's headed to Darkwood.' She looks to Hansel. 'What do we do? We have to warn them. Can you use your witchy powers, or…?'

Hansel tries to contact Gretel again. Still nothing.

He shakes his head at Daisy.

'Then we'll have to warn them the unmagical way,' Daisy tells him. She starts hurrying along the road towards Nearby and the Darkwood's edge again, pulling Hansel behind her by the hand.

The sound of the great machine in the sky rumbles closer. Whatever it is, it's moving much faster than they are. Darkwood is still barely a smudge on the horizon, Nearby nothing but a thin line of smoke as its residents start the chilly autumn morning by lighting fires and stoves. It's a full day's walk away. They're never going to make it; whatever it is up in the sky will likely overtake them within minutes. In desperation, he tries to get through to his sister yet again, to no avail. The thick, crackling magic swells within him again in his panic. Initially he tries to bottle it in as he always does, but a realisation hits him. Daisy already knows, and there's nobody else about. There's nobody to hide the magic from, not right now.

Still hurrying along, he focuses, controlling his breaths, and the magic with it. He doesn't try to swallow it all down this time, but instead he makes an attempt at channelling the power, rather than just letting it all spill out. He sucks in light as he breathes in, and as he exhales, allows the magical tendrils to sink smoothly into the ground. He'd be very pleased with how well he's able to direct his magical power when he concentrates, were it not for the detail that as soon as the tendrils of magic burrow into the ground, they cause a short tremor directly under his and Daisy's feet, causing them both to topple over, mid-run.

'Sorry,' he says, helping Daisy up. 'I thought maybe I could make use of some other powers, but no. Not with that thing above the clouds and us stuck down here.'

Daisy nods. 'I noticed your magic often affects the ground.'

'Not on purpose.'

Daisy takes a couple of steps along the road again, then stops, looking at him curiously. 'What if it *was* on purpose?'

'I don't… what?'

'Do you think if you really concentrated, you could control *how* the ground moved?'

'Possibly? I haven't really tried. What sort of thing did you mean?'

'Well, could you perhaps get this bit of road we're standing on to move over to that bit of road, where we're headed to?' Daisy points to the distant smoke that marks out Nearby's early morning hot breakfasts and ablutions. 'Really fast?' she adds.

'Er.' Hansel frowns. Trousers. Maybe he can. Or maybe it'll all go horribly wrong. Maybe the magic would accidentally throw them off their feet at great speed, or cause the ground to swallow them whole. The sound of whatever it is in the sky is getting closer. He puts his arms firmly around Daisy.

'Ooh,' she manages, 'that's nice.'

He takes in a deep breath through his nose, concentrating on the road towards Nearby. The dull grey light dims for a moment, as if somebody has briefly thrown dawn into reverse. He parts his lips slightly and exhales through gritted teeth. He thinks about the danger his sister is in, about the debt he owes to the Darkwood residents who helped free Nearby, about the fear of the hidden Citadel witches and the hatred of the huntsmen. He collects all the anger and sadness and horror and pictures it pushing him, driving him to a place where he can help. The magic burrows into the ground under his and Daisy's feet. It rumbles – not unbalancing them, but vibrating deeply at a pace that steadily increases. In front of them, the road begins to crack and split in a long, thin line. There is a shudder underneath them. A circle around them on the dirt road breaks away and begins to push forwards with them on it, along the cleft track, at walking pace at first, speeding up to the tempo of a jog.

'Hansel, you're doing it,' cries Daisy.

Hansel breathes the light in and the magical energy out once more. The tendrils find a pace, plunging into the ground outside their circle and heaving them along. Still, they accelerate. Running speed. Sprinting speed. Faster. The speed of a galloping horse. Faster. Hansel has never travelled so fast before in his life. He wishes he could spare the breath to scream. Daisy is screaming, but it's one of those excited, happy screams other people do on Ferris wheels. Hansel doesn't do happy screams on Ferris wheels. He's not been on one since that time in Goosemarket when he threw up. He is aware that he might throw up again now. At the speed they're going, it would make an almighty mess. He tries not to think about it, to remove all the thoughts from his head except for the ones driving them ahead of the huntsmen's hidden flying machine.

Still, they speed up. Wind, dust and goodness knows what else buffets Hansel's face. He has to partially close his eyes against it, and ends up not seeing Nearby rushing up upon them until it's a little too late for a gradual deceleration. Hansel brings them to a sudden stop just outside the village, so that they tumble over one another.

'Sorry,' says Hansel.

Daisy pushes herself up. She's giggling with thrilled delight.

'You did it! That was amazing! I think I've got a fly stuck to my teeth but that was *amazing*!' She squeezes his arms. Hansel still feels sick, but not altogether in a bad way now.

'Oh!' shouts a distant, elderly voice. 'Hello there!'

Hansel looks up towards the source of the voice. Gregor Smithy is up on the village's main lookout tower.

'Hi,' says Hansel weakly, hoping Gregor didn't see them arrive.

'Didn't even notice you arrive, kidders,' calls Gregor, swinging a telescopic spyglass over in their direction. 'Ooft, the state of that road these days. Well, that's the huntsmen for you, isn't it? Only ever fund the Citadel and their stupid witch hunts. That ain't what I pay them my taxes for.'

'You aren't paying them any taxes right now,' Daisy calls to him. 'None of us are; we're rebelling, remember?'

'Oh aye,' replies Gregor. 'Well, fair enough about the roads then, I suppose. Anyway, welcome home, you two.'

'Thank you!' Hansel thinks for a second. 'Gregor, could you quickly call the village to a meeting in the square? We've got some things we need to say.'

Gregor nods down at them both gravely. 'Is it about how you lost Ethel Wicker's best handcart?'

'Oh,' mutters Daisy. 'I forgot about that.'

24
The Breakfast Run
That Never Was

'My best cart!' cries Mrs Wicker. 'And all those baskets!'

The entire village has indeed gathered in the square as per Hansel's request. Only ten minutes have passed since they arrived, although almost all of them have been spent on the question of what happened to all of Ethel Wicker's stuff.

'We had to leave it all, Mum,' Daisy tells her, yet again. 'Isn't it better to have us back safe and sound…?'

'That is beside the point, young lady; that was my favourite cart.'

'You know, Mum, I'd find it easier to believe that you really are cross at us about the cart if you weren't still hugging us both.'

Ethel Wicker gives Daisy and Hansel one more quick squeeze before releasing them. 'Hush up, you gobby child. Your poor old mother might be relieved that you're both OK, but you're still in big trouble.'

'I did make fifty silvers,' Daisy tells her, jingling her money belt.

Ethel Wicker considers this. 'You're still in moderately sized trouble.'

'It can wait,' Daisy tells her. 'There's something more urgent. There's a new head huntsman, and she's even worse than the last one. She's sending flying machines over to attack the Darkwood as we speak—'

'"She"?' interrupts Mother Goggins.

'Yes,' says Daisy. 'Her name's Morning Quarry; she was just elected. She's kind of new-fangled, she wants to move away from masks and abomination lists, but she's going to wipe out Darkwood straight away, and—'

'And you found all that out just from going to the Citadel for a couple of days?' asks Carpenter Fred sceptically. 'What happened to that monster you said was going to attack it?'

'She's the monster,' Hansel says. 'Or, her hatred of magical beings is.'

'So, you tried to fight her and failed?'

'Ah.' Hansel looks at his feet. 'Actually, we sort of… accidentally helped her win.'

'You what?'

'You don't understand; she had this friendly smile, and there was this dog, and…' Hansel sighs. 'We messed up. I'm sorry. We thought she was the way out of all this hatred. She said such nice things.'

His stepfather pats his back. 'Huntsmen lie, son. You're not the first to be taken in by one and likely you won't be the last.'

'Darkwood needs us,' says Daisy. 'Whatever Morning has launched, it's big, and she means business. They came to our aid twice; the alliance works both ways.'

Hansel's stepmother nods resolutely. 'Hear hear. We'll stop that thing before it even reaches the forest. Catapults, everybody!'

The villagers hurry to the catapults. There are over twenty of the defensive weapons now. The original dozen Gretel built are still lined up facing the road towards the Citadel, from the battle for Nearby only a few weeks ago. Adding to them at the village's perimeter, newly fixed, stand the machines abandoned by the huntsmen on their retreat – more catapults, trebuchets and a huge ballista, as well as three weapons Daisy was made to invent while in captivity. Daisy's inventions are the ones that get the most people squabbling over who gets to use them. They're by far the most powerful, and her latest prototype even uses explosive powder, which several of the younger villagers think is very exciting.

Thankfully, the arguments are short-lived. Most of the villagers who've quickly trained themselves to work the large weapons have a favourite one to man anyway. Daisy settles herself in catapult four, affectionately called Big Greenie by nobody but her, and to the confusion of most villagers, since catapult four is neither particularly big compared to the newer weapons, nor particularly green any more. With the argument over who's going to use the explosive artillery finally won by Bilberry the candle lad and every machine now manned, Hansel leads the remaining villagers in loading them with bolts and missiles.

'We don't know what it looks like,' Daisy calls, 'but it's high, and it's big. Suggest lightweight projectiles that'll pierce it, let's try to bring it down slowly enough for anyone on it to parachute to safety. No setting anything on fire, Bilberry!'

'Aww,' Bilberry complains.

The machines are loaded, and a quiet falls. Everybody watches the sky, and waits.

And waits.

And waits some more.

'Should I go and do a breakfast run?' asks Hansel's stepfather after about half an hour of waiting. 'I could murder an egg butty.'

'Ooh, and a cup of tea,' agrees Mother Goggins.

'There's that big tea urn in the village hall,' adds Ethel Wicker. 'I could run off and fetch that. Obviously I'd need someone to help me bring it out here once it's full, since *somebody* lost my best cart...'

'Let it go, Mum!'

'Shan't!'

'Shush,' says Hansel suddenly.

There it is again. The rumbling of a machine, somewhere up in the distant sky. The flying machine is catching up with them again.

'I hear it,' says Daisy. She calls out to Bilberry, and the others at the newer, more powerful machines. 'You'll have it in range first; wait for my mark.'

The wait continues. Minutes pass. The noise above the clouds grows louder and closer. The villagers watch Daisy for a sign. In his mind's eye, the Hydra flaps lazily towards Hansel from a distant spot, ignoring him, its multitude of eyes fixed on some unfortunate prey far beyond where he stands.

'Look,' cries Gregor Smithy, a little unfairly, since he's the only one with a telescopic spyglass to hand.

The others all have to make do with squinting in the direction he's pointed. Sure enough, something is slowly emerging from the sheet of cloud. It's long, dark, wide and flat, like a huge paddle slowly dipping down out of the clouds.

'Now?' cries Bilberry, but Daisy shakes her head. It's still too far.

'What's it doing?' she mutters. 'Is it landing…?'

In his magical vision, the Hydra gives its mighty wings another ponderous flap. The gaze of one of its heads shifts onto Hansel, meeting his eyes. It looks at him for a moment. Its monstrous lips slide back into a knowing smirk.

'No…'

The Hydra tips, and turns.

'It's turning,' cry Hansel and Daisy, realising at the same time.

We're not stupid, the Hydra tells Hansel in his vision. *You're disloyal troublemakers, and you have projectile weapons. Darkwood is big. Nearby is not the only way in, or over.*

'It's going north,' calls Daisy. 'Trousers! It's keeping out of range!'

There is a loud explosion, and a smoking iron ball screams into the air from Bilberry's artillery machine. It sails noisily up and up towards the dipping wing of the great aircraft, far further and faster than any of the other weapons could send a projectile, before gently arcing downwards again, missing its target by a least a thousand yards.

Daisy turns to him. 'What did you do that for?'

Bilberry shrugs. 'Thought I might as well try.'

They all watch the wing continue to peacefully turn the hidden aircraft, before rising back up into the clouds. The sound of it begins to grow more distant.

'There's loads of places between here and Slate where they can get to the north of Darkwood unchallenged,' Daisy frets.

'Prolly headed straight to Bear Mountain,' says Mother Goggins grimly. 'There's witches up there. Old 'uns. Living off scraps, so they say. Doubt they'd be able to put up much of a fight.'

'What do we do?' Daisy asks.

Hansel notices that everybody is looking to him.

'We can't fight the huntsmen,' he says quietly. 'Not from the air. Not this time.' He thinks. 'But we can still help the Darkwood. We can put out fires, we can free people from collapsed buildings and caves, we can supply first aid, food and water... This isn't a battle, this time. It's a rescue mission.'

Carpenter Fred looks uneasy. 'What do you want, a refugee camp in the village or something?'

'Maybe eventually.' Hansel nods. 'We'll have to see what damage that flying machine does. For now, we need to go into Darkwood, bring buckets and bread and bandages, and...'

A worried hush has descended.

'*Into* the Darkwood?' Ethel Wicker asks, worried.

'Yes.'

'Now? As it's being attacked?'

'I'm afraid so.'

'But...' Hansel is surprised that even his own, caring, stepfather seems to be having trouble with this concept. 'But all those witches and beasties, Hansel...'

'You lot all just had a party with them, Stepfather!'

'Aye, on our turf, not in the accursed forest!'

'It's just a few trees! Gretel does all right out there.' Hansel takes a deep breath. 'In fact,' he adds, 'once we've finished this relief effort, so will I.'

Daisy blinks at him. 'Wait, what?'

'I'm sorry, Daisy,' he tells her. 'I'm sorry, all of you. You all know there's been something witchy about Nearby for years. It's what got Gretel sent away. But she isn't a witch.' He takes in one more calming breath, inhaling the light for a second, before exhaling slowly, pushing magic into the earth so that it rises smoothly beneath his feet, creating a short, muddy pedestal for himself. 'I am,' he tells them. 'I'm so sorry for not telling any of you sooner.'

The whole village gazes at him for a moment. It's Mother Goggins who speaks up first.

'Yep,' she says, 'so am I.'

'What?' cries Lisbet Grief.

'Oh come off it, Lisbet, you suspected. It's how comes I always knows so many secrets.'

'I think what we all meant to say,' says Mrs Mudd pointedly, 'was "Thank you for telling us, Hansel".'

'Oh, so he gets his moment, but I don't?'

'It's going to be all right, son.' Hansel's stepfather squeezes his hand as Mother Goggins mutters reproachfully about the fact nobody's really paying attention to her.

'But what do you mean about "doing all right out there"?' Daisy asks him.

Hansel takes her hand sadly. 'What I'm doing isn't fair, Daisy. Leaving all those other witches to fend for themselves in the wilderness while I get to hide away in comfort; letting Gretel be sent off into the woods in my stead; bringing suspicion and danger to the village in the first place... The huntsmen know I'm a witch now. If I stay here, they'll come back later and do to Nearby what they're planning to do to Darkwood today. Since it's out in the open that I'm a witch, then I'll stand with the other witches in Darkwood.'

'No, son,' says his stepmother. 'We'll *all* stand with Darkwood. That's what allies do, isn't it?'

'You can't *all* live in the Darkwood, Stepmother.'

'We'll cross that bridge when we come to it,' his stepmother tells him. 'But for now, we'd best be getting a wriggle on.' She turns, and starts marching back towards Mudd Farm, with the hurried gait she uses whenever there's a crisis or an animal in pain there. The rest of the villagers fall into her wake, several having to jog to match her urgent speed. 'I'll fetch my medicines bag; Coriander, I'd advise you to do the same.'

'I'm not a medic,' frets Coriander, 'I'm a midwife.'

'And I usually do pigs,' Hansel's stepmother replies, 'but there's no time to be picky. Roger, you fetch the veterinarian.'

'Aye.' Her husband nods, scuttling off.

'Mother Goggins, go and fetch some of your herbal remedies...'

'Those are just for headaches and such,' complains Lisbet Grief. 'We're going to be dealing with proper injuries here.'

Mother Goggins narrows her eyes at Lisbet. 'Who's to say some of those injuries won't include aches to the head?'

'Headaches, pah,' replies Lisbet. 'Some "witch".'

'The herbal remedies are nothing to do with my witching, I'm just good at 'em!'

Hansel's stepmother continues to scour the crowd for makeshift medics. 'And Farrier Ned. You amputated a finger once.'

'Not on purpose,' says Farrier Ned.

'Stitched the stump up nice and neat, though, didn't you? One-handed and all. Didn't get infected or anything.'

'Aye,' sighs Ned, regarding his stumpy finger.

'Right, well, you're our field surgeon, then.' She claps her hands. 'Rest of you, get cracking. Food. Buckets. Blankets. Bandages.

Chop-chop.' She stops, meeting eyes with Carpenter Fred. 'If you want to, of course. If you're not too scared of the Darkwood.'

Carpenter Fred glares at her, then at the forest, then at his wife, already rushing towards his workshop for supplies. He sighs. 'I'll fetch buckets, then.'

25
The Mudd Witch

Patience manifests again. The others are still waiting at the border with the northern territory, having all turned out pockets and rolled up sleeves, just in case.

'Well?' asks Buttercup desperately.

Patience shakes her head. 'Gilde must have salted the whole perimeter after we left; I can't get in there to look for him.'

'But *we* salted the cottage when you started haunting us, and you still got in easily,' Buttercup wails.

'I know,' replies Patience in a tone that shows she's trying her best to be kind, 'but your Ghost-repellent mixture wasn't very good, and hers is. Sorry.'

'We have to go back,' frets Buttercup.

'But the bears,' whines Scarlett, setting the rest of her pack off into scared whimpers.

'But Trevor,' Buttercup replies. 'I know you might not think he's much, just a spider, but...'

'You're right,' says Hex quietly. 'Nobody's nothing. Trevor's one of your... one of *our* group. We need to go back.'

Jack smiles at him. Hex looks down at the ground nervously.

The wolves still haven't stopped whimpering.

'What's that noise?' asks Scarlett, flattening faintly pointed ears backwards against her head.

'It's your big, brave pack having a massive cry about the prospect of rescuing the littlest of our friends from an old woman and a few sleepy bears,' snaps Snow.

Gretel frowns, and looks around. She can hear it too, a low sound, like a distant steam engine, high up.

'No,' she says. 'There's something coming.'

The others stop and listen. A couple of Dwarves mutter ominous 'yummy's.

'What *is* that?' Gretel mutters.

Suddenly, it looms into view above the trees. A massive machine, like a boat, but shaped almost like a dragonfly, flying above them, just below the clouds.

'What *is* that?' repeats Gretel, her voice a scream above the roar of the great overhead machine.

'I… could fly up and take a closer look?' Hex offers hesitantly.

As they watch, a soaring blackbird suddenly loses control in the air rushing around one of the machine's great wings, smacks into its hull and flutters towards the ground in a limp tatter of feathers.

'Raspberries,' curses Snow through gritted teeth.

'Yeah, maybe not,' Jack tells Hex. 'For starters, you'd be harder to clean up than a blackbird.'

Gretel tries her best to ignore the Dwarves racing each other to catch and dispose of the dead blackbird. She continues to watch the massive machine.

'Huntsmen,' she says. 'Has to be. But what are they doing? Where are they…?'

Something is fired out of the front of the flying machine. The trees make it hard to see what it is or where it goes, but the ship is pointed straight in the direction of Bear Mountain.

'Trousers!' She starts running straight towards the northern territory again.

'New Girl,' begins Snow, 'where are you…?'

Everybody hears the explosion. It must be about a mile off to the north.

'Trousers,' repeats Gretel.

There's another explosion. Everybody's running with her now, in the direction of the sounds and smoke. It's on instinct. Gretel imagines that, like her, nobody else knows what they're actually going to do once they get to the devastation.

'Wait,' shouts Scarlett from the rear.

Creatures start pouring from the trees, running in the opposite direction, magical beings stampeding in panic alongside non-magical. Jackalope and rabbit, Gnome and fox, Satyr and deer. The air starts to become thick with smoke.

Gretel trips over a Leprechaun, and apologises. It scrambles to its feet, not even bothering to pick up the gold that spilled from it when it tumbled. 'Gettoutevit,' it mutters, fleeing. 'Runyerbeggars.'

A couple of Dwarves slow at the sight of the gold, scooping it up as they go with excited 'hi ho's, and get scrambled over by a panicked Gorgon, who has, at least, taken a moment to cover her eyes in order to avoid making an already terrible situation much worse.

'Wait!' Scarlett shouts again over all the noise and confusion. 'Wait! Something else!' Her face is frozen somewhere between wolf and human, a low, worried growl issuing from the back of her throat, and many of her pack. 'Coming from behind. The ground.'

Gretel stops. She can feel it too, underneath the chaos and the fire and the flying machine. Scarlett's right; it's deep in the ground, and it's big, and it's coming from home.

From home.

Home…

It's catching a glimpse of a long-lost loved one across a crowded thoroughfare. It's hearing a snippet of the voice of somebody thought gone forever. It's the gasping, life-reviving breath of a dear one brought back from the brink of oblivion. It is that sudden burst of hope and joy and adoration which floods Gretel's heart in a rush, making it thunder in her chest.

He's here. He came for her. She can feel him, his magic pulling him to her like a magnet.

'Hansel!'

'Ooh,' mutters Jack, 'yes, I feel it too. It's like the magic that drove the huntsmen out of Nearby. How did he manage to send his magic all the way out here?'

'It's not just his magic.' It isn't just a sensation any more. It's a palpable shaking and cracking of the ground, audible even over the sound of the stampede fleeing the explosions. Gretel takes a couple of faltering steps in the direction it's coming from, although she knows it's pointless to do so. He's coming to her, and he's doing so at a speed she couldn't hope to match. 'It's him.'

'Loud, isn't he?' asks Snow. One of the Dwarves is trying to stuff its own hair into its ears, which Gretel feels is a bit rich, considering how noisy Dwarves usually are.

'The Mudd Witch,' breathes Hex. 'The real Mudd Witch. Is he here to save us?'

The sound of roaring earth is upon them. Thick trees splinter and topple like matchsticks. Jack hurriedly rots a few of the bigger ones to keep the trunks from falling on the creatures escaping in the other direction. Cutting through them comes a very large, flat wedge of rock, somehow ploughing itself through the forest floor, big enough to carry over a hundred villagers on it. Gretel knows it's this big, because it in fact has over a hundred villagers on it, carrying buckets and supplies, hanging onto one another for dear life and all looking monumentally wind-lashed and dishevelled. As it grinds to a stop in front of them, Gretel notices that it is not actually a single piece of rock, but bears the worn, muddy brick slabs of Nearby's village square. It even has half of the old hopscotch grid still painted onto one of the sides.

'What is this?' manages Snow.

'Is… the Mudd Witch a whole village?' asks Hex.

'What is this?' asks Snow again, since nobody answered her the first time.

Gretel is too surprised to move. She can't see Hansel amongst the tightly packed throng of queasy-looking villagers.

'Hiya,' manages Daisy, picking leaves out of her hair. 'We're here to help.'

For a moment everybody stands stock-still, too surprised or travelsick to move, save for the terrified creatures of the northern woods still streaming past. Lisbet Grief throws up delicately, just missing a cursing Gnome.

Gretel breaks the pause. She starts striding forwards, towards the villagers. 'Hansel?' she croaks, still not quite daring to believe that he's come back to her, after being separated for so long. The crowd parts, and there he is. He looks exhausted. Moving the whole village must have drained huge amounts of magical energy. Their step-parents have him by the shoulders, keeping him upright, but his gaze is glassy. He doesn't seem to be able to focus on her, or on anything.

'Hansel,' she says again. She reaches her hand out to him.

His eyes settle on hers at last. There it is. That spark of recognition. He takes in a gasp of breath.

'Glaaaaaah,' he says, and passes out, collapsing forwards out of their step-parents' grip and onto Gretel, knocking her onto her back and landing on her like a massive, heavy blanket.

'Oh for the love of trousers,' she manages, winded, 'not again.'

26
Everybody Hates Big Cave

Gretel's step-parents help lift Hansel off her.

'Why does this have to happen every time?' Gretel moans. 'Every chance I get to actually see him, he's used up all his strength getting to… oh!'

Hansel's eyes flutter open again. 'Gretel?'

'You're awake! You're here!'

'I know!' Hansel pauses, still giddy. 'So are you!'

'Of course I am, you knew I was here!'

Hansel hugs her tight. 'I found you! I concentrated my magic! By the way, the village knows about the whole witch thing now.'

'Yes,' wheezes Gretel through her brother's embrace, 'I imagined they might, considering.'

'We came to give aid,' says Mother Goggins, before dipping into a low curtsey in Snow's direction. 'How might we humble servants assist you, Your Majesty?'

'You can pack that in, for a start,' snaps Snow.

The exodus from the north is starting to thin now. There have been no more explosions and the flying machine has passed almost out of hearing range. Still, smoke plumes and fire crackles from the trees beyond.

'We all have to go north,' Buttercup tells her, 'put out the fires and find Trevor.'

Snow frowns at the burning forest. 'No.'

'No?'

'I'm sorry, Buttercup. I can't be sure that that flying machine won't come back.'

'Chances are, it will,' adds Patience. 'If the huntsmen have decided to attack the forest, we can't expect any mercy.'

'Then, we should prioritise making the residents as safe as possible,' says Snow.

'But Trevor's a resident,' pipes up Buttercup.

'We'll go back for him,' Snow tells her softly. 'I promise. But we can't do that at the expense of the whole forest. I gave a pledge to protect this place and everyone in it.'

'What did you do *that* for, Majesty?' grunts Carpenter Fred.

'Because I asked her to,' replies Buttercup. She sighs. 'Snow's right.'

'Seriously?' Jack asks. 'The whole forest? How are we going to shelter them all?'

'We're going to have to open up Big Cave,' Snow announces.

'Yummy?!' cries a Dwarf, in protest.

'I know,' Snow replies, 'but it's the only place that's safe from bombardment and big enough to fit everyone.'

'But the whole forest?' Hex frets. 'With half of them already running scared? How are we supposed to round everybody up?'

'Er, there's loads of us?' Snow gestures around at the crowd. 'And at least half a dozen of us are magic. You can start by flying the perimeter, seeing who's where for me. You can keep in contact with me via the jackdaws. You speak jackdaw, right?'

Hex pulls a face. 'I have trouble with their dialect, and they're always swearing.'

'Don't care. Chop-chop.'

'Please?' Jack asks him gently.

'Fine.' Hex transforms, shaking off his clothes as he does. He takes off, in a great rush of inky black feathers.

'Oooh,' gasps the watching crowd.

'Jack's boyfriend is a rook,' breathes little Tiler Hill in admiration.

'A raven,' corrects Jack, picking up Hex's shirt and breeches. His mouth twists with a strange, bitten-down smile.

'Oi.' Snow snaps her fingers at one of the Dwarves. 'Oi. You lads go ahead, start corralling.'

'My pack can help,' adds Scarlett, pulling up her hood for a controlled transformation.

'Werewolf!' shouts Gregor Smithy, delighted. He watches her run off towards the south, along with the other wolves and Dwarves. 'Haven't seen one of them since the Littles moved out, way back when.'

'Aye,' says Mother Goggins, thoughtfully. 'The Littles…'

'The rest of us can spread out and do a sweep,' Gretel tells them. 'As far north as the fires will let us go, and then back towards this cave of Snow's.'

'It's not my cave,' Snow replies. 'Wouldn't set foot in there usually, it's too big for Dwarves. It's all echoey, puts the wind right up the lads.'

The search of the northern woods is hurried yet gruelling. A few villagers are able to fill buckets from a nearby stream, but they quickly run into a wall of fire and smoke. A few pails of weedy water are going to be about as effective at stopping carnage of this scale as a damson plum would be if hurled in the path of an apocalyptic meteor by an overconfident dinosaur. A couple of the villagers courageously fling their water at the fire anyway. It evaporates with a hiss. They only manage to rescue a dozen or so creatures, trapped beneath collapsed trees, or unconscious from the smoke, before the fire stops them. They do run across many more for whom it's already too late. Coughing, eyes stinging and with Buttercup still fruitlessly calling for Trevor, they turn back. Hansel's several attempts to magically put out the fire fall flat: his magic is still too drained from getting the village into the woods. On Gretel's suggestion, Jack uproots as much foliage in the path of the fire as he possibly can, in an attempt to stop it spreading. Even then, Gretel really isn't sure if it'll actually work, or if the huntsmen's airship will reappear at any moment to continue burning the forest. Once out of the northern woods, they head in a wide sweep towards a large canyon, ushering Darkwood creatures as they go.

Gretel notices that Buttercup has stopped calling for Trevor. She can't remember ever seeing the Cake Witch so downcast before. If Gretel's being honest with herself, it's a bleakness that she shares, reunion with her family aside. Here they all are, standing together, the witches of the south and the north, along with the people of Nearby Village, and for what? To pick up the pieces when the huntsmen crush the Darkwood on a whim. To cower in a cave that even Dwarves find unpleasant. And then there's Trevor. They can't even protect the littlest of their own family.

As they draw nearer to the canyon, Gretel sees other groups of creatures, either approaching or already making their way down it along a narrow path. The wolf pack shepherds one set; another lot of creatures are being rudely hassled towards the crevasse by the Dwarves. Gretel can spot Charles the Magnificent amongst other Unicorns in the unhappy herd, as well as Henrietta the Centaur, clutching the Mirror protectively. Hex swoops down and lands next to Snow, a multitude of smaller birds and a couple of very annoyed-sounding Harpies circling overhead.

'That seems to be everyone,' he tells them, gratefully receiving his clothes back from Jack. 'I caught sight of the airship turning back, but the good news is, the fire seems to be quite a thin band. Bear Mountain looks untouched, from what I could tell.'

'That's something,' says Jack. 'Gilde might have been a pain, but nobody actually wanted her to burn to death.'

'And, hey,' adds Gretel hurriedly, 'if Trevor's still at her cottage, that means he's probably still all right.'

'Hmm,' adds Buttercup glumly. 'Let's get to the cave before the flying machine comes back.'

'I don't like the thought of the cave,' mutters Hansel, frowning. 'Something dangerous about it.'

'Everybody hates Big Cave,' Snow tells him. 'It's just really…
big.'

Still, Hansel frowns. 'I must be sensing the flying machine. It
must be close. Closer than we think.'

Gretel squeezes his hand. 'Let's hurry, then.'

They file down into the canyon. It has, Gretel notes, a large
gash in the rock. It's tall and wide enough for even an Ogre or
Wyvern to squeeze through, and the blackness inside it looks very
deep indeed.

'Yummy,' complains a Dwarf, clambering down the face of the
canyon to land on Snow's head.

'I know,' Snow replies. 'Well, then – everybody in.'

'No,' says a friendly voice from within. 'Everybody out, in fact.'

'Oh, trousers,' chorus Daisy and Hansel.

'What?' Gretel asks.

From out of the cave's wide entrance steps a figure – she's
dressed in the black robes of a huntsman, but her hood is down
and her mask is missing. A wild shock of dandelion hair and a big,
buck-toothed grin greets them with sunny cheer.

'Morning,' breathes Hansel.

Behind him, Jack looks confused. 'It's, like, three in the
afternoon.'

27
Afternoon, Morning

'Hello, Hansel.' The huntsman beams. 'Daisy. And you must be little Gretel Mudd, I've heard so much about you. The name's Morning Quarry.'

She holds out her hand, in a friendly manner. Gretel just frowns. As her eyes grow accustomed to the gloom beyond, she notices that there are many armed huntsmen behind this interloper, their weapons raised. Scarlett trots up to join Gretel, her hands instinctively on the hood of her cape, her lips snarling at the sight of the huntsmen, exposing slightly elongated teeth.

'Oooh, the Werewolf's back, is it?' Morning smiles. She addresses the huntsmen behind her. 'Such a weird, confused creature. I mean, I usually love dogs, but what *is* that thing? Man or beast?'

'She's neither.' Snow scowls. 'If anyone's confused about her, it's you.'

'Oh! And Your Majesty, what an honour.' Morning dips her shaggy blonde head at Snow in an approximation of a respectful greeting. 'Sorry about all that dreadful business with your parents. Your mother really took *so* long to die, didn't she?'

Snow smiles a dangerous smile. 'So did your head huntsman, from the remains we found.'

'Oh, he was an idiot. Had good maps of this accursed forest, though; I had a feeling you'd all try to hide in this big horrible cave if I flushed out some of the woods. Seems like all the huntsmen really needed after all was some fresh new thinking from a fresh new head huntsman.' She points to herself, proudly. 'Yours truly, by the way, as from today, thanks to Hansel and Daisy's help.'

'What?' Snow asks Daisy, through gritted teeth.

'It's a long story,' Daisy replies. 'There was a dog. Needless to say; sorry.'

'It's a good thing, Daisy,' says Morning. 'I meant every word I said about doing things differently from now on. Gretel, you'll be pleased to hear that you're free to return to your home village. No recriminations, and no more abominations. Man or woman, boy or girl, all of you are free to pursue whatever interests, hobbies or careers you please. No more need to turn to the wicked witches in order to escape the Citadel's rules. The huntsmen are on your side. *I'm* on your side.'

'Just as long as we're not witches, right?' Gretel replies coldly.

'The witch problem is a threat to our way of life, I'm afraid.' Morning doesn't drop her cheerfully matter-of-fact tone whatsoever. If anything, it makes her message sound even more upsetting. 'It doesn't have to be a problem that concerns you any more, though. We will eliminate them, to protect you. You can go home – all of you humans – you can live happily ever after, in comfort and freedom.'

Gretel draws herself up to her full, tiny height. 'No, I can't.'

'If this is about your brother, I'm sure we can come to some—'

Gretel meets Morning's eye steadily. 'I can't, because I'm a witch too.'

'Aww.' Morning barks out a loud, good-natured laugh. 'No you're not, but aren't you sweet for trying to stick up for them? In time, you'll see how they brainwashed you into that.'

'I am a witch.' Still Gretel refuses to break eye contact with Morning. 'I made half a village disappear and turn up somewhere else. I magically escaped death on the bonfire. I'm a witch.'

'So am I,' chimes Daisy, taking Gretel's free hand. 'That's how I escaped the rack. I'm a witch too.'

'I see what you girls are doing,' Morning says with a smile, 'but I'm sure your parents will talk sense into you before—'

'I'm a witch,' says Gretel's stepfather quickly, stepping forward next to Hansel.

'So am I,' adds her stepmother.

'Me too,' says Ethel Wicker, linking arms with Daisy.

'I'm a witch too!' cries Coriander the midwife.

'We're witches,' call out Tailor and Tiler Hill in unison.

'So am I,' shouts their mother Dollis.

'So am I!' adds their grandfather Gregor.

'I'm a witch,' shouts Lisbet Grief.

'I am *actually* a witch,' shouts Mother Goggins over her, but gets drowned out.

Morning takes all of this in, smiling and nodding in understanding. 'I see. Are there any of Nearby's residents who *don't* want to admit to witchcraft right now? Knowing what the penalty for it is?'

There is a pause. Carpenter Fred shuffles towards her awkwardly.

'No,' he tells her. 'No, we're all witches. We can't take your crumbs of a slightly better life if it's at the expense of thems that live in the Darkwood. So, anything you want to do to witches, you're going to have to do to us, too. Due to us being witches.'

Morning nods again, and her face splits into a beautiful, warm, toothy grin. 'OK.'

'Uh oh,' says Scarlett, her voice turning canine as she transforms as a reflex.

'Oh,' Carpenter Fred says, realising. 'Hang on…'

But no, the huntsmen will not hang on. They come pouring out of the cave, melee weapons at the ready, and Gretel is suddenly aware that none of the huge group of villagers and Darkwood refugees is armed. Her own knapsack of devices is still in Gilde's cottage way up in the mountains behind a river of fire, as is Snow's armour and all of her axes. Even her precious new 'secret weapon' was lost along with Trevor.

'Run,' she cries.

'*No,*' calls Hansel over her, in a voice that carries further and holds far more authority than hers. 'The flying machine's doubling back. If we leave the crevasse, we'll be easy pickings for it.'

'So, what do we do?'

The huntsmen are only a few yards away from them. Dwarves and wolves push forwards to form a defensive line in front of the other creatures, sharp teeth snapping. They're joined by a few of the Unicorns, horns lowered, ready to stab. A couple of Ogres stomp forwards as well. Gretel notices that they too are unarmed – nobody would have had time to grab anything as they were being herded to the crevasse.

'Jack,' she calls, 'we could do with some lumber here.'

'Gotcha.' Jack sweeps with his arms, causing a tangle of thorns to grow between the huntsmen and the Darkwood creatures and villagers. As huntsmen swear and hack at the thicket, Jack pulls up a small copse of birch trees for the Ogres to pull up and use as weapons. They swiftly rip branches off the trees and pass them down to the villagers as smaller makeshift clubs. Some of the Dwarves clamber to the top of the thorny barrier and start throwing stones down at the huntsmen on the other side of it, which considerably increases the volume and strength of the swearing.

Hex flutters his wing nervously. 'Should I fly over?'

'Not yet,' Snow tells him, selecting the sharpest bit of branch that she can. 'I saw crossbows. You'll only make yourself a target…'

Beyond the thicket, there is the sound of a thick crossbow string's release, followed by a dull, meaty sound. A Dwarf tumbles from the thorny barricade, a crossbow bolt in its belly.

'No,' screams Snow. She races to the stricken Dwarf, the other Dwarves howling in horror and outrage.

With the swipe of a broadsword, a huntsman breaches the barrier of thorns, and is met with the bared teeth of the wolves.

The huntsman stumbles when he's nipped in the leg, but another huntsman clambers over him to take his place, followed by another, and another.

'Oi. Oi.' Snow pats the Dwarf's cheek tenderly, and for the first time, Gretel realises that 'Oi' must be this particular Dwarf's name.

'Oi, come on. We'll get you stitched up, you'll make it.'

Gretel's stepmother kneels down next to Snow. 'I can deal with this, Majesty. You get back to fending them blighters off.'

'But…'

'I've brought newborn piglets back from death's door, Majesty,' snaps Gretel's stepmother, 'but I can't do it while being stabbed by a huntsman, so get to it, please and thank you!'

Gretel barely has time to be proud of her stepmother before the breach in the thicket completely collapses and huntsmen pour towards them once more. Wolves snap and bite, Unicorns charge, villagers, Ogres and assorted other beings swing tree trunks and branches. Above the noise of all of this comes the sound of the flying machine again, approaching them from behind. Trapping them in the narrow crevasse.

Snow spots it too, and whistles a low note. Thousands of birds take off, flying in the direction of the airship's engine noise. The Harpies and Manticore start flapping as well, and Hex begins to change.

'*No*,' comes Hansel's curiously loud voice again, travelling through the ground and up into the soles of people's feet rather than through their ears.

Hansel is standing quite still in the middle of the fray. He hasn't picked up a branch, or one of the few dropped huntsman weapons. He doesn't need to – the fight so far has managed to avoid him entirely. He stands in the middle of an untouched circle of calm, as the ugly, chaotic brawl rages all around him. Shadow fills the circle, with little dark tendrils spilling outside its radius, like roots, foraging for light to sap. Hansel, Gretel realises, is about to do something really cool.

'Oh.' Morning beams, watching Hansel as she easily brushes off Patience's valiant attempts to haunt her. 'He's about to do something.'

Hansel takes in one great gulp of light, plunging the already shadowy crevasse almost entirely into darkness for a moment, and then he releases.

It isn't like it was in the liberation of Nearby, when the whole of the ground turned into a churning sea. This time it's much more focused. Great mounds of rock thrust upwards, underneath the feet of the huntsmen, some of them missing Darkwood creatures and villagers by mere inches. Huntsmen are thrown against the crevasse walls, or dozens of feet up into the air, only to plummet back down onto the hard ground again, with bone-breaking, consciousness-losing thuds. Hansel turns and glares at the approaching flying machine sailing into view above them. Shadows swiftly grow and thicken around it, in huge, dark tentacles. The flying machine slows and stutters, as if the shadows are physically holding it back. The birds around it scatter with startled squawks. Hansel grits his teeth. Gretel can see that he's struggling. She tries to move towards him, but with one last rush of magical energy, he sends a boulder hurtling upwards towards the straining flying machine. The magical missile smacks into one of the machine's wings, smashing it in two. The shadows dissipate, leaving the flying machine to make a very lopsided and undignified three-winged emergency landing in the forest beyond. Exhausted, Hansel sinks to his knees.

'OK,' Morning tells her army, or at least those of them who can still walk, 'now.'

Morning and around half a dozen huntsmen start running straight towards Hansel's collapsed form. In a sickening instant, Gretel realises what their attack was about. All of this – herding and trapping them in an enclosed space, provoking them to fight back – all of it was in order to identify and eliminate the most powerful witches in the Darkwood. And Morning is only a few strides away from making it happen.

Gretel starts running towards Hansel herself, branch aloft, but she's too far; there are too many people between her position and where her brother sits crumpled and prone. She isn't going to make it. She isn't going to…

There is a great flap of black feathers ahead. Hex, in full raven form, lands heavily between Morning and Hansel, mighty wings outstretched, sharp beak open.

Morning and her posse stop suddenly. She stares at Hex, and then… she laughs. Head back, eyes bright, her merry, guileless laugh is so incongruous in the closed-in battlefield of the crevasse that it causes the others to stop fighting and watch what's going on.

'I'm sorry,' she calls after a moment. 'I imagine lots of you won't get the joke. You're either too young or you don't know enough about Ashtrie to understand why it's so funny you actually got one of the Glass Witch's victims to protect the very same degenerate race that did this to him.'

Hex doesn't change back, doesn't respond. He stands firm in front of Hansel.

'This lot must have done a real sweet-talk number on you,' Morning tells Hex. 'Oh, I'd know the Glass Witch's handiwork anywhere; any senior huntsman would.' She addresses the crowd again. 'What the Glass Witch did to Ashtrie is the whole reason we huntsmen had to intervene and save Myrsina from the witches in the first place,' she tells them. 'And you'd better believe that once we've worked out the best way to eliminate magicals through trial and error on you lot, we'll be moving on to the real challenge of clearing out the eastern woods.'

Hex looks aghast. He changes back into mostly human form. 'No! You mustn't go east. If she catches you—'

'Oh,' interrupts Morning conversationally, 'a nettle-shirt charm, is it?' She nods at his remaining wing. 'Doesn't work very well, does it? Hey ho.' She reaches forward and rips the scrap of nettle from around his neck.

Hex doesn't get the chance to say anything else. He is instantly turned back into a raven – not a man-sized one any more, but a completely ordinary-looking raven.

'Hex!' Jack cries, locked in hand-to-shrub combat with a much larger man, and unable to get any closer to the raven.

Morning strides towards Hansel with her posse once more, shredding the dried nettle between her fingers. Hex has to flap out of the way to avoid being trodden underfoot. Gretel makes a lunge for one of the huntsmen, but is punched to the ground. She sees Daisy struggling with another huntsman, and both of her step-parents kneeling next to the bleeding Dwarf. Snow is sprinting towards them, a branch swinging above her head, but one of the huntsmen has already reached the helpless form of Hansel, a dagger unsheathed.

'And now…' says Morning.

Whatever the Head Huntsman was about to say is cut off by an almighty roar. It echoes along the canyon; too deep to be a wolf, or even an Ogre or Manticore.

Everybody stops, and stares. Leaping down the canyon at a ferocious speed is a little old lady, in silver armour about twice her size, and absolutely covered in axes and mechanical weaponry. The two bears flanking her are intimidating on their own, but her mount is what causes several of the huntsmen, including the one within a knife-slash of Hansel's life, to step back with a gasp. She is riding a bear the size of a brick shed.

'Tally ho!' cries a familiar little male voice from somewhere near the giant bear's head.

Amongst the tableau of fear, horror and the carnage of skirmish, Buttercup throws up her hands in glee.

'Trevor's OK!'

215

28
Secret Weapon

With the huntsmen suitably distracted by the immediate and significant threat of a colossal bear heading straight for them, Gretel manages to scrabble towards her brother and throw herself between him and the huntsman with the dagger. Gilde, barely visible underneath Snow's oversized armour, tugs at Baby's fur, bringing him to a stop in the middle of the frozen fray. Mamma and Papa spread out a little to flank her, keeping as many huntsmen as possible at close range to at least one bear. This doesn't particularly embolden any of the villagers or Darkwood creatures, who are understandably just as anxious about the arrival of a family of very hungry-looking bears in their close proximity.

The whole canyon of combatants remains awkwardly still for a moment, watching the bears, mouths agog in worried confusion.

It's Morning who breaks the stand-off. 'Gilde Locke?' she asks pleasantly. 'Could it be? The old Bear Witch of the mountains, come out of hiding after all these years?'

Gilde peers at Morning imperiously – quite a feat, considering that she's only visible from the nose up under Snow's gorget.

'Do I know you, missy?'

'Oh, no. But I know you. I grew up in Slate. They say you were from round there too, before you walked into the mountains and never came back... except to steal food from us, of course.'

'Didn't do nobody no harm.'

'Didn't you, though?' Morning shrugs blithely, with a grin. 'You didn't think maybe a town might have needed that food more than you? Or needed our granaries and meat stores to last a few weeks at a time without being smashed? Didn't think we'd starve?'

Gilde grunts. 'All of us have had to grit out through lean winters, lady.'

'Yes, you can certainly say that again.' Morning clasps her hands together, addressing Gilde as if she's just having a perfectly normal, relaxed chinwag. 'And now the famously insular Bear Witch of the mountains is here, apparently to the rescue of the south-western territory and a human village; what an exciting about-face.'

'You just set fire to my territory.'

'Only a little bit. I'm sure you could have hunkered down, waited for it to burn itself out.'

'Spitting fire down from the sky itself in that infernal flying contraption!'

'Oh, do you not like my new tech? I suppose not; after all, it's very modern. You wouldn't be the type to appreciate that sort of thing, demographically speaking.'

The visible bit of Gilde narrows her eyes dangerously. 'Oh, I can appreciate new-fangled doohickeys just fine, lady. Why, only last night I had some houseguests who left behind all sorts of interesting contraptions. I appreciated those a lot.'

In spite of the situation, Gretel raises her eyebrows at this.

'So much so, in fact,' continues Gilde, 'that I was persuaded it'd be a crying shame to let 'em go to waste, instead of bringing them here to teach you a lesson in manners.'

'Ooh, you've brought your own tech to the table.' Morning beams. 'What fun, I'd love to see.'

Gilde tosses Gretel her knapsack.

'Girlie's got some real nasty stuff in her bag, there. She's got a stick that'll zap you.'

217

Gretel pulls her modified electrical light stick out of the knapsack and does her best to hurriedly wind the dynamo while brandishing it at the nearest huntsman.

'Axes for you, Majesty,' adds Gilde, hurling Snow's and the Dwarves' blades in their general direction, somewhat unwisely. Several villagers have to duck out of the way of the more poorly aimed ones. 'Not "new-fangled" as such, but they work. This, however…' Gilde pulls out a small, sleek oblong of wood, covered in tiny hinges. Gretel sucks through her teeth quietly. The secret weapon. She'd hoped that Gilde wouldn't find that. She knew that the Bear Witch was bound not to like it.

'This,' Gilde continues, holding the tiny contraption aloft, 'I love. I'm keeping it.'

Morning cocks her head with a giggle, ignoring the fact that Gretel, Snow and several Dwarves are now properly armed. 'You funny goose. What in Myrsina even is it?'

Gilde unhinges one of the secret weapon's many blades. 'It's a doohickey. See? It has an adorable little saw.'

All the better to cut ropes and wooden bars with, thinks Gretel to herself.

'And teeny scissors,' Gilde adds.

All the better to snip off bits of magically draining nettle.

'And a compass…'

Well, I just put that there out of common sense.

'And the whole thing is so itty bitty…'

So I could hide it until the time was right.

'So's it can fit perfectly in my ikkle hands,' concludes Gilde triumphantly. She attempts to demonstrate this, but sadly the effect is rather ruined by the fact that she's trying to hold it in Snow's oversized gauntlets. She gives up on this, and instead pulls out another sharp implement from the secret weapon, and waves it at Morning. 'So, what's it to be, lady? I saw your nasty ole flying machine crash, half your gang look like they've been thrown against the rocks, we got bears, we got wolves, we got dragons or whatever those guys are...'

'Wyvern,' Trevor tells her, crawling out from Baby's fur. 'Hi, guys!'

'We got witches, and we got weapons,' Gilde continues. 'What do you say? Cut your losses?'

Morning casts a long, speculative gaze around the canyon. 'Yeah,' she says amiably, 'OK then.'

'What?' asks the huntsman nearest to Hansel and Gretel. 'You were going to go all in on these freaks; are you giving up just because one of them's got a few bears and... what *is* that she's waving at you? A corkscrew?'

'Ooh, I like that you feel comfortable backchatting me like that,' Morning tells the huntsman. 'It really highlights how far we've already come in reforming our organisation, and believe me, your punishment will highlight how far we have yet to go, which is just as important.'

'Thank you,' replies the huntsman, before adding, 'hang on, "punishment"?'

'This was always going to be a case of trial and error,' Morning tells the huntsmen. 'We've gained a lot of really useful information today, about our enemy's allegiances and shared territory, about their strengths...' She beams at Gretel, still shielding her brother, her little electrical stick aloft. 'And their weaknesses. We should put this down as a win, brethren, even if our only actual kills were the odd Dwarf, this time.'

'What was that about the Dwarves?' asks Trevor.

Morning either doesn't hear him, or ignores him. She claps her hands at the huntsmen like a mum chivvying a muddle of children along. 'Come on, this fight's over. Find a buddy to help; looks like there's a lot of broken legs about and our lift home was crashed, so it's going to be quite a trek.' The huntsmen do as she says. Morning turns and gives another little bow to Snow. 'Wonderful training exercise, your Majesty, thank you so much, you've given me loads to work with.'

Snow hasn't lowered her axe. 'Give me one reason why I shouldn't kill you right now.'

'Well, for starters, the likelihood of one of my army stopping and killing you before you got that axe anywhere near me is very high,' Morning tells her. 'And on the off-chance that you did manage to kill me, not only would you make a martyr of me the way we made a martyr of Patience Fieldmouse… do stop trying to haunt me by the way, Patience, it's not working…'

Patience stops hovering malignantly over Morning's head and floats down to ground level sulkily.

'But also,' Morning continues, 'I'd only be replaced by someone even more hard-line, just like the last head huntsman was replaced by me.' She pulls a sympathetic expression. 'Don't be glum, you've got plenty of positives to take away from this, too. Look how unified you all are! It's very sweet. You even managed to crash my flying machine. You are all worthy opponents, and as such you have my respect, and my word that someday, very soon, I *will* come back and kill you. All of you, including everybody who chose to identify themselves as a witch to me today, so you might want to get cracking with beefing up those village defences. It won't help you at all, but it'll make you feel as if it could.'

'I can't believe I ever trusted you,' Hansel tells Morning weakly.

'Neither can I.' Morning grins. 'I *am* a huntsman, after all. It was the dog, wasn't it? People always go soppy over a nice dog, witches doubly so.' The other huntsmen are starting to limp away. 'You'll be letting us all leave in peace today,' Morning tells the witches and villagers. 'None of you are prepared for an escalation right now, "doohickeys" or not.' She peers at the secret weapon in Gilde's hand as she walks past. 'That *is* a corkscrew, isn't it? On a little hinge, how novel. I'll have to get my own boffins to come up with something similar. Until next time!' She stops, thinking of something, and momentarily turns back. 'Oh, and probably don't try fleeing into the eastern woods. Firstly, we'd find out, secondly, we can also reach you there but most importantly, I'd quite like the pleasure of being the one to wipe you all out; I'd hate for the Glass Witch to get to do it after I've put all the work in. OK, I really am going this time, take care, byeeeee!'

'Well, she's awful,' says Trevor, as Morning leaves. 'Did some of you really trust her because of a dog?'

'We are never going to live this down,' sighs Daisy.

29
Oi

Gilde nods triumphantly at the retreat of the huntsmen.

'You're very welcome, folks.' She folds her corkscrew back away.

'You came for us,' says Buttercup gratefully, patting Baby's huge side, 'after we hurt your feelings.'

'After you smashed up my house,' Gilde corrects her. 'I was persuaded to, um… how was it you put it, little spider?'

'To stop moping over the mess, and do something to try to fix it,' Trevor tells them all, hopping onto Buttercup's shoulder. 'We had a long chat about controlling behaviour and mutual respect in friendship, I think it was really healthy.' He pauses. 'I *have* committed on your behalf for all of you to go up and help rebuild her cottage, though, when all this is over. Sorry. It was a negotiating tactic. Although the biggest incentive for Gilde came from the huntsmen.'

'If they're sending those beastly machines overhead to burn up my forest when I *do* keep my head down, then they ain't giving me no reason not to push back instead.'

'You did really well,' Hansel tells her. 'Thank you.' He pokes Gretel's arm and whispers, 'Who is she?'

'Pleasure, kiddo,' Gilde tells him. 'Pretty sure my poor bears are way too tired to have put up much of a fight, but the whole tactic was to scare the enemy away by making ourselves look big. It's a bear thing.'

'It's actually a wolf thing,' says Scarlett.

'Pretty sure you doggies copied it off us,' Gilde tells Scarlett, looking around the crowd. 'Good to see you, I guess, ungrateful bounder though you are. Where's Sweetiebird?'

Gilde's eyes fall on Jack, kneeling on the rocky ground, clutching a raven. Only its dejected stillness and general lack of flappy panic at being hugged by a young man give away the impression that there's anything unusual about this bird whatsoever.

'Oh, tarnation,' breathes Gilde.

'She did something to him,' Jack tells her. 'Ripped up his leaf. Is it fixable?'

'Sorry, loverboy.' Gilde does look genuinely sorry. 'What was did to him in Ashtrie can't be undone. The nettle shirt was the best fix his witch of a sister could come up with, and that took all her powers for six years. Near killed her. Once the last nettle's gone, so's the last of her magic holding back the curse.'

'Maybe we can find her, ask her for another...'

'She died. He told me that that was the last straw, his reason for leaving Ashtrie and pushing nor'west into the forest.'

'Then we can go to Ashtrie, find who cursed him, get them to reverse it...'

Gilde snorts out a bitter laugh. 'That there's a Glass Witch curse. That ain't never getting reversed, and the only thing you could expect from begging her mercy is for you to get yerself turned into a toad for your trouble.'

'There has to be *something*,' argues Jack.

''Fraid not, loverboy.' Gilde gives the raven a sad little nod. 'Sorry, Sweetiebird. The witches'll make sure you're looked after, I'm sure.'

'There *has* to be something,' repeats Jack, more to himself than anyone else.

'Of course we'll look after him,' Gretel says. 'Right, Buttercup?' Gretel looks around. '…Buttercup? Snow?'

Gretel sees Buttercup and Snow in a low huddle with her stepmother. Their voices are low. None of them look up. The Dwarves clutch one another at Snow's side, pressed tight together in a strangely still and silent hairy mass.

The injured Dwarf!

'Oh no!'

Gretel and Hansel rush towards the group. Their stepmother is beaded with sweat, despite the chill air. The surgery bag she usually keeps at the farm for emergencies with the livestock is open by her side. Her hands and wrists are stained with Dwarf blood.

Their stepmother is sewing up a large wound in the Dwarf's abdomen. The Dwarf is still alive and awake, whimpering with pain through gritted fangs. Snow and Buttercup are both kneeling by its head, stroking it gently as if it were a distressed pet.

'Worst's nearly over now, Oi,' Snow tells the Dwarf in hushed tones. 'You've got through it, you'll be all right.'

Gretel's stepmother doesn't look so sure. Gretel's dealt with injured animals enough to know that this creature isn't out of danger yet.

'You're being very brave,' Buttercup tells the Dwarves. 'All of you.'

'Yeah, you'll have to be gentle with Oi for a bit once all this is over,' Snow chides the other Dwarves softly. 'No biting your mum, eh?'

Gretel blinks. '"Mum"?'

'Yes, obviously,' replies Snow in the sort of tone that suggests Gretel just asked her whether the sky is a horrible shade of dingy grey. 'They're a litter. Oi's the mum, the rest are juveniles. Don't reach maturity till they're fifteen, Dwarves. They were all still babies when Oi found me, that first night.' She pauses, running a hand over Oi's brow. 'I owe her everything.'

'Oh,' Gretel breathes. 'I never knew.'

'You never asked.'

'Yes I did! Repeatedly!'

'Oh.' Snow frowns. 'Yeah. Fair enough. Well, I never fancied telling you, I suppose.' She indicates over to the juvenile Dwarves. 'Stinky, Stabby, Scourge, Claws, You There and Gitface. Scourge and Gitface are boys, rest are girls.'

'If five of them are female,' asks Patience, manifesting overhead, 'why do you call them all "lads"?'

'Force of habit, I suppose,' replies Snow. 'Are you just going to go around materialising to make snarky comments or are you going to make yourself useful?'

Patience tuts. 'Fine, I'll go and haunt the fire out then, shall I?' she mutters, drifting away.

'Or organising a fire crew would be helpful,' Snow calls after her. 'Ugh. Dead people are the worst.'

'Well,' Mrs Mudd tells them, 'that's why we're here. To make sure the huntsmen create as few dead people as possible.'

'And we appreciate it,' Trevor tells her, from Buttercup's hair.

Mrs Mudd shrugs. 'You helped us when we needed it. I just hope we made enough of a difference.'

It does make enough of a difference. Hansel's earlier attempts to contain the fire mean that it's reasonably easy for a team of villagers and Darkwood creatures to extinguish the worst of it before Hansel and Jack return to rot away trunks and smother with overturned earth until the last of the fire is completely out. With the fire and the flying machine gone for now and the caves no more secret or safe from the huntsmen than any other part of the Darkwood, the decision is made not to bother seeking emergency shelter after all, but to return home and improve defences there instead. Gretel suspects that this is largely because the caves are horrible, dark and damp, but she's not going to be the one to bring that up. She just wants to go home, at last.

30
Home, At Last

'Home, at last!' Buttercup bursts gratefully through the cake cottage's biscuit door, and into the sugary kitchen within. 'Henrietta, you did a smashing job of looking after the place; only seven broken plates.'

'I did my best.' The Centaur smiles shyly, leaning the magic Mirror safely against a wall.

'No way,' breathes Scarlett, following the others inside. She takes in deep nosefuls of the place.

'Welcome to your new home,' Trevor tells the Werewolf. 'You too, Gilde, I'm sure the quadrupeds can scooch beds and chairs around to make room. Plenty of nesting places for Hex, too, and Snow can tell you where the wolf pack and the bears can rest safely.'

'This isn't my new home,' Scarlett tells them, a strange smile on her face. 'Buttercup, how did you get this place?'

'Just sort of found it,' Buttercup tells her, wrapping the tattered remains of her skirt around her hands to safely load logs into the stove. 'It was already abandoned when I got out here.'

'This is Little Cottage,' Mother Goggins exclaims, looking around. 'Old wood lodge. Or at least, it's a rough approximation of Little Cottage, made out of marzipan. We used to come down here all the time, back in the day. There was old Mrs Little the

Werewolf, had a cape a lot like that one.' She indicates Scarlett's tatty cape. 'With her grandson, the woodcutter lad. But then he went missing…'

'She was never a "woodcutter lad",' Scarlett says quietly.

Mother Goggins regards Scarlett thoughtfully. 'Aye,' she says after a moment. 'I imagine you'd know best, bein' her… granddaughter, is it?'

Scarlett nods. 'I moved north after she passed. People were starting to get funny about us. Starting rumours and stuff.'

'Oh!' Buttercup straightens up, regarding Scarlett awkwardly. 'I didn't… um… I hope you don't mind my being here. And accidentally turning a lot of it into cake.'

'It's fine. It's nice to be back.'

'Did…' Buttercup flounders. 'Did you want it back?'

'Oh!' Scarlett cringes at the very idea. 'Oh, no, I abandoned it, it's your home now.'

'It's fine.' Buttercup smiles politely, even though it definitely would not be fine. 'It would be no problem at all.' It absolutely would be a massive problem.

'Honestly no, I insist,' frets Scarlett, desperate to out-polite Buttercup, 'I wouldn't dream of it.'

'Oh. Well.' Buttercup relents. 'Of course, you're welcome to stay with us, at least. Permanently. Trevor was right, we can all scooch…'

'She can have my bed,' says Gretel.

Buttercup's face crumples a little. 'Oh. Oh, yes. Right. You'll be wanting to move back to… yes, of course.'

'We'll still see each other all the time,' Gretel tells her. 'We've got defences to build and a regime to topple. But if the huntsmen now see Nearby as just another part of the Darkwood, there's no reason why I shouldn't go back there, to the farm.'

'Yes,' sighs Buttercup. She still looks crestfallen.

'I'll be around every day,' Gretel adds. 'I just… miss my bedroom.'

'...the bedrooms,' says Gretel's stepmother, entering the cake cottage midway through a sentence. She and Hansel have Oi on a stretcher. 'Hansel, you can stay with... wait, isn't this Little Cottage, only more spongey?'

'Yes, Stepmother, we've just been over that.'

'Ah.' Mrs Mudd turns to Buttercup. 'Do you have room for a big lad, Miss Buttercup?'

'We've always got room,' Buttercup tells her. 'Why?'

'There's all together eight badly wounded that I need to keep an eye on for infections and such,' Mrs Mudd tells her. 'I'm going to have to make an infirmary out of the farmhouse bedrooms for the time being, I thought Hansel could share with his sister here.'

Gretel deflates. 'So... I can't go home?'

'It's only a bedroom, Gretel Mudd,' her stepfather tells her. 'You'll get it back when the injured are better. No being a fusspot, please.'

'I'm not being a fusspot! I've already been stuck out here two months.'

'Gretel Mudd!' snaps her stepmother. 'You'll stay here with your brother and you'll be grateful.'

'I already *am* grateful, Stepmother.'

'It's a beautiful home, Miss Buttercup,' Mr Mudd tells Buttercup graciously. 'Love what you've done with the place. Very original décor.'

And Gretel *is* grateful, truly she is, once the pang of disappointment at not being able to go back to the farmhouse just yet has evaporated. Before long, she's just glad to be alive and unharmed and comparatively safe with her family and friends. The cake cottage isn't *that* bad, really. Things start looking up even more when Scarlett, Carpenter Fred and Lanky Joe the thatcher make plans to fix the cottage's leaky sponge roof.

Soon, Gretel is busy organising relief camps for the creatures made temporarily homeless by the fire, and creating teams to deal with medical care, food and water supplies and improving their defences against the next huntsman attack. It takes her a little while to notice that many of the queries coming to her from Darkwood creatures and villagers alike are questions that would usually be asked of Snow. That's when she realises that Snow hasn't been seen for hours.

Gretel makes her excuses and steps outside. She passes by Jack, who is sitting quietly amongst a large thicket of nettles, concentrating on a bit of fiddly needlecraft.

'Seen Snow anywhere?' she asks him.

He looks up at her briefly, doesn't reply, and gets back on with his work.

Gretel tuts. 'What's up with you?'

'Nettle-shirt spell,' says Gilde. She's curled cosily against the fur of Baby's giant, sleeping frame. She doesn't even open her eyes. 'Fer Sweetiebird. I told him it won't work, but he ain't listening.'

Gretel steps a little closer to Jack to take a look at what Gilde means. Jack is slowly, delicately stitching stinging nettle leaves together by hand. His fingers are already red with angry raised welts.

'Jack, your hands…'

'Best you don't try to make conversation, girl,' Gilde adds. 'From the first stitch to the last, he ain't allowed to speak, nor cry out, nor nothin'.' She smiles sweetly, her eyes still closed. 'You're welcome for all the peace and quiet in the next few weeks or however long it takes.'

'Weeks?' Gretel frowns.

'Took Hex's sister a full year per shirt,' Gilde tells her. 'But then she was only allowed to work at nights in secret, the situation bein' such as it was, and she had to pick the nettles special like; she couldn't cheat like this 'un.'

'Maybe if more of us chip in with the work it can be done quicker?' Gretel suggests. 'It would be nice to get Hex back to his old self as soon as possible, if we can…'

Gilde shakes her head. 'That'd only take the spell from "almost def'nitely not going to work" to "absolutely positively not going to work". Nettle shirts only block a curse if they're stitched by hand, in silence, by a witch who loves you.'

'Oh,' sighs Gretel.

'Not "you" specifically,' Gilde adds, 'but the person who's been cursed. You know what I mean.'

'You're in love with him,' breathes Gretel.

Jack shoots her a quick, embarrassed glance.

'Oh, don't be like that, Jack, I'm proud of you.'

Jack looks even more embarrassed and concentrates back on his painful sewing.

Gilde snuggles deeper into Baby's fur. 'By the bye, Her Majesty went thattaway.' She points off in the general direction of the Dwarf cave.

Gretel thanks her and follows her pointed finger.

She finds Snow a hundred yards or so into the trees, sitting on a stump and ruffling the fur of either Stinky or Claws or Gitface... Gretel honestly can't tell the difference between the Dwarves just by looking at them.

Gretel sits down next to her. 'You all right?'

Snow pulls a face. 'About what you and your village did, back there. Lying to that huntsman about being witches.'

'A united front.' Gretel smiles, proud of Nearby's residents. 'You're welcome.'

'Yes, I get what you were trying to do, but being a witch still isn't a costume you get to put on; I'd appreciate it if you didn't, in future.'

'Oh,' huffs Gretel, deflating.

Snow continues to scowl off into the distance. 'We lost, today.'

Gretel shrugs. 'Not really. The huntsmen's goal is to kill us all, and they haven't managed it yet. Today was more of a draw.'

'They'll come back,' says Snow. 'With more weapons. They have flying machines!'

'We'll have flying machines too,' Gretel assures her. 'I saw enough of that prototype to be able to work out how to recreate something like it. We've got full use of the village's workshops and craftspeople now; we can start knocking out inventions much faster...'

'It won't be enough,' says Snow quietly. 'The northern witches... Gilde and her bears need to hibernate, Scarlett and her pack are limited in terms of what they can do, and as for Hex...'

'Jack's on the case, with Hex.'

'Nevertheless. Even with your brother learning to focus his power, I'm not confident that we can beat a whole army, change the whole system. At least, not without more good people getting hurt. Or worse.'

'Stepmother says that Oi's odds are getting better all the time,' Gretel assures her. 'The farm has medicines that minimise the possibility of infection, we have never lost a single pig to sepsis.'

'I'm not taking that chance again,' says Snow. 'Not with my lads. Not with any of you.'

Gretel frowns. 'You sound like either you're about to give up...'

'Never.' Snow spits on the ground.

'Or,' Gretel continues, 'as if you're thinking of doing something reckless.'

'It's not reckless. It's part of the wider plan. We need every possible ally onside before we take on the Citadel.'

Gretel stares at Snow. 'You want to go east.'

Snow glares off into the trees. 'We talked the Bear Witch round. It should be possible to persuade the Glass Witch to join us too. Her territory's under just as much threat from the huntsmen as the rest of us.'

'Are you sure? Just, from everything that's been said about her...'

'Oh, she's just a witch, same as us,' replies Snow dismissively. 'She's going to turn out to be another sad, lonely, half-starved soul stuck out in a shack in the wilderness, just like all the rest, you wait and see.'

'But, didn't Hex and Gilde say…'

'Hex and Gilde were rumoured to be so ferocious that we didn't dare to stray into the northern woods for thirteen years,' Snow reminds her. 'We have to stop listening to the stories telling us to fear what's in the Darkwood. We *are* the Darkwood.'

Gretel nods. 'When do you want to go?'

'Soon,' Snow tells her. 'I should rest first, and make sure Oi's on the mend. I'd hate for her to take a turn for the worse while I'm away.'

'Well, while she's healing I'll get as many blueprints as I can over to the workshops so that they can start building while we're gone…'

Snow turns to Gretel. 'Oh, you think you're coming with me?'

'I assumed we were going as a team again.'

Snow shakes her head. 'I'm not having another Oi on my hands. I'm even getting the rest of the lads to stay behind on this one, aren't I, Scourge?'

The Dwarf she's petting mutters a very unsure 'Yummy'.

'Buttercup isn't going to like this, you know.'

Snow manages a small, fond smile. 'Why do you think I'm out here? I've got to work out how I'm going to tell her.'

'You really do love each other, don't you?'

'Wow, that's none of your business, New Girl.'

'I think Jack's fallen in love with Hex, too.'

'Yeah. I noticed he was going all soppy. Good for him, I suppose, even in spite of… you know.'

'The fact that Hex is currently a bird? I told you; he's working on that.'

'I meant more the age difference. Still, each to their own.'

'*And* I think my brother's started stepping out with my best mate from back home.'

232

Snow pulls a face. 'What are they – ten?'

'Thirteen and fourteen!'

Snow's expression of distaste doesn't change. 'Who's even interested in making smoochy-eyes at that age? Hope you're not, New Girl.'

Gretel shudders. 'Bleh. No. Who needs kissing when you've got spanners?'

Snow gives her a gentle punch on the shoulder. 'That's what I like to hear. Bit of common sense around here.'

Gretel walks back to the cottage, thinking. She walks past a pack of wolves slinking away to find somewhere to rest. She walks past the sleeping bears, with Gilde curled into the warmth of their bellies. She walks past the nettle patch where Jack still silently stitches, as Hex beadily watches him from a nearby tree. She walks past some of the northern wood creatures setting up a temporary camp far from the fire damage of their own territory. She walks past a group of villagers carrying stretchers back towards Mudd Farm. She walks past Scarlett and a handful of villagers surveying the cottage's roof. She walks past Daisy bent over a slate, sketching out designs as Patience hovers over her, making comments that are only occasionally helpful. She enters the cottage, and hears Buttercup and Trevor upstairs, cheerfully discussing how they're going to move things around to fit in all the new beds. Hansel gives her a cup of tea and a big smile.

'This is nice,' Hansel tells her. 'I like your new friends.'

'Yeah.' Gretel takes a sip. It's disgusting. She can't believe she's forgotten in these few months away just how terrible her brother is at making a simple cup of tea. She grins down into the revolting brew. 'I've been pretty lucky so far, all things considered.'

'Here's hoping it holds out.'

Gretel nods, taking another sip of horrible, beautiful tea. 'I might need it. I'm going to go with Snow to see the Glass Witch. Whether Snow likes it or not.'

'Oh,' says the Mirror from its corner, softly.

An odd expression crosses Hansel's face. For a moment, the shadows in the cottage seem darker, more tangible, somehow.

'You all right?'

Hansel snaps out of it. 'Yeah. Sorry. Don't know what happened there. I thought I was getting a vision, but then it just… went. It's like… you know when you think you need to sneeze but then it sort of goes back in?'

'Hmm.' Gretel turns to the Mirror. 'Sorry, what were you going to say?'

'The Glass Witch,' says the Mirror. 'I'm not sure… No, sorry, it's gone. Forget I said anything!'

'Do you know anything about the Glass Witch?' asks Gretel.

'Um…'

Gretel sighs. 'Mirror Mirror, please do snitch, what know you of the Glass Witch?'

'I *did* know something,' the Mirror tells her, unsure. 'Reports from Ashtrie, from back when I was king. But now… I must have forgotten it all. I'm sorry.'

'Oh.' Gretel frowns faintly. 'Well, I suppose it can't be *that* bad, then.'

And so, the residents of Myrsina, within the Darkwood and without, go about their days. To the west of Darkwood, word of the new head huntsman gets around. The abomination lists and ducking stools are torn down. In the Citadel, and in towns and villages from Slate up north-east near the mountains to Goldenharbour in the south-west, kissing the Golden Sea, people celebrate, free at last from the tyranny of abominations. The witches hiding amongst them celebrate along with the unmagical, swallowing down their terror at being caught out. Morning Quarry and her huntsmen, unmasked and smiling out at the world, return to the castle and begin making plans for the final push to completely purge the Darkwood.

To the east of Darkwood, there is a river. It's quite small, just a trickle really, but it officially creates the border between Myrsina and Ashtrie. In the Ashtrian side of Darkwood, all is quiet and still.

Utterly quiet. Utterly still. No chirp of a bird, no rustle of a rodent.

Deep within the silence, a smile splits, cold and sharp as glass, beautiful as crystal. The Glass Witch, queen of all she surveys, shares her stunning white smile with the glittering walls of her empty palace. A new opportunity is approaching. An opportunity for more praise, more worship, more power. More *fun*.

A new opportunity for revenge.

Acknowledgements

Thanks to Dom Lord & Abbie Headon for all their support and help. Thank you to everybody who read and recommended *Darkwood*, especially Jess, Paul & Lucy. A huge thank you to The Lovely Nathan, and thank you to my mum, whose name is Rory (it's a long story).

About the Author

Gabby Hutchinson Crouch (*Horrible Histories*, *Newzoids*, *The News Quiz*, *The Now Show*) has a background in satire, and with the global political climate as it is, believes that now is an important time to explore themes of authoritarianism and intolerance in comedy and fiction. Born in Pontypool in Wales, and raised in Ilkeston, Derbyshire, Gabby moved to Canterbury at 18 to study at the University of Kent and ended up staying and having a family there.

Also available

Magic is forbidden in Myrsina, along with various other abominations, such as girls doing maths.

This is bad news for Gretel Mudd, who doesn't perform magic, but does know a lot of maths. When the sinister masked huntsmen accuse Gretel of witchcraft, she is forced to flee into the neighbouring Darkwood, where witches and monsters dwell.

There, she happens upon Buttercup, a witch who can't help turning things into gingerbread, Jack Trott, who can make plants grow at will, the White Knight with her band of Dwarves and a talking spider called Trevor. These aren't the terrifying villains she's been warned about all her life. They're actually quite nice. Well… most of them.

With the huntsmen on the warpath, Gretel must act fast to save both the Darkwood and her home village, while unravelling the rhetoric and lies that have demonised magical beings for far too long.

Take a journey into the Darkwood in this modern fairy tale that will bewitch adults and younger readers alike.

OUT NOW

Note from the Publisher

To receive updates on new releases in the Darkwood
series – plus special offers and news of other humorous
fiction series to make you smile – sign up now to the
Farrago mailing list at farragobooks.com/sign-up.